1,260 Days

ENOCH'S STORY AS TOLD TO CONTE

Conte

iUniverse, Inc.
Bloomington

1,260 Days

iUniverse books may be ordered through booksellers or by contacting:

iUniverse
1663 Liberty Drive
Bloomington, IN 47403
www.iuniverse.com
1-800-Authors (1-800-288-4677)

ISBN: 978-1-4759-3893-7 (sc)
ISBN: 978-1-4759-3895-1 (hc)
ISBN: 978-1-4759-3894-4 (e)

Library of Congress Control Number: 2012913924

Printed in the United States of America

iUniverse rev. date: 8/9/2012

Dedicated to Madre and Padre

"Remember Him before the silver cord is broken and the golden bowl is crushed, the pitcher by the well is shattered and the wheel at the cistern is crushed; then the dust will return to the earth as it was, and the spirit will return to God who gave it." *Ecclesiastes 12:6-7*

ACKNOWLEDGEMENTS

Thank you, Diana Fabio for editing the book. I appreciate everyone who journeyed with us to Europe and the Philippines as the book was being posted online. Your presence was a motivating force to push us forward during difficult times. A special thanks to Rich Marotta, Greg Tortell, and Scott Hartstein for their positive reviews.

Table of Contents

Chapter 1: Sex & Dying in a High Society

Part A: Thailand
01 Arrival in Thailand 7/5/08-7/5/08
02 Khao Yai National Forest 7/6/08-7/9/08
03 Asian Horse of Bangkok 7/10/08-7/11/08
04 Phuket 7/12/08-7/17/08
05 Bachelors Party in Pattaya 7/18/08-7/22/08
06 Pattaya Reflection 7/23/08
Part B: I Must Not Think Bad Thoughts
07 Ko Samui Island: The Lord of a Trip 7/24/08-7/27/08
08 Back in the U.S.A 7/28/08-7/29/08
09 Where Am I? 7/31/08-8/29/08
10 Either/Or You'll Regret it 8/21/08-9/6/08
11 Economic Meltdown 9/10/08-11/10/08
12 Death & Disease 11/11/08-12/27/08
13 Goodbye Uncle Jim 12/28/08-2/8/09
Part C: The Decline of Western Civilization
14 In the Name of Allah... 2/7/09-4/5/09
15 Lukewarm 4/6/09-5/13/09
16 Running with the Devil 5/14/09-5/30/09
17 A Higher Calling 5/31/09-6/16/09
18 Pride 6/17/09-7/5/09
19 The Fall of the West 7/6/09-8/13/09
20 Bob Marley, Joseph Smith, & the Rapture 8/14/09-9/28/09
21 Sports Addiction 8/29/09-9/27/09
Part D: The Unheard Music
22 Post Office Shooting 9/28/09
23 Prayer, Meditation, & Loving One Another 9/29/09-10/24/09
24 Death Throes by the Train 10/25/09-11/22/09
25 The Path of Least Resistance 11/23/09-12/5/09
26 Yin Yang 2009 12/6/09-12/27/09
27 Pornography 12/28/09-1/10/10
28 Infidelity 1/11/10
29 Sex Slaves 1/12/10-1/23/10
30 Forty-Two 1/24/10-2/14/10
31 Suicide 2/15/10-3/1/10
32 Baggage in my Head 3/2/10-3/23/10
33 Attack Upon Christendom 3/24/10-4/12/10
34 Usury 4/11/10-4/22/10
35 Shakespeare, Success, Evil, & the Lord's Return 4/23/10-5/2/10
36 Fame, Fortune & Everything Else in Between 5/3/10-5/15/10
37 Foul Ball 5/16/10
38 Scratching the Itch 5/17/10-5/25/10
39 Here's the Place... Now Saving Away 5/30/10-6/14/10
40 Mercy 6/15/10-6/28/10

Chapter 2: 40 Days & 40 Nights in Europe

Day 01 Lost Luggage 6/30/10
Day 02 The Fall 7/1/10
Day 03 The Monricans 7/2/10
Day 04 Fez, Morocco 7/3/10
Day 05 1992 Vs. 2010 7/4/10
Day 06 The Thrill is Gone 7/5/10
Day 07 Lisbon 7/6/10
Day 08 Welcome to the Machine 7/7/10
Day 09 Purgatory 7/8/10
Day 10 Church 7/9/10
Day 11 Highlights 7/10/10
Day 12 Espana, World Cup Champions! 7/11/10
Day 13 Grapevine 7/12/10
Day 14 Running with the Bulls 7/13/10
Day 15 Come on Down & Make the Stand 7/14/10
Day 16 Sabbath 7/15/10
Day 17 Faced Away 7/16/10
Day 18 Hangover 7/17/10
Day 19 For Freedom 7/18/10
Day 20 Love Your Neighbor as Yourself 7/19/10
Day 21 The Venetians 7/20/10
Day 22 Prost Austria 7/21/10
Day 23 Krakow, Poland 7/22/10
Day 24 The Holocaust 7/23/10
Day 25 Eating, Drinking, & Screwing 7/24/10
Day 26 Environmentalist & Disease 7/25/10
Day 27 The Application of Pot 7/27/10
Day 28 Music 7/28/10
Day 29 Zbigniew Paul 7/28/10
Day 30 I Met Mary - Hell No 7/30/10
Day 31 Real Mary - Hell No 7/30/10
Day 32 Ménage à Trois 7/31/10
Day 33 Preaching Science 8/1/10
Day 34 Lourdes, France 8/2/10
Day 35 In the Train to Overcoated Thinking 8/3/10
Day 36 ... 8/4/10
Day 37 Modern Conveniences 8/5/10
Day 38 The Meaning of Life 8/6/10
Day 39 Caesar's Rome 8/7/10
Day 40 Forty Day Fast 8/9/10

Chapter 3: Visions of the Absurd

01 The Clock is Ticking 8/9/10-8/30/10
02 Beating Fetus Witness 8/31/10-9/7/10
03 Written in Stone 9/8/10-9/14/10
04 Absurdity 9/15/10-9/20/10
05 Was Jesus a Murderer or a Maniac 9/21/10-9/25/10
06 Death, Reduction, & the Unknown Soldiers 9/26/10-10/3/10
07 Fall of the White House 10/4/10-10/9/10
08 My Only Friend... The End 10/10/10-10/23/10
09 Liberty & Anarchy 10/24/10-10/31/10
10 The Closet 11/1/10-11/12/10
11 Repentance 11/13/10-11/23/10
12 Holy Bible Atomic Hell Fire Heat 11/24/10-11/29/10
13 If I Had One Year to Live 11/30/10-12/5/10
14 Passing 12/6/10-12/15/10
15 Drought 12/21/10-12/22/10
16 Retirement 12/23/10-1/12/11
17 Alternate Realities 1/13/11-1/17/11
18 Gadzooky 1/18/11-1/23/11
19 Sick until Summer 1/24/11-1/31/11
20 Farmer 2/1/11-2/7/11
21 Vanilla Sex 2/8/11-2/13/11
22 Dark Side of Love 2/14/11-2/28/11
23 The Rapture 3/1/11-3/9/11
24 Roots: Radicals, Rockers, & Reggae 3/10/11-3/14/11
25 Greenbelt's Dying & It Won't Be Long 3/15/11-3/23/11
26 Forever & Ever 3/26/11-4/4/11
27 The Jester 4/5/11-4/10/11
28 Zachariah 4/11/11-4/17/11
29 Israel, Israel 4/18/11-4/24/11
30 Zachariah, the Prophet 4/25/11-5/1/11
31 Nascent Mischief & My Nanosthesex 5/2/11-5/8/11
32 Juvenile Delinquents 5/9/11-5/17/11
33 Mirror 5/18/11-5/22/11
34 Repentant 5/23/11-6/31/11
35 Politics 6/1/11-6/6/11
36 Rich Man's Blues 6/6/11-6/26/11
37 Welch Hunt 6/9/11-6/16/11
38 Laughter 6/17/11-6/19/11
39 Fading Vision 6/20/11-6/22/11

Chapter 4: The Philippines

Day 01 Typhoon Landfire 6/23/11
Day 02 Disaster Delight 6/24/11
Day 03 Family, Family, Family 6/25/11
Day 04 Abraham Lives! 6/26/11
Day 05 From U.S. to a Boner 6/27/11
Day 06 Life of Leisure 6/28/11
Day 07 Sunshine, Rain, & in the Middle of Nowhere 6/29/11
Day 08 Tequila Sob & Risk Takers 6/30/11
Day 09 A Cebu Story 7/2/11
Day 10 Sad Day 7/3/11
Day 11 The Beat on the Street 7/3/11
Day 12 The Glass 7/4/11
Day 13 Missing 7/5/11
Day 14 Humidity 7/6/11
Day 15 Life in the Fast Lane 7/7/11
Day 16 Less for Words 7/8/11
Day 17 Snapped? 7/9/11
Day 18 Out of Gas 7/10/11
Day 19 Hypocrites & Unbelievers 7/11/11
Day 20 Under the Weather 7/12/11
Day 21 Gambling in the Backroom 7/13/11
Day 22 Teaching English Abroad 7/14/11
Day 23 South African Robbery 7/16/11
Day 24 Karaoke Follies & Burning Charcoal 7/19/11
Day 25 Demon Possessed Boy 7/17/11
Day 26 Take a Walking Girl 7/18/11
Day 27 Jealously Accident 7/19/11
Day 28 Slow Goo 7/20/11
Day 29 Eastwood's Tale 7/21/11
Day 30 Education & Vices 7/22/11
Day 31 Acmen & Realtree 7/23/11
Day 32 Hash Run 7/24/11
Day 33 Luke & the Lost 7/25/11
Day 34 The Prodigal Son 7/26/11
Day 35 Company, Culture, Food, & Language 7/27/11
Day 36 So Far Away 7/28/11
Day 37 Certified & Saying Goodbye 7/29/11
Day 38 The Meaning to Hell 7/31/11
Day 39 Highway to Hell 7/31/11
Day 40 Goodbye Emerald Islands 8/1/11

Chapter 5: The End

Part A: Anger, Analysis, & Anarchy
01 Post Travel Haze 8/2/11-8/5/11
02 Fickle, Cynical, & Frozen in Stupor 8/6/11-8/12/11
03 The Sermon 8/13/11-8/14/11
04 Beyond Good and Evil 8/15/11-8/29/11
05 Frolic Pussy 8/21/11-8/25/11
06 Exodus 8/27/11-8/29/11
07 Writing Well Memorial 8/29/11-9/2/11
08 September 9/3/11-9/7/11
09 Discord 9/8/11-9/11/11
10 Sickness Unto Death 9/12/11-9/17/11
11 Harvest Time 9/18/11-9/23/11
12 Questioning the Omnipotent? 9/24/11-9/28/11
13 Angry & Unresolved 9/29/11-10/2/11
14 True Sounds of Liberty 10/2/11-10/9/11
15 Sex, Marriage, & Multiple Relationships 10/8/11-10/11/11
Part B: Broken & Parting
16 Running Death Dream 10/12/11-10/14/11
17 Balled Out 10/15/11-10/16/11
18 Freedom of Speech 10/17/11-10/19/11
19 Overcome 10/20/11-10/23/11
20 It's a Wonderful Life 10/24/11-10/28/11
21 Halloween 10/29/11-10/31/11
22 Romans 11/1/11-11/3/11
23 Mercy, Mice & Jest 11/4/11-11/7/11
24 Clarification 11/8/11-11/10/11
25 Veteran's Day 11/11/11-11/12/11
26 VW Bug 11/13/11-11/15/11
27 Subterranean Rhapsody 11/16/11-11/18/11
28 Letter to the Americans 11/19/11-11/23/11
29 Controversialist Corner 11/22/11-11/24/11
30 Prayer 11/25/11-11/27/11
31 Gospel 11/28/11-11/29/11
32 We see the Light 12/1/11-12/4/11
33 What If... 12/5/11-12/6/11
Part C: The Holy Land
34 (Day 1): Friday, Dec. 9th
35 (Day 2): Saturday, Dec. 10th
36 (Day 3): Sunday, Dec. 11th
37 (Day 4): Monday, Dec. 12th
38 (Day 5): Tuesday, Dec. 13th
39 (Day 6): Wednesday, Dec. 14th
40 (Day 7): Thursday, Dec. 15th

PROLOGUE

In the *Book of Revelation* there are Two Witnesses who appear in the spotlight and perform great miracles upon the earth during the apocalypse (see Rev.11). Who are these two prophets? There has been much debate over this issue among theologians, but no one knows for sure. Most scholars believe that one of the witnesses is Elijah. As for the second witness, there are many possibilities. Some people think Enoch is one of the prophets. Others think Moses is the second witness. And some believe it could be John, Zerubbabel, or someone else. Personally, I believe the second witness is Enoch who was taken by God in the *Book of Genesis*. This book is about Enoch's testimony before the dark and terrifying Day of the Lord.

1,260 Days is the continuing saga of Enoch's prophecy to mankind. It began long ago in the *Book of Enoch*, an ancient text found within the Dead Sea Scrolls that dates back to 200 BC. This book was considered authoritative by many of the early church fathers, but today is considered a pseudepigraphical text by most of the Christian community. Today only the Ethiopian Orthodox Church accepts the *Book of Enoch* as the inspired Word of God. This book is broken up into five sections, but after years of studying the manuscript, I personally believe that only the first section (Chapters 1-36) should be considered for inclusion in the Bible. The rest of the book is highly speculative and should continue to be excluded from the canon of scripture.

1 Enoch retells the story of the Watchers (fallen angels) who sleep with women and bare offspring called Nephilim (giants). Due to the Watchers' wicked deeds, the Nephilim cause much trouble and turmoil on the earth, so God decides to destroy them. As for the Watchers themselves, they ask Enoch to speak with God on their behalf asking for forgiveness, but God does not exonerate them. Instead the Watchers are bound on the earth for seventy generations then judged for their crimes. The rest of *1 Enoch* takes the prophet on a wild journey, and he is shown many magnificent and dreadful revelations by God's holy angels.

Thousands of years later, Enoch returned to the earth in the winter of 1968. Details of his early exploits and his prophetic visions were chronicled in my second book, *Disciplined Order Chaotic Lunacy*. A few years after the book was published, God spoke to Enoch in a dream and informed him it was time to finish his testimony unto the world. It began on July 3, 2008 and was completed 1,260 days later. These are Enoch's writings during that period, and I have chronicled them in this book.

Sincerely,
Craig Conte

Chapter 1:
Sex & Dying in a High Society

PART A: THAILAND

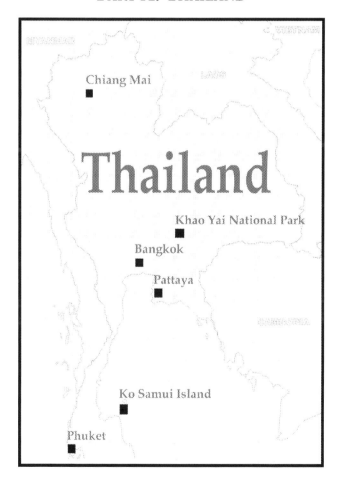

01 Arrival in Thailand 7/3/2008-7/5/2008

After spending eighteen hours on a plane and a short layover in Hong Kong, I arrived in Bangkok. Did I have high hopes? Did I see hookers on every corner waiting to offer me their services? No, I did not. There were some hookers, but mostly I saw what you will find in any city. There were bums. There were beggars. There were people running around trying to earn their Baht (that's Thai money), and there were odd sites to view and gawk at.

Right now it's 5:00 A.M. in the morning. I can't sleep. Neither can my traveling companion, Kiana, my wife. Today we are going to see the temples and do touristy things in Bangkok. I then plan to get a Thai massage afterwards with a happy ending. In other words, the massage girl will jerk me off into orgasm, and I'll go back to the hotel with a smile on my face. Then again…maybe these are my "Great Expectations." Now you see how my mind works.

In Bangkok, I'm sure I'll see the Emerald Buddha. Apparently, it's this giant statue/idol of the Great Buddha. Ninety-five percent of Thailand's 65 million people are Buddhists. Does that mean that 65 million are going to hell because they don't believe in Jesus Christ? I don't know. I'll leave the judgment part in His hands. I do know He's a just God, so why worry about inconsistencies in Christianity???

There is one element of Buddhism I truly respect and honor; it's called Karma. It means good actions bring good results and bad actions bring bad results. If we all believed this, we probably would have a better society. At least it does show that there are consequences for one's evil deeds. As for the "rebirth" after death, I think most Buddhists will be surprised. If the *Bible* is true, they will not come back as a prince or a peasant. They will find themselves at the pearly gates or end up in the bottomless pit. But how will God judge them if they have not heard the Word? No one knows for sure, but I think God will judge these people based on their Karma. Did their good Karma outweigh their bad Karma? If it does, they will go to heaven. If it doesn't, they will go to hell. As for evidence to support my claims, I'd suggest you read Ezekiel 18 and Romans 2:12-16. These scriptures seem to suggest that God will judge us based on our good and evil deeds. I know this belief is not in accordance with the scripture that reads, "I am the way, the truth, and the life; no one comes to the Father but through Me," (Jn.14:6) but it does seem to be just and fair from the human perspective.

As for me, what am I doing out here in the Orient? Why did I begin my testimony here? I suppose it could have begun anywhere, but I chose Thailand because it's supposed to be one of the wickedest places on earth. Also, I've never been to Thailand before, and I heard it was the place to go if you're looking for decadence and immoral behavior. I couldn't resist my inquisitive nature, and I wanted to see if the stories were true or not. Isn't that my job? Isn't it my duty? Probably not, but here I am anyway.

02 Khao Yai National Forest 7/6/2008-7/9/2008

Right now I'm looking out at Khao Yai National Forest. It's a giant jungle with all sorts of interesting looking creatures. We've seen monkeys, elephants, snakes, centipedes, leeches, and everything else in between. Seeing so much life makes me wonder what life must have been like before mankind destroyed the Garden. The earth must have been a place of beauty and peace, a place where birds were free to roam and sing. Someday the whole earth will return to its natural beauty, and we can start all over again. In the meantime, we must make do with the city noise of Bangkok and deal with the hedonistic lifestyle of places like Phuket. But this age is coming to a close. A new sun is rising in the east. It's called the Millennial Reign. I hope you will join me on this trip. "Everyone aboard! Noah's Ark is departing! All are welcome!" But I know how it is. It's difficult to leave the things of the world behind, but you know and I know that none of it will bring us peace of mind. Be that as it may, we still hold onto it like a giant treasure. But in the place I see, gold and diamonds hold no wealth. Only love matters over here. Once again I holler, "The boat is leaving port! All aboard!" I'm only here by sheer grace. Won't you join me? This ship is heading home...

03 Ashen Horse of Bangkok 7/10/2008-7/11/2008

The last two days have been a bit odd to say the least… On the 10th, we had a bunch of time to kill before our flight left from Bangkok to Chaing Mai, so we watched the newest Hollywood hit *Hancock*. The movie was alright, but the man sitting behind me in the theatre was far more interesting. He was coughing pretty hard and the stench given off from his body was horrendous. At first I wanted to move away from him, but as the movie proceeded, the Lord revealed to me through His Spirit that it was the Ashen horse of pestilence sitting right behind me in the disguise of a man. *Well, maybe it was just a figment of my imagination, but please humor me and go along with me on this trip...* It made me come to realize that this is how the angel plans to spread forth his disease. He plans to come to an international city like Bangkok and get everyone sick. These businessmen and tourists will then return home and spread the disease in their homelands. Before the world knows what to do, we will have a plague set loose upon the earth that will kill one-quarter of man. (Rev.6:8)

On the next day, Kiana and I met a couple from New Zealand. They had left everything behind and decided to travel the world during their retirement years. They had come to the conclusion that the pursuit of wealth and material goods was a waste of time, so they decided to pick up shop and live abroad. My oh my, the gall of this older couple! I love it! I could never see my mother and father doing something like that. It's too risky. They would never leave the creature comforts of home to pursue these wild dreams. Instead they are rotting away unto death, and they will never experience life outside their hemisphere of the world.

Later in the evening, we had dinner with the Kiwis. We talked politics, travel, and finally the conversation landed on the issue of God and religion. They were both "Universalists," especially the woman. They believe there are many ways to God, so she sort of encompassed a little bit of each religion into her belief system. She then started talking about how we are all gods and that you will find God by looking within. Instantly it made me think of Matthew 24 and the "inner rooms," and I realized she was mislead. It made me think of the lie the Serpent fed to Eve in the Garden. "You will be like God." (Gen.3:4) She had bought into this dogma. So after listening to her talk about how God is in everything, even the metal pole and tree, I told her I disagreed and explained why YHWH is the only true God. Of course, many of the old arguments came into play, and I did my best to defend my position. I've been having debates for decades on apologetics, so my responses are pretty solid. Nevertheless, I did try to listen and understand her perspective in a loving way. In the end, we agreed to disagree, and we just laughed over a pot of tea. I've learned over the years that the only way to pass on the message of Jesus Christ is to listen and laugh with them. Then when the time is right, come in with the message of hope and put all the naysayers and doubters to shame with the evidence that proves the Judeo-Christian God is the way and the truth.

04 Phuket 7/12/2008-7/17/2008

Phuket is everything that it's supposed to be, and it's everything that it's not. Patong Beach is a cesspool of tourists with vendors and conmen and hookers and ladyboys. Now I see why God sent forth a Tsunami to wipe the place clean, but He didn't do a good enough job because the streets and hotels are filled again. Maybe next time "a real rain will come and wash all the scum off the street," (Taxi Driver) but for now commercialism and capitalism reigns supreme. I've seen this scene before. It's at every tourist trap across the globe, and the whole world would be better off if we colon cleansed it out of our system and washed it all down the sewer. For the time being, the wife and I headed south to Karon and Kata Beach to get away from the Holiday Inn umbrellas. It's much slower there, and I felt like I truly was on vacation and not being shoved into the meat grinder. In another decade or so, I'm sure the area will be overrun like Patong, and there will be no quiet place to get away from the masses. And in another century, nothing will be left. We will have drilled, mined, deforested, and polluted every nook and cranny on the earth. And you ask me why I say the end is nigh??? The end is coming, but the world is going about their business. Everyone is buying and selling, but when the storm of judgment hits, there will be no time to flee to the mountains.

Note: Kiana went home last night. She had to go back to work, but I'm staying for another ten days to hang out with the guys. One of them is getting married on Ko Samui Island, and there's a bachelor party on the mainland before we fly over.

05 Bachelor Party in Pattaya 7/18/2008-7/22/2008

In Pattaya, I must have gotten into trouble every day. When I first arrived in the city, I was a bit worn out so I decided to get a massage at one of the parlors down the street. On the corner were about ten girls dressed in skimpy clothing calling out to me, "Massage…massage…massage…" I made the fatal mistake by giving them eye contact, and the next thing I knew they were crowded around me. At this parlor they were offering a special, the "4 Hands Massage." So I looked at the group of girls, picked the two cutest ones, and went to the back room to get my massage.

Initially, when I set out that afternoon I planned to get just a massage, but the two girls had other intentions. At first, it started off quite innocent. I was lying on my belly with a towel covering my butt. Instantly, one of the girls removed the towel and started rubbing my back, my neck, my shoulders, my legs and other inappropriate places. Before I knew it, one of the girls had completely stripped naked and was lying on my back rubbing her breasts and body up against mine. What was I to do, make her stop? That's like asking a drug addict to not have another hit? Well, I don't need to go into all the intricate details about this massage, but there is something special about being with two women at the same time. Later that night, I went out on the town and hung out at the strip joints with the guys. I had strippers all over me, and I was giving out 100 Baht (about $3 dollars) like it was candy.

The next day, I hung out by the beach, but was hounded by solicitors every five minutes, so I headed back to my hotel. On the way back, I stopped off at one of the massage parlors and received a deep tissue massage for about $10 dollars. Oh, this girl was good! I'll take a high-quality massage over a hand job any day. For one hour, I was in total bliss. This girl was walking on my back, pressing real hard with her feet, and she managed to get all the kinks out of my back. This was far better than any happy ending. Afterwards, I went back to my hotel room and took a nap.

Later that night, I went out to the bars and strip joints again. At one place the girls shot darts out of their vaginas and hit balloons on the walls twenty feet away. It was hilarious as hell and the best marksmanship I had ever seen in my life. At another bar, the girls were doing magic tricks with ping-pong balls. You'd be amazed at how many ping-pong balls a woman can put inside herself. At one of the other discotheques, some of the girls were tied up and being whipped by dominant women in bondage outfits. In general, the whole night was filled with other circus acts, but these ones stick out as being the most memorable. I have to admit I had a great night of entertainment. Everyone was drunk and laughing. There were hordes of naked women everywhere, and it felt like I had entered fornication heaven.

To sum up, I could tell you the rest of the story, but I don't want to incriminate anybody. Let's just say Pattaya is like Vegas except for the high price tag. You can also touch the girls everywhere and do whatever you want. So I suppose, Pattaya is nothing like Vegas. It's superior in every way and makes Sin City seem as tame as cable television.

06 Pattaya Reflection 7/23/2008

There is an old saying in the scriptures, "Resist the devil and he will flee from you." (Ja.4:7) This is all fine and dandy in theory. Putting it into practice is something that I have not done so well because my fleshly desires have ruled me. Have they ruled you too? It might be a click away on the computer, a shifting of stations on the TV, or it might be something more sinister. In Pattaya everything is out there in the open where anyone can see. The hustlers on the outside draw you in, and beyond the next door are hordes of women fulfilling your every wicked kink. For me, my downfall has been lechery. For others it might be homosexuality. To some it's drugs. To others it's every sin written about in the Holy Book. Do I have the power to resist my personal lusts? No, I do not, and I have fallen on many occasions. Therefore, I assume you are in the same position. Over the years, my passions have only become more deviant. And I call myself a Christian??? How can I be a Christian when I'm so overcome? Others have seen my example, and I have done more damage than good. Is there hope for me? Is there hope for you? Even my own wife said, "Enoch, you're more inclined towards evil than good." She might be right. I always thought I was somewhere in between. It's too bad there is no purgatory. I can't buy my way out. I can't earn my way into heaven by doing good deeds, so I must rely upon the cross. I must put my faith in Jesus Christ and hope that He will bail me out. I suggest you do the same because if your sins are as black as mine, we're going to burn when the reaper calls our name. Pattaya, you've brought me to open shame. I've given into my temptation.

07 Ko Samui Island: The End of a Trip
7/24/2008-7/27/2008

After being on the road for almost a month, I'm weary and tired. My body is covered with mosquito bites, and I think I may have lice. I've been bitten by bed bugs and spiders. I don't think I have malaria, but I'm sure I've picked up some infectious disease. Oh Thailand, you know how to ruin a man. You play on our desires and we westerners pay with our wallets and our souls. "It's so cheap!" we say, but it starts to add up over time. It makes me think of my sins. They've been adding up. There are far too many to count. I'm only left with regrets. I thought I headed out on this mission to help my fellow man escape the abyss, but before I knew it, I was caught up in the whirlwind. Now what? Where do I go from here? I'll get on the next flight and head back to the States. For some odd reason I thought I wasn't ever coming home, but I am. There must be some unfinished business out West. Does it really matter anymore where I rest my head? After all, the world has gone global. With the Internet and satellites, everybody knows what everyone else is doing anyway. And if you don't know what's happening across the world, maybe it's time to open your eyes. We all speak a little bit of the universal language called English. It doesn't matter what corner of the globe you are from. No one can escape the fire and brimstone on the way. As for the priests and the prophets, they're all the same. They've been corrupted like you and me. There are no holy men to lead us because there are no holy men. I'm sure there are a few out there somewhere, but I haven't found them. And please don't look at me as a guiding light. I'm as screwed up as you are. I've just been given a little insight. And man, I've fallen hard. Do you feel me? Do you understand? Anyway, I'm checking out for now. I need to put my house in order. I need to live a holier lifestyle. Until then, my testimony ain't worth the feces I've been walking on. I'm a hypocrite, and I deserved to be spewed out of His mouth.

PART B: I MUST NOT THINK BAD THOUGHTS

08 Back in the U.S.A 7/28/2008-7/30/2008

After being gone for a month in Thailand, it's hard to get back into the treadmill lifestyle of L.A. For a brief moment, I forgot about the attitudes and the chopping block of people trying to look like models and the actors on TV. It's like America is trapped in fast forward, and everyone is waiting for the next big thing. I'm still having flashbacks from Thailand. I wake up in the middle of the night not knowing where I am then suddenly realize that I'm back in the good ol' U.S.A. I must say I'm happy to be back. The States are a great place to live, and I'm proud to be an American. But in a way, I sort of feel sorry for us. We're caught up in the rush hour traffic, and everyone is going this way and that. I believe we are missing out on things. We are not seeing the greater picture. There could be purpose to our lives, but we are caught up in the madness of the American Dream. I'm afraid we are going to end up like my Aunt B who died while I was away. The email read, "Aunt B went to the hospital. She died hours later. The funeral is on the 25th." And that was it. She is gone forever. I don't want to end up like my aunt because I'm not sure she had joy in her life or brought joy to others. Truthfully, I think her life represented the opposite. I'm a lot like her too. I've fallen short, and my focus has been on me instead of my neighbor. America, you have been blessed with so much as well, but when was the last time you've looked up from your troubles and saw the affliction and poverty across the globe? It's time for us to love our neighbor as ourselves. If we do this, we will be one step closer to understanding Jesus.

09 Where Am I? 7/31/2008-8/20/2008

Here I am on the last leg of my testimony, and I can't seem to get my feet back on the ground. I'm lost in vices, and I'm in bondage to a busload of pleasures and pain. It's unbelievable. It's been three weeks since I last wrote, and I don't know what's happened or where I've been. I suppose I've been passing the time like everyone else. I've been ignoring the warning signs and pushing them to the recesses of my mind. But it's there lurking in the shadows. The plagues, the wars, the disasters have not gone away. They will come. They will destroy. The bombs will go off and billions will die. I even joke about it as others mock my warning cries. Yet I'm not crying wolf, and I never have. Still, I can't hear my own words. I'm lost in a labyrinth, and I don't know why. Of all the people you'd think the person with the gift of prophecy would be able to perceive, but my ears have become dull. I can't hear the voice of the Lord anymore. The Internet and the TV are drowning Him out. There's so much commotion in the background that I can't hear the running stream. The crickets have all died. Instead, I hear the hiss of electricity. O Lord, free me from the chains that bind me! Free your people before it's too late! Is there anyone left out there? Or are you all caught up in the game like me? I'm racing this way and that. The Clash said, "Are we going backwards or are we going forwards?" All I know is that I'm not on the path I should be on. I'm guessing your road is as crooked as mine. If so, we need to get back on the straight and narrow highway. I can't even remember which exit it is. I've been lost in the freeway lifestyle for so long that all I'm seeing is red lights and traffic jams. Father, send me a cloud by day and a pillar of fire by night, so I can find my way back home. Then maybe if I get back on track, I can help others who are also lost.

10 Either/Or You'll Regret It 8/21/2008-9/9/2008

I've been thinking about a lot of different things lately. Mostly I've been thinking about the past. The wife and I are trying to get through my past indiscretions, but there are still a lot of tears. We're doing the best we can. We're trying to stick it out like every other marriage that's gone through turmoil. We're making a valiant attempt to keep the bond together. I hope we pull through. I truly have reaped what I have sown. I wish I never would have put Kiana through this misery, but I can't change the past. I've always been one to play with fire, and this time we both got burned.

With regards to the Lord, I've remained faithful to Him in my own way, even though I haven't been a stickler to the Law. I haven't denied Him, and I've preached His word through my books and my music. I wonder if anyone's receiving the message??? I've been trying for over two decades, and I'm not sure if anyone's listening. Am I coming in? Are you picking up my frequency? Since I became a man, my dream has always been to be that voice in the wilderness. I've always wanted to be the John the Baptist to my generation, but I've failed miserably. I have many defects and shortcomings, and I have not lived the sanctified life. My church has been in the bars. I've been hanging out with bookies. I drink with the unbelievers and cynics. Still, through it all, my God and I have remained intimate with one another. No one can take that away from me, and no one will. Yes, I've been a hypocrite. I've been a liar. I've been a fornicator, but I've also been a faithful friend to my Lord and King. One day in the Kingdom Age, I'm going to eat and drink with Him. We'll smoke the peace pipe together and be one.

I'm on the last leg of my journey, and I'm earning my degree to keep busy. It probably won't have any long-term benefits because I'll be dead and gone before that money kicks in. Then again, I might be wrong. I've been wrong before. It's the same old story for most of us down here. We never become rich and famous. We never attain our dreams and ambitions. We die trying, and I'm dying over here. Are you dying over there? As Bono once said, "I still haven't found what I'm looking for?" Glimpsing back at my time on earth, in some ways it's true, but in other areas it's not. It just feels like my whole life and testimony has been a failure.

11 Economic Meltdown 9/10/2008-11/10/2008

Over the last two months, the financial systems of the world have collapsed. Almost everyone who made money on stocks has taken a financial drubbing. There's a lot of uncertainty, and people are wondering if we're headed for another great depression. Who knows what the future will bring? The Lord has not given me any new revelations. But I do believe this economic meltdown was necessary to bring us one step closer to receiving the Mark of the Beast. (Rev.3:16-18) A numbered system would make it a lot easier for all of us. A simple mark or chip on the right hand or forehead seems logical. This way every nation and state would know who has what and everyone would be more accountable. It's all a prelude organized by the powers that rule the world. Am I worried? Yes and no. I've lived securely all my days, and it's hard to watch my family and friends lose their retirement and their securities. As a teacher, it hasn't affected me yet, but I'm sure it will when the cutbacks start kicking in. Right now, I still have all the things that have made me comfortable for years. I've also traveled as a vagabond, and it's made me realize that I can probably live through anything. I still have food on the table, shelter, and energy to light my stove. In the future these luxuries might fall by the wayside. Meanwhile, I'm waiting around to see what's going to happen next.

Receiving my Masters Degree in education is just around the corner, and I'm also working on getting citizenship in Europe. The degree will mean my paycheck will go up a little bit and that I'll be able to pay off some of my dues. An EU passport will mean I'll have an escape plan just in case something terrible happens to America. If I'm one of the lucky ones who survive, I'll consider it a sign that the Day of the Lord is around the corner. Until then, I'm going about my business. I'm working, doing my time, and pretending that everything's okay. I'm watching the baseball playoffs and football on TV. But deep down inside there's a gnawing sense inside me that's saying, "Everything's not okay." Do you sense it? At any rate, it might be a good idea for both of us to get right with God. I'd hate to find us at the final judgment with all our sins upon our souls.

Note: We have a new president. Many Americans see Obama as a glimmer of hope after many years of war and corruption. Is he going to be the one who solves all our problems and restores our country's reputation abroad? Probably not, but maybe he'll be a just president, and he'll do what's right for the people and not for the lobbyists. I suppose miracles can happen, yet I'll have to wait and see like everyone else.

12 Death & Disease 11/11/08-12/27/08

My dad is dying. Apparently he had some malignant bacteria in his leg that turned into a flesh eating disease. Within a day or so, it had spread from his calf, and it went all the way up his leg. It looked like gangrene. So the doctor tells him, "We either remove the skin or you die." They removed the skin from his toes all the way up to his hip, and now he's hooked up to life support fighting for his every breath.

He's survived heart attacks, open-heart surgery, a stroke, pancreatic cancer, diabetes, and a multitude of ailments, but I don't know if he's going to beat death this time. It comes for everyone, and it's looking like his time is up. It's the same with the planet earth. It's sick. It's dying, and mankind is the bacteria that's killing the planet. We'll either kill everything on earth, or the earth will spit us out like a disease and erupt with a volcanic rage of anger. It's coming! Oh, believe me it's coming! The signs of disease are on every corner of the globe. Look around! Open your eyes! Even the scientists are predicting doomsday scenarios. Mankind is a flesh eating disease, and we are killing the planet.

I'm forty years old right now, and I can't live forever. Ultimately my body is going to fail like my father's. He's sixty-seven. As for mankind, I'll give us thirty or forty years, at most, before there's an all out nuclear confrontation. I hope I'm wrong, but that's what I'm predicting. Hell, I've been wrong before. I thought we were on the brink of destruction during Reagan's reign as President, and that was decades ago. So maybe there is hope??? I'm preparing for the worst just in case. I have my flask of oil filled to the rim, and I'm waiting on the Lord. I have my passport, my backpack, my traveling *Bible,* and all my important paperwork ready to go. On the other hand, why bother? I'd almost rather go out with the first nukes. It would save me a lot of time and suffering. You might think differently on this issue, and that's okay. Maybe nuclear winter will be like a trip to the Bahamas or something??? But if you do survive, pack up all the canned goods you can find. Put your gun inside your holster, and get ready for the rollercoaster ride of your life. Be prepared for anguish and misery. No matter what you do, don't take the Mark of the Beast! It will be on your right hand or forehead. And if you give into your hunger pangs, you'll have all eternity to ponder what you've lost. Best of luck, and may the Lord be with you!

13 Goodbye Uncle Jim 12/28/08-2/6/09

They buried Uncle Jim two days ago. A week before he passed away I visited him. I was sort of like Isaiah, the prophet, visiting Hezekiah and telling him to "put his house in order." (2 Kings 20) I told Uncle Jim the same, but I didn't give him any hope that he was going to live fifteen more years on earth. I did tell him about Jesus and our eternal hope in heaven. I think my uncle was really listening, and I do hope he made peace with God before he passed away. At the funeral, I was one of the speakers. I tried to comfort those mourning that death is not the end. I told everyone that we live on forever and ever-some with God and some without. I truly hope Uncle Jim is one of the ones who made the right choice in the end. Heaven wouldn't be the same without him. He was such a character and a great man.

As for the rest of you, I hope you don't wait until you're on your deathbed to believe in God. There's no guarantee you'll see death coming. It might sneak up on you and take your life away when you least expect it. Who knows, we might have lung cancer like Uncle Jim and not even know it; hence, we all need to put our house in order and listen to the small still voice of God before it's too late.

My dad's been in the hospital for over a month, and they had to chop off his leg due to disease. He's recovering, and he'll probably have to live out the rest of his days in a wheelchair. Someone asked me, "Enoch, what's your take on all this?" I'm not sure what to think. In some ways I feel it would have been better if he passed onto the next life instead of enduring all the pain he has gone through. If he survives, he'll be dependent on my mother, and it seems rather cruel in a way. But maybe it will give him more time to repent and believe. And maybe none of it will matter. Maybe he's doomed for the Lake of Fire. I'll leave it in God's hands because I've tried many times to reach out to him with the Gospel, but it seems like he doesn't want to hear it. I want him to have that house by the beach and a mansion in heaven because I love him, but he's going to miss out on everything if he doesn't accept the Lord.

Yes, this is what's been happening over the last month. Death and disease are making their presence known. I try to comfort those in need, and I'm constantly at the hospital. It's a drag. The place smells like medicine and puke, and everyone tries to be so positive. Even the doctors say, "We're going to try this," but we all know the patients are guinea pigs, and the odds are stacked against them. I do believe they are trying their best, but it makes me realize we're still living in the Dark Ages, and we'll probably be there for a long time to come.

PART C: THE DECLINE OF WESTERN CIVILIZATION

14 In the Name of Allah… 2/7/09-4/5/09

The prophecies seem to be falling into place. The G20 Summit and the cry from Russia and China to bring about a new world currency to replace the dollar are signs that the number of the beast is lurking beyond the horizon. When will Lucifer get the balls to try and pull this thing off? C'mon…bring it on! There are many of us who've been waiting for the real deal for years. And I'm one of them. Are you? I'm tired of living in this fallen world. Let Lucifer have his fifteen minutes of fame because Christ's reign will last forever and ever… Don't get me wrong, I'm all for preserving the environment and trying to salvage what's left, but at the rate we're going, there will be nothing left in a century or so. Even today everything's dead and dying and now the Muslim world is going to get nukes. These are dangerous times, and there's no turning back! As Yeats once wrote, "Things fall apart. The centre cannot hold. Mere anarchy is loosed upon the world."

The Iranians might have nukes already, and if a crazy terrorist gets their hands on one, we can be sure of one thing, they will be the ones who are stupid enough to open Pandora's Box. "In the name of Allah, the merciful, and you're all gonna die! Ahhhh!!!" It should read, "In the name of Allah, a false god and Muhammad, his false prophet." They're just like the Beast and the False Prophet spoken of in the *Book of Revelation*. That's right, the Nation of Islam, you've been worshipping a false god all your life. Wake up, Islam! Read your *Bible* and pay attention to the contradictions with the *Quran*. The *Old Testament* outdates the *Quran* by thousands of years, and the *New Testament* by 600 years. The *Quran* is false, and Muhammad lied to you long ago. Yeah, I know I should be killed and all that other propaganda you've been fed your whole life. All I'm asking of you is to research the facts yourself. I'm trying to help you, Islam. I'm telling you the truth. If at the end of the day you still want to chop off my head, then so be it. If that's your solution, then you've already proven my point.

As for everything else, I received a financial blessing by getting my house payment lowered. Phew…I can finally breathe again and not have to constantly think about money. As for the poor and helpless, hang in there! Your time in prison is almost up. During the Millennium, you'll never have to thirst or hunger again, and you won't have to be afraid no more.

Note: I'm at peace with the House of Islam. I just disagree with Muhammad's teachings. I believe YHWH is the one and only true God.

15 Lukewarm 4/6/09-5/13/09

It's easy to slip back into the doldrums as you're waiting for the world to end. So what do you do? You go back to business, work your 9 to 5 job, and sit around twiddling your thumbs. You're not hot or cold but compromised with your dick in your hand, masturbating to Asherath or some other foreign god. Oh, wait a second! That's not you, it's me, and that's what I've been doing for the last month or so. You know, come to think about it, I've been worshipping these foreign gods not for months but for years. In fact, I think a decade has passed already. Burp, I'm full. I think I'll have some more dessert. Wasn't I supposed to be in a race or something? Isn't that what the hare said to the tortoise? Or maybe that's what Paul said to the Church of Corinth? Hell, I don't know. I know I read it somewhere? Maybe it's the *Book of Hebrews*??? Lately my mind is not as sharp as it used to be. Truthfully, I can't remember a lot of things. I suppose that's why I keep making the same mistakes over and over again. It's like I'm caught in a time loop, and I'm Captain Pickard or something on Star Trek. Are you following me? If not, go back and have yourself another latte or maybe a diet Coke. I know it will come back to you eventually???

In the meantime, I keep thinking about what Stoner, the mathematician, said. If Jesus fulfilled only 8 out of the 300 or so prophecies written about Him in the Old Testament, the odds would be 1 in 10 to the 17th power that He could fulfill them. That's 1 in 100,000,000,000,000,000. Jeez, that's a lot of zeros. I wonder what the odds would be if he calculated all 300 of them. The odds would be astronomical. It would be like trying to win the California lottery multiplied by a trillion or something. But I still donate my dollar every week. You never know??? I'll tell you what though, you and I are both suckers, and it's time for us to wake up! But why do we keep finding ourselves heading back to the crap's table? Do we think we're finally going to have a run? Honestly, it's been a long time since I've been on a hot streak. And it's not like I'm crapping out all the time either. I'm just a lukewarm shooter. Of course, I'm talking figuratively here. I hope you're still following me. Sometimes I get lost in metaphors when I really need to speak literally. Maybe if I put on an old DK's record I'll find some inspiration. Where's Jello when you need him? I need something to get my blood pumping again. How about another earthquake or a pandemic flu or an economic meltdown? Man, those terrorists got us running in circles. Excuse me, I mean the news media. Oh just bomb us and get it over with already! I'll ride the mushroom cloud with Holden Caulfield and be raptured up to heaven!!!

16 Running with the Devil 5/14/09-5/30/09

Summer approaches. It's usually a time of travel and leisure for me because I'm a teacher. This year, however, I'm out of funds and trying to pay off my debts like the rest of the country. At least I haven't lost my job or my home yet. I suppose those go hand in hand. So what am I supposed to do with my spare time? I know I'll be occupied for at least a month with a summer school class. After I pass this class I'll have my Masters Degree in Education. "Now ain't that special???" Not really. It simply means I put the time in sitting on my ass and was willing to write a whole bunch of essays and process worthless information. Sure, some of it was enlightening, but most of it doesn't apply to real life situations. I only got this degree so I'd get a bump up on the pay scale. Yes, I know it's vain, but that's how the system works. I'm just playing the game like the rest of you. I'm meeting the standards, so I can move up the ladder and retire comfortably. In truth, I'm not counting on my retirement funds to be there, but I'm planning for it anyway. I think by then something disastrous will occur, and I'll be shit out of luck. Meanwhile, I'm plodding along. By the end of the year I'll be completely out of debt if I'm disciplined, and I'll be able to travel somewhere in 2010. Maybe I'll go to Europe or South America or Thailand again??? I could teach over there and make enough money to pay off my dues. That's what I keep telling myself, but you know and I know that I'm only thinking about foreign pussy. Yes, there's something to be said about exotic cuisines, and I'm not talking food here. Even right now, my mind is filled with evil deeds. My dick is getting hard in my pants, and I'm all over the place. Phew Lord, you have to tame the devil in me before I'm swept away in sin. Van Halen said, "I found the simple life ain't so simple when I jumped out on that road," and I have to agree with them. Being good is not easy, especially after being where I've been. I've engaged in too many wicked deeds, and I've gotten a taste for them. How about you? Are you "Running with the Devil" too? I know it's a dim-witted question, but I thought I'd throw it out there anyway. So what can we do? How are we going to escape the abyss? In my case, I know if I leave it in my hands, I'll be wandering to the whore's den, so I guess I'll have to trust the Lord and pray that He bails my ass out of jail again. He hasn't let me down even though I've failed Him on many occasions. God's still cool with me though. I'm family, and we go way back. Does that mean I can get away with murder like David did? No, it merely means I have a friend in high places, and I'm covered for my sin. "Peace out" as my students always say and try to take the high road as often as you can.

17 A Higher Calling 5/31/09-6/16/09

School's out for summer, so I went up to Big Bear for the weekend with my cousins and some of my brother's friends. It was fun. We went mountain biking, wake boarding, played horseshoes, ping pong, and poker. I got really wasted though and was stoned out of my mind one night. In fact, I couldn't even count correctly or keep my thoughts straight. It was a really bad testimony, and I feel horrible about it. Two times during the trip people asked me questions on my faith, but I was too out of it to answer properly. It made me realize that I need to cut out the drunken behavior in my life and act more like a man of faith. In reality, I might have to cut out marijuana altogether because I can't seem to function properly when I'm under the influence, and I'm around a lot of people. I'm not a chronic user either, but those few times a year are still too much. It's making my testimony impure, and it's stumbling others. So from now on I'm going to try and do things differently. By God's grace I'll be able to keep it altogether. Personally, I don't think ganja or alcohol or having a good time is evil, but it does seem to be a stumbling block for others. If these substances are used in moderation and only on special occasions, I believe it's in accordance with God. But is it for kings and priests and prophets? I don't know. Maybe we're supposed to be like the Nazarites who don't drink from the vine? I'm not for sure, but I definitely need to make some changes after looking back at my boisterous, drunken behavior last weekend. So if I offended anyone, I'm sorry. I'll try to do better next time.

As for the last two weeks, nothing major has happened. I turned in my grades and completed another year of teaching the *Bible as Literature*. I held to the Word and did my best in reaching these students. I hope it will make a difference in their lives, and they'll come to the knowledge of the truth someday. Regardless, their blood is no longer required of me, and I can wash my hands saying, "It's up to them now." I just wish I could do the same. I'm a much better teacher of the Faith than one who lives by its laws. In reality, I break the law all the time and pray that I don't get caught. I'm not saying I've done any heinous crimes, but I am one to step over the line when I see all the stupid laws being made by our legislators. The U.S. and the State of California are so bogged down by red tape that I don't know if we can call ourselves the Land of the Free anymore. But I do know the Millennial Reign will be better. We won't have to live by laws anymore. We'll just say, "Know the Lord," and everything will be understood.

18 Pride 6/17/09-7/5/09

If for some reason my name becomes one that everyone recognizes, I want to make myself perfectly clear that I am not a holy man. I do not deserve to be worshipped or even idolized. I don't want to be "Nobody's Hero" as the Stiff Little Fingers used to say. I'm a sinner. I have many vices, and if you hear some deviant story about me someday, it might be true. I figure I better come clean now before the vultures eat me alive. I do try my best at being meek and modest, but be aware, it's all a front. I'm as proud as anyone else, and my evil deeds far outweigh my good ones. I am only here because the Lord has lifted me up. I have no supernatural powers. I cannot see into the future. I'm merely stating what the Lord has revealed to me. He deserves all the honor and praise even though I like to hear the sound of clapping hands and cheering.

Other things: I went to the Angels game last night against the Orioles and saw a fireworks show after the game for the 4th of July. They were playing all these patriotic songs, and I have to admit I'm damn proud to be an American. I've seen a lot of countries in the world, but there's still no place like the good ol' U.S.A. It's too bad our power is waning. As I think about it, tears come to my eyes knowing that my country once stood for truth, justice, and freedom. Now I'm not sure what we represent. How about greed, gluttony, and imperialism? I believe we got lost somewhere along the way, and we're going to have to pay for these crimes that we've committed.

19 The Fall of the West 7/6/09-8/13/09

During the early Punk Movement, there was a record titled *The Decline of Western Civilization*. That era foresaw the direction that we were headed in as a society. They were right. We have lost our moral values, and we have lost our conscience. No longer can we decipher between right and wrong because according to Nietzsche everything is "beyond good or evil." We have been seduced and have veered off the path of truth. Thus, the Lord has taken the visions away from the prophets, and our pastors are no longer feeding us bread from the Word because there are no holy priests to set us on our way. They've all become talk show hosts and porno queens. "This is who we are" as spoken from the doomsday television series *Millennium*. We are on the path of destruction. I see ashes and dead bodies and scorched streets. I see drought. I see famine. I see disease. In my comfortable shelter in the suburbs, it all seems unreal. It couldn't happen here? Could it? Could an entire city burn down, and its populace be laid to waste? It's all beyond comprehension as I drink my bottled water and eat my processed food. To me, it all seems like footage from one of those old war documentaries. But it's 1945 in my head. I'm in Hiroshima, and everything's alright. The madman on the corner said, "Get out of town!" but I spit in his direction laughing with the crowd. Yet if one reads the prophecies, it seems so clear. Everything is lining up. It appears as if one domino could bring it all tumbling down. My buddy once asked me, "Enoch, give me an example. Give me proof." So I quoted Matthew 24, Ezekiel 37, and several of the 300 prophecies that Jesus fulfilled in His lifetime. But my friend rationalized everything away. He said, "That could apply to any generation. Your so-called prophecies are irrelevant to me." To an extent, I understand his opinion, but at some point you have to say, "That's pretty amazing." In any case, I have little doubt these are the latter days. I believe the Day of the Lord is just around the corner, and if it doesn't happen in my lifetime, I will be surprised. There are too many so-called "coincidences" falling into place.

"Place your order. Place your bet. As you play poker the time clock ticks. The thief ain't coming or summer's near. Roll them dice or flee in fear."
Misconceptions by the Faithful Church

20 Bob Marley, Joseph Smith, & the Rapture
8/14/09-8/28/09

Summer is coming to a close. I'm out of funds, so I'm not as downtrodden about the approaching school year. In fact, I'm sort of expectant. At least I still have a job, food on the table, running water, and electricity. Most people throughout the world don't have these luxuries, so I'm not complaining. It's a shame that not everyone has these basic necessities. In the Kingdom Age we'll have all this and more. Yes, it's going to be glorious during the 1,000-year reign. In the back of my mind I wonder if it's all a pipedream. One thousand years of peace and prosperity??? C'mon, how gullible are you making me out to be? Homo sapiens are not a peaceful race. I'm hopeful though. I'm waiting for the coming Messiah and trudging along during these pre-apocalyptic days. I suppose if I lost everything, I would wander the earth like Caine. I'd let the Lord supply my basic necessities and make my final stand. In the meantime, I'm biding my time. I'm preparing for death and destruction. I'm keeping a watchful eye out for the Man of Lawlessness, and I'm searching for Elijah. What about you? Are you twiddling your thumbs? Do you have your flask of oil ready? Are you expecting God to miraculously lift you up in the clouds, so you won't have to suffer during the Tribulation? Maybe it will happen, but it probably won't. Most likely, you're going to have to suffer like the early church and die for your faith. So if you find yourself suddenly "left behind," you can come over to my house and share some of my rations.

As for other stuff, I've been studying the Rastafarian religion lately, and I must say their doctrine is as messed up as the Mormons and Jehovah Witnesses. Sure, Bob Marley stood up for justice and righteousness, but he believed that Haile Selassie was the Messiah. Did you know that? Most people don't. Sorry to stir the boat, but the former Prince of Ethiopia was just a man. He was not the incarnation of God (Jah) or the second coming of Jesus Christ. So in a way, Bob Marley was a false prophet like Joseph Smith and the Watchtower Society. Yes, I loved Bob Marley's music too, and he's still on my Top 10 list, but with regards to his faith, the Rastafarian Prophet was deceived. As for the Mormons and Jehovah Witnesses, I've met so many good and honorable people who've been raised in these religions; however, their beliefs are as skewed as the Scientologists.

21 Sports Addiction 8/29/09-9/27/09

Going back to work and football season seem to overwhelm me with too many distractions. I don't have much time for the Lord, and this distresses me. I'm running around going here and there putting on hold the profitable things about life. I just wish I could keep my focus. There are so many idols that take up a majority of my time. In fact, one could argue that sports are my religion, not Christianity. I spend hours upon hours watching the NFL, college football, Major League Baseball, the NBA, and the NHL. Then there are the television programs, the DVDs, and the Internet. Sometimes I feel overwhelmed by these technological distractions. The Devil has us so entertained that there's no time for the Lord. Are you following me? Do you feel the same? Anyway, I thought it might be a good idea to point out the obvious. Sometimes we need to tune out the madness of this world and find time to meditate in prayer. It's easier said than done, but at some point we need to ask ourselves, "Whom do we serve?" For example, it's like the life of my retired father. He's in gambling pools and fantasy football leagues like everyone else in the family, and he spends 24/7 in front of the television set waiting for the next fix. One would think being so close to death he would spend more time thinking about the greater picture. Well, I guess it's a lesson for us all. We need to put down our knick-knacks and ask ourselves what's truly important. It will all be tested by fire in the end. Are any of our hours in front of the television beneficial to our souls? I believe 99% of it will be burned as stubble. And if the average American household spends about eight hours a day watching TV in a 24-hour period, think of what we could accomplish with those hours if we used them more profitably. The possibilities are endless…

PART D: THE UNHEARD MUSIC

22 Post Office Shooting 9/28/09

It was about 6:00 A.M. in the morning, and I had stopped off at the post office before driving to work. I had just put my mail in the drive through mailbox and started to turn into the main road when this guy sped by and honked at me. I didn't see him coming, but I thought he was driving too fast, so I honked back at him. The man in the car didn't like that, so he stopped his car about fifty meters away and looked out his window. That pissed me off. I put the pedal to the floor, stopped right next to him, and rolled down my right window. His window was already down, and he was yelling obscenities at me, so I cursed back at him. It was getting uglier by the moment because neither one of us was backing down. He screamed, "Get out of the car, you pussy," waved at me to follow him, and pulled over to the side of the road. Suddenly, I came back to my senses. I thought to myself, "Do I really want to get in a fight with this guy over something so stupid?" and I drove away slowly. The man, however, didn't let up. He pulled up next to me. He was hanging halfway out of his car, and he started calling me a pussy again and all sorts of other names. This angered me, and it flipped my switch. I pulled out my 9mm handgun I kept hidden under my seat. I popped in the clip, pulled back the barrel, and shot about ten rounds in his direction. The man's face changed from anger to fear in half a second, and he ducked back into his car to get away. Meanwhile, my finger was on the trigger firing. I think I shot him, too. He was so close. I then pushed down on the gas pedal, ran a red light up the road, and scurried onto the freeway.

On the drive to work I had this cold sweat, and my mind was racing about a hundred miles per hour. "Did I shoot him? Did anyone see? Maybe I killed him." I can't be for sure because I sped out of there so fast. Luckily, it was still dark when the incident occurred, so I don't think anyone saw us. And even if they did, I doubt they could read my license plate. In reality, I don't know for sure.

For the next month, I kept reading the fine print in the newspapers to see if anything turned up, but there was nothing written. I was too scared to research the hospitals myself, so I didn't make any calls. Instead, I laid low and hoped I got away with it. Luckily, I was prepared. In my guns, I always make sure all the bullets are clean and that there are no prints on them. I do that every time I reload my guns because I know how short my fuse is.

Looking back, it's been almost five years since the post office incident, but I still think about it all the time. I'm not sure if I killed someone or not. I hope I didn't. I've thought about turning myself in to get rid of the guilt and make amends, but what purpose would that serve? I would probably go to jail and destroy my entire life in the process. Thus, I've remained silent about the whole confrontation until now. It's almost like a burden's been lifted off my soul by telling all of you. As for God, I've confessed my sin to Him many times over, and I think He's forgiven me. I suppose I won't know if I really committed murder until I'm standing at the judgment seat of God. If I did, I'm sure there's going to be some retribution.

Since the post office incident, I don't carry a gun in my car any longer. I had to learn my lesson the hard way. Also, I try not to push people's buttons anymore when I'm driving. This incident has taught me a lesson in humility. I now try to remain calm and blow it off when I'm on the road and I encounter bad drivers. Sometimes it's difficult to keep my anger in check, but over the years, God has been teaching me how to turn the other cheek and let it go.

23 Prayer, Meditation, & Loving One Another
9/29/09-10/24/09

They say "Idle time is the Devil's playground," and it's probably true because lately I've been idle with the Lord. I've been keeping myself busy with this and that, but what have I done to edify others? What have I done lately that's going to last eternally in the heavens? Very little. I imagine many of you would answer the questions the same way. Don't get me wrong, I'm not teaching one of those works based ideologies. I'm just saying we could do a lot more with our time for the Lord. Number one would be more prayer time with God. That means more interaction and interpersonal communication with the Creator of the universe. We need to be more intimate with the Lord. We need less "Our Fathers" and "In the name of the Lord Jesus." We need to replace this dialogue with words that come from the heart. We need to communicate with the Lord like we would with an intimate lover. That means anything goes, and there's no holding back. If we do this, we will truly be the bride at the marriage feast. Number two, we need to spend more time in the Word. That means reading, listening, and getting the *Bible* into our heads by any means necessary. This will help us on our walk and give the Lord a platform for speaking unto us. Of course, He will always do that through our reborn spirits, but this is one of the best avenues for speaking to us directly. The third action I think we need to do is start loving one another. We need to set aside our ambitions, our goals, our forked, witty tongues and sincerely start to care about one another. Personally, I've noticed this with my own students. I spend far too much of my energy on discipline and order, but when I just love the kids, these things seem to fall in line. It's true, discipline and order are important, especially with rebellious and disruptive teenagers, but the best way to influence their behavior is to love and care for them. And if we apply the principle of "love your neighbor as yourself" to all aspects of our lives, we truly will be following in Jesus' footsteps.

Wow! I wasn't really planning on writing about these topics, but the Lord sort of took my pen today like he does sometimes with his pastors and overseers. He directs their thoughts in the middle of a sentence, and the whole congregation feels like the Lord truly spoke to their hearts that day. Everyone leaves the meeting refreshed and ready to take on the day or week inspired. I hope my short message does the same.

24 Down There by the Train 10/25/09-11/27/09

Thanksgiving Day weekend. Some people are here. Some are not. Some friends have moved on and some are with us. In any case, we're all getting older. Our time will expire like those who have passed away. We may die young or we may die old. We may die in the Tribulation or of natural causes. All I know is that the time clock is ticking for us all. At some point death will find us, and we will meet our Maker like every generation that has gone before us. So we must be prepared. We must be ready. For the believers, this is your reality check. It is time to make amends and repent of your sin for you know not the day or hour that you will die or when the Lord will come. As for the unbelievers, there's still time to make a choice for the Lord. If you wind up in hell, don't blame it on fate. You've had many chances to believe in God, but you have held onto your freedom and pride instead. I know you are your own man or woman, and you will not bow down to any god, but what have you bowed down to instead? Pleasure? Sex? Money? The idols of this world? Well, I've bowed down to them all as well. And what did it get us? Nothing, emptiness, it was all vanity. And now that I'm getting older, I can see my folly and the light is becoming clearer. Will you be shrouded in darkness until the end of your days, or will you join us in heaven? There isn't much you have to do but simply repent and bow your knee unto Jesus. Yeah, I know it all sounds so corny. I laughed too, but I didn't make up the rules. God did. The rule is you must believe in Jesus if you want to be saved. Not Buddha, not Allah, or any other religious leader or teaching. Jesus is the "way, truth, and life." (Jn.14:6) I know it seems unfair, and I've heard all your objections. I object with you!!! The fact of the matter, however, is that this is the only way to inherit the Kingdom of God. This is the agreement He made with humanity. He is our sacrifice and Savior. So where do we go from here? I suppose it's all up to you. Make a choice for Him or continue down the same dissatisfied path you've always walked. It's not my job to convert or persuade you. I'm just a messenger, a prophet of God, sent out to proclaim His Word and the impending Day of the Lord.

25 The Path of Least Resistance 11/28/09-12/05/09

Another project finished. Now I suppose it's time to hibernate for the winter. It's amazing I've been in numerous bands and recorded many CDs. I've written tons of literature, and I've accomplished much artistically in my life. Academically, I've earned my degrees, and I've been teaching for over sixteen years. Now what do I do? I suppose I'll finish this testimony. It will take me to the end of my days. Hopefully someone will read my writings and listen to my music and I can influence or help someone along the way. At least now everything is available to the public. It's funny though. We run this way and that our whole lives and almost all of it's insignificant. All that will matter in the end is what we did for the Lord. The rest will burn like Southern California.

Looking back at my life, I'm not really sure what will make it through the fire. I've tried to "walk the road less traveled," but many of those unpaved roads led me nowhere. I've discovered that there are consequences for every bad trail we take. Usually it ends in misery and pain. Still, I wouldn't change a thing. Well…most things. I know I was supposed to take the straight and narrow path like it says in the scriptures, but if I did that, I really wouldn't have any stories to tell. For a writer, this is worse than death. You just have to take the good with the bad and live in the gray every now and then. Haven't we all compromised a little? Aren't we all like the Church of Laodiceans? (Rev.3:14-22) I'm not saying that that's okay. I'm just saying we all have our shortcomings. Thank God there is forgiveness for sins! So now what? What advice do I have to offer? Solomon would say, "Fear God and keep His commandments,"

(Ecc.12:13) but I say, "Seek the Lord for help and avoid the path of least resistance."

26 Yin Yang 2009 12/6/09-12/27/09

2009 was a rough year for many Americans. Lots of people lost their jobs and their homes. The economy is still in the dumps. Hopefully things will get better, but I don't know if it will. People with the gift of prophecy don't usually predict economic outcomes. They simply edify, exhort, and console. I do know one truth; however, people typically turn to God during rough times. Others blame Him for everything. I suppose we have to accept the yin yang of everything and go forward with our lives. No one said life was going to be easy. And if they did, they lied. This applies to the rich and the poor. You have to accept both the good and bad times. This is all insignificant though. The real test is to see which way we go during our trials and tribulations. A bigger test is to see how we fare in times of plenty. In both areas, I have to give myself a "C" average. I'm not the worst, and I'm not the best. How have you fared? I imagine most of you are a lot like me. If you fared better, keep doing what you're doing. If you fared worse, maybe it's time to make a change. There's no reason to repeat the same mistakes over and over again. Am I preaching to myself or am I preaching to you? Both I suppose.

As for the last month, it's been pretty much the same on my end. I'm still working my job. I haven't been fired yet. My work record is not pearly white, but I do think I'm helping the 175 teens I teach each year. I'm planting seeds in the next generation and hoping that they will bear some fruit in the future. As for the Devil and his minions, they show their face from time to time. They're trying to tear me down, but God has a hedge around me. His holy angels won't let me down. Fight on brothers! Let's have a drink sometime. I'll see you on the road to heaven.

27 Pornography 12/28/09-1/10/10

The last couple of weeks, I've gotten off track. In fact, I've been walking in a trance. First of all, sports, TV, and movies have me completely mesmerized that they are occupying my soul like a roaming legion of demons. Second, I've spent far too much time looking at pornography. The Internet truly has added a new dimension to the porn industry. Wait 'till they get holograms! I may never leave my 8x10 abode! Is anyone else having the same struggles as me? I don't think I'm making the cut. Trying to remain faithful to one woman is like riding a bicycle with no hands as you dodge in and out of traffic. There's bound to be an accident or misstep. My whole life has been a giant misstep, even though the Spirit has given me the gift of teaching and prophecy. I've been so blessed that I could probably pastor an entire church, but I know I'd probably lead many astray like Brother George did when he committed adultery. Please don't blame the Lord when you see Christians fall from grace. I've seen more than my share over the years, and my name is near the top of the list. I've been a fool and a failure. Even at this moment, I can't keep my mind and flesh in check. It's like I'm in a hypnotizing trance, and I can't seem to wake up. I can't escape this flesh of mine, and I'm always getting into trouble. I'm a poor witness. Sure I can speak the words about what's wrong and right, but I can't put it into action. Are you falling short of expectations too? Lord, help me out of my abyss and anyone else who is going through the same turmoil. Eve's waving that apple in my face, and I swear I'm going to take a bite out of it!

Note: Brother George was a lead pastor in a Fullerton, CA church.

28 Infidelity 1/11/10

It was Back to School night and one of my former students came by to visit me. She was a nerdy Latina girl with a perfect ass, and she had a niece who was now attending the school. Anyway, it was a slow Back to School night, so Lucia and I reminisced about the old days. She told me how she was at Long Beach State now, and how she was one year away from completing her B.A. in Psychology. Lucia then told me how she had a crush on me back when she was a senior, and she came by the school tonight so she could pay me a visit. At first, I laughed and said, "You're kidding me. I'm old enough to be your father." She flirted back, "No you're not. You look like you're still in your thirties." I said, "Thanks a lot, but I'm almost 40." Anyhow, the two of us continued talking like this for a while until a parent walked in and we had to part company.

A month later, I saw Lucia again at Long Beach State because I was also attending the school working on my Masters Degree. We crossed each other's path in one of the halls, and we struck up a conversation. We then decided to go get a beer at the campus pub. Before we knew it, one beer turned into two beers, and two beers turned into three, and the conversation started to heat up. She told me how she had a teacher-student fantasy that she masturbated to all the time. I said, "Oh really, and who is the teacher you're fantasizing with?" She leaned over in her chair, revealed a little bit of her cleavage, and whispered in my ear, "You,

Mr. E." She kissed me on the cheek and laughed lightheartedly saying, "You want to live out that fantasy?" My dick instantly rose in my pants. I tried to shuffle in my chair to hide my erection, but she noticed and smiled. I shook my head and stuttered, "Lu…Lu…cia…the girl in the front row with straight A's. Who would have thought you were so forward?" Time froze for a moment. We both looked each other in the eyes. Neither of us spoke as we both sat contemplating her last words. I was just about to say something to kill the silence when Lucia spoke up abruptly. She said, "What do you say, Mr. E? I live close by and my roommate works nights. How about you come over? I still have one of my uniforms from back in the day. I could put it on for you."

At that point, I really didn't have a choice. This enticing young woman had seduced me. Twenty minutes later, we were at her place having another drink. We started making out on her couch, and we were both getting pretty aroused. She whispered, "Wait here. I'll be right back," and she drifted off into the back room. I sat impatiently on the couch awaiting her return. Finally, Lucia came down the hallway, and it was definitely worth the wait. She was wearing a Catholic schoolgirl uniform, and she was holding a ruler in her hand. She said, "I've been a very bad girl. I need a spanking…" The rest of the night got even more out of control, but I'll let you fill in the blanks about what happened next.

Looking back, I have to admit this first encounter with my former student was one of the best sexual experiences of my life. At the time, I was completely entranced by this provocative, young woman. She was beautiful and seductive. On the other hand, Lucia was one of my greatest downfalls. The two of us had a brief affair that lasted throughout the semester. It was something I tried to keep hidden from my wife, but she became suspicious and found out. I was telling too many lies to her, and eventually they caught up with me. After that, everything unraveled. Lucia and I broke up, and the wife and I talked about separating or getting a divorce. In the end, we worked through my unfaithfulness and decided to stay together.

Overall, it's been hard. At first the pain and tears were endless, but now that a couple of years have passed, the tears come less often. We're still dealing with the trust issue, but it's getting better. As for Kiana, she had every right in the world to leave me, and Biblically, she would be justified to do so. There would be no mark on her record. I hope she doesn't change her mind and decide to take that path because I still love my wife, and I want to grow old with her.

In retrospect, I was a fool to break my vows. I was caught up in my fleshly desires, and I never thought about the ramifications until it was too late. Despite the consequences, I learned a valuable lesson, and I found out the hard way why adultery is listed as one of the Ten Commandments. God put it in the Law to protect his children from all the pain and misery that follows infidelity. It is also one of the main reasons why God judged the Hebrew people. They were disloyal to Him and served other gods. I am like the Nation of Israel and David their king. I have been unfaithful to my wife and my God.

29 Sex Slaves 1/12/10-1/20/10

Isaiah walked about naked for three years. Jeremiah walked about with a yoke of bondage on his shoulders. Both of these were signs of a future outcome to befall the people of Israel. Is this what's next for our generation? I hope not, but I do know I've been degraded and exploited by online entertainment. I just can't seem to get enough lately. Have you fallen into this trap as well? If so, we have become slaves to sin. We serve the sex god of Asherah. We spend hours upon hours lost in the labyrinth of sex and pornography, and we cannot escape her Web. We have been freed and bought with a price by the Lord, but we still find ourselves slipping back into bondage. We look back longingly towards Egypt, and some of us have turned to salt like Lot's wife. But this is not the Days of Egypt or Sodom. These are the Last Days, and we are about to be judged for our crimes. Yet we still grovel upon our knees and serve our master obediently. We are subjugated and broken for all the world to see. We are laughed at, mocked, and put to open shame because of our disobedience. We will be like Haiti after the earthquake of 2010. We will have dirt on our faces. We will prostitute ourselves for food and water, and we will ask why this happened to us? It occurred because we have been disobedient for months, years, and even decades. We have turned our backs upon the Lord willingly knowing that the path we've chosen is the wrong one. The Lord cries, "Where are you, my prophets? Where are you, my priests?" They have forsaken the people. Their lives are compromised, and the people walk about like lost sheep in the wilderness. Yet there's still time before the dark days come upon us. It's time to truly turn from our sin and start anew. The Lord will forgive. He will give us strength to resist the desires of our flesh, and we will be one with our Maker once more. If not, we will be slaves to sin until the end of our days, and God will bring a strong judgment upon us.

Note: Asherah was the Queen of Heaven, an Old Testament god.

30 Forty-Two 1/21/10-2/14/10

It's my birthday today. I'm forty-two. I'm sitting here completely naked and writing about what's transpired the last few weeks. Nothing of magnitude has taken place because it's been a series of repeat episodes in my neck of the woods. I have a lot potential as do all of you, but I squander away my gifts and abilities on fruitless entertainment. Yes, I know it's true. I'm a middle-aged man whose body is more out of shape. My mind is not as sharp, and my soul is not where it needs to be. I look down at my decaying body and realize I don't have forever. The sands of time move forward, and soon the hourglass will be empty. I'm sitting here rocking back and forth reminiscing about the old days. I should be seizing the day with what time I have left.

I've come far over the years, yet I should be further down the road. There's so much more I could have accomplished in the time I've had, but I've squandered it away on unprofitable pursuits. I just need to keep my eyes focused on the Lord instead of giving into all the temptations of the world. In the West, we have everything, so it makes it much easier to get off track. At times I wonder if our cross is more difficult to bear than the cross of those living in poverty. When you're down-n-out, you have nowhere to turn but upward. But when you have it all, you get waylaid by this and that and you forget to call upon His name. So what am I trying to say??? I'm saying it's tough to be a believer on both sides of the tracks.

As for the last three weeks, my walk with the Lord has been weak. I'm still tripping over the same old sins. And sometimes I just don't give a damn. Some of these sins I've been doing so long that I don't even feel guilty when I'm doing them anymore. Yes, I'm in a fallen state, and I can't seem to find my way back home. His Spirit has not been strong within me, and I'm in Sheol.

31 Suicide 2/15/10-3/1/10

One of my students committed suicide yesterday. He hung himself over a girl. Seth was a senior. He was in my *Bible as Literature* class, but his life has come to an abrupt end. Last week, we had been discussing Judas and his betrayal. We went into detail about how he hung himself, and his bowels came out. I wonder if our readings affected Seth's method of execution. I hope not. That would truly bum me out. It's so sad. The event greatly upset the emotions of many of my students. We talked about it in class today, and I had the students write a letter of comfort and edification to the family. Apparently, he was also a believer. According to the Catholic Church, suicide is a mortal sin, and you automatically go to hell. There's no evidence of this doctrine in the Bible. It's true that one of the Ten Commandments states that "Thou shall not murder," (Ex.20:13) but is suicide considered murder? Does Seth deserve eternal separation from God because he did a rash act in a moment of extreme depression? In my opinion, I don't think so. The Bible states that "whosoever believes in Him shall not perish but have eternal life." (Jn.3:16) Therefore, I believe that if Seth genuinely believed, he is with the Lord at this very moment. Still, I think he will lose out on many rewards due to his impulsive action, but he will not lose his salvation. As for suicide itself, I think it's a terrible option. It leaves everyone wondering why they didn't see the signs. It makes you feel like dung on the ground that you weren't there in Seth's darkest hours. "If I only did this…If I only said that…" Damn it, Seth! What were you thinking? He was a good kid too. He was respectful, kind, and he looked like he had a bright future. Presently, those who knew Seth best must go forward with their lives and stop blaming themselves. He was young. He was foolish. One day we will meet up with him again in heaven. For now, the mourning has just begun for those who truly loved him.

32 Baggage in my Head 3/2/10-3/23/10

Teaching the Bible to others is really teaching the Bible to oneself. The warnings and exhortations are a lesson in humility. For instance, the other day I was teaching in James about how we need to be "doers of the Word" (Ja.1:23) not just speakers or hearers of the Word. This truly hits home for me because I'm really good at preaching the Word, but living the Word is a whole different matter. I'm still walking around like the heathen instead of putting on the "new self" (Col.3:10) like I was told. And sometimes I get so caught up in my vile deeds that I forget about God altogether. As of late, my communion with the Spirit has not been strong. At times I cannot feel Him at all. This made me realize that I need to put my house in order. I've really made a mess of things, and it's time for me to start throwing out the baggage. Once again, it's easier said than done. I have so much baggage swimming in my head that my mind is drowning in riffraff. I suppose I'll have to tackle each vice one at a time. Where to begin??? For me, I suppose it's in the area of fornication. If I can get that under control, I might actually be able to get some things done instead of wasting my talent on worthless entertainment. It's all going to burn in the end, and I'll have nothing to show for my labor. Yes, it's time to clean house and move on.

Right now, it's Saturday night. I'm alone like the old days when I was single. Back then I filled the void by being with someone, anyone, instead of being in solitary. It makes me realize how insignificant our lives are. If I died, there would be some tears from those who knew me, but they would quickly move on without me. Not much in life really matters. We're just passing through for a spell. At one moment it's spring then summer is upon us. To me, it feels like I'm in the fall of my life, and there are signs that winter is coming. I'm dying. My body's decaying, and I'm breathing hard with all my strength to live another year. Father, I'm tired. Is there hope for tomorrow?

33 Attack Upon Christendom 3/24/10-4/10/10

In the last century there seems to be a lot of people on the attack against Christianity, but what I keep hearing on the streets is the same old arguments being repeated over and over again. Sure, there are many reasons to shun the Christian faith; nevertheless, the evidence to prove there is a God and that Jesus truly is the Messiah is overwhelming. If you are a cynic, I would simply ask that you give both sides equal weighing and not taint your conclusions on the biases of the day. This will not be easy because there is so much bad representation out there that the true message of Jesus is getting lost in the shuffle. All I ask is that you look at the prophecies pertaining to Jesus yourself and see if they are credible. That means you will have to read the *Old Testament* prophets to see if it's true or not. And if you don't have the time, make time! I'm tired of listening to the same old excuses. Your eternal outcome may be at risk here.

As for the Big Bang Theory, I only have one thing to say, there had to be a Prime Mover. For example, if I showed you a computer, you would have to agree that someone made that computer. It didn't just come into existence all by itself. Someone had to make the intricacies of the machine just like someone made the universe and the human race. To me, it seems logical that God is the Creator of matter. He is the X factor.

Now there has been a lot of debate over the heaven and hell issue. How could God cast someone into the eternal flame, especially someone who has never heard the Word like the Indians or someone brought up in another religion? As the *The Who* once sang, "How can the deaf, dumb, and blind kid ever be saved?" To be honest, it doesn't seem fair does it? Of course, it doesn't. I do know God will be just though. He will be fair. He will be righteous. He will be far more righteous than any of us will ever be. I'm going to leave it in His hands. I hope you do the same.

To sum up, there are many other reasons to discount the God of the Bible, but I don't have enough time and space to cover every disputed issue. If science is your conundrum, research science, but please read the arguments by the scientific elite on both sides of the fence. If there is some other issue blocking your way to knowing God, please let down your guard and listen to the other side for a change. If at the end of the day you still don't believe, at least you can say you tried with all your heart and mind. Prophesy, archaeology, and historical evidence were the proofs that convinced me, but to be candid, I don't really understand why some people have faith and others don't. I suppose it's a blessing from above.

34 Usury 4/11/10-4/22/10

About five years ago, the wife and I bought a home. I was proud and happy about my venture into the real estate market, but after I saw how much we'd have to pay each month, my elation turned to sorrow when hard times came down upon us. As for my home, I bought it for $650,000, and today I still owe $650,000. How is this possible? It's because I have an interest only loan. I can't afford a loan that will pay off my balance, but I have paid over $150,000 in interest over the last five years. Is this just? Is this fair? I don't think so. In addition, I've used credit cards for over twenty years, and I have finally paid them off after shifting money around for years and years and skimping by on nickels and dimes like a poor man. And I have a good job. I've worked hard since I was 15 years old, and I've always paid my dues, but why can't I seem to get a piece of the American Dream? It's because the banks and credit card companies are using an unjust usury system against us.

In the Law of Moses, it states, "You shall not charge interest to your countrymen/brothers: interest on money, food, or anything that may be loaned at interest. You may charge interest to a foreigner, but to your countryman you shall not charge interest." (Deut.23:19-20) This means that if you are a Hebrew you cannot charge interest against another person who is of the same race, but a Jew may charge interest against a Gentile. So it does appear there are some loopholes where interest may or may not be used based on the *Old Testament* Law. Does that mean that the banks and credit card companies need to charge interest at an accelerated rate? No, it does not, but that's what has happened in the United States and abroad. The bankers have the populace by the balls, and they function like loan sharks. This is unjust and the practice needs to be rectified. If not, I believe God will bring a strong judgment against companies and people who practice inflated usury.

A simple solution to the problem would be to make it illegal to charge exaggerated interest. This law would apply to Jew and Gentile alike. Ideally, I wish we wouldn't have to charge interest to anyone, but I don't think this policy will work until the Millennial Reign where people will be just and fair with one another. Today there is too much corruption, and if we allowed people to borrow money at no interest, the lenders would have no financial justification for loaning money at all. My solution is we make it illegal for banks and credit cards companies to charge interest above 1%. Yes, you heard me correctly one percent! That seems just. That seems fair. This is not an insane decree of lunacy. It's a reasonable resolution. Let the revolution of our financial markets begin today!!!

35 Shakespeare, Success, Evil, & the Lord's Return 4/23/10-5/2/10

This school year is coming to a close. Another year added onto my tenure of teaching. It's been sixteen or seventeen years now. Can you believe it? Time surely flies. In a couple decades, I'll be retired and gray. Death truly has a way of sneaking up on you. My parents' generation is at that cusp now and already we've lost some people we love. Have you lost some too? Earlier this year I mentioned one of my students committed suicide, and I've spoken previously about the death of Uncle Jim. Two difficult loses to take. What else can you do but simply move on and make the best of the time that remains. I desire to attain my dreams before my time is up, but I may or may not shine in the spotlight. I don't know if I'm a credible witness. As for success, I think Linda Perry said it best. She said, "Will success fail me? Will it make me free? What they tell me I should want; is it what I need?" Success is not really my bleeding heart's desire, but it would be nice to be recognized once in a while. I just want to fulfill my calling and get the hell out of here. The 1,000-year reign awaits me and an eternity with my Father in heaven. That's what I'm looking forward to. I'm sure fame and success would be just another letdown anyway, so I'll continue down this desert road alone.

Some of the movies I've been seeing and the press that's been coming out lately has been pure evil. In the old days, good would always win and the villain would be exposed, but nowadays directors are suggesting that sometimes the bad guy wins. Yes, it's true; evil wins a good percentage of the time, but it's only a temporary victory. In the long run, they will lose their eternal souls. I believe Shakespeare would not have approved of the Hollywood scripts coming out today. Sure he wrote a lot of tragedies that were filled with blood and death, but right always won in the end. The press isn't helping either. The stories they bring to our doorsteps is more depressing everyday. There's earthquakes, oil spills, the killing of innocent children, hurricanes, tsunamis, terrorism, war, more blood, more death, more famine, more distress. It's driving everybody crazy. There's no security, and things are getting worse with each passing generation. Lord, isn't it time to set things right? It's time to count the stock and say enough is enough! I'm not too sure if you are saving more new souls or you are losing more to apostasy??? What's the purpose of it all? O Maranatha, O Lord come!!! When are you returning? Haven't you let us rot in hell long enough? Look at your creation. The planet and all that dwell within are sick and dying. Mankind has not been a good steward. We need the righteous Son of Man to lead the way. We need you, my Lord! Come down from the clouds and guide us! Be our sovereign King!

36 Fame, Fortune, & Everything Else in Between 5/3/10-5/15/10

Last weekend I played a gig to about 200 people. I played for about 45 minutes intermixing covers with original material. It was fun but a little stressful. I wonder what it would be like to go from town to town playing music every night. I know for sure my voice wouldn't hold up. I only have about one lecture in me a week before my voice is gone. Back in the day when I sang all the practice sessions with my old band, I survived on hot tea to get through the sweat filled sets. Now I'm older. I still drink tea, but I think I've damaged my throat and vocal chords beyond repair. As for my hearing, I damaged it long before I ever picked up an amp and guitar going to live gigs and listening to loud music. I try to tell the next generation to turn it down and to wear earplugs, but they think I'm an old coot talking out of my ass. So if anyone's listening, take care of your eardrums before it's too late.

It's funny. Every time I get out in front of a large crowd, I think this time it's going to be my big break. In my wild fantasies, I think some music executive is going to be there and someone from *Rolling Stone Magazine* is going to do a story on me, but it's never happened. I've been playing for years and years with my heart on my sleeve, but I've never had a break or a headline. I'm just another struggling artist-the unheard music. Whether I make it or not, this is my last hurrah. 1,260 days of rambling babble! Maybe when it's all said and done, God will lift me up into the heavens, but in the meantime, I'm going to continue my walking blues.

How about you? Do you have any dreams, any hidden secrets? Yes, I know you want to be rich, and I know you want to be famous. Some of us are rich in lots of things already. It's just not fame and power. I've heard some of you talking about a mansion in heaven. I dream about a Kingdom of truth, justice, and righteousness. I have acres and acres of land near the shoreline and generations of loved ones around me. We till the land when we want to. We work and play at our leisure. There's no fear. There are no worries. We are one with Mother Nature and God is with us…

37 Foul Ball 5/16/10

It was Saturday night. The wife and I had no plans for the evening, so I said, "Why don't we go watch the Angel's game tonight?" She said, "We don't have tickets." I said, "I know. We'll just buy them at the box office." She said, "Okay," and off we went. When we got to the ballpark, all that were left were nosebleed seats, so we bought them and entered the stadium; however, we didn't sit way up on top. We snuck passed one of the ushers and sat about fifteen rows back from the dugout on the aisle. I figured, hell, why not give it a try? Anyway, the game started right on time and the A's batted first. They went down 1…2…3 as we tried to look inconspicuous in our seats. I said, "We are so close we could get hit by a ball if we're not paying attention. Maybe we'll get one tonight." Sure enough Erick Aybar, the Angels lead off man, fouled one off in our vicinity and both of us paid closer attention. On the next pitch, Aybar fouled another one and it ricocheted off one of the scoreboards in our direction. The ball was going about 80 miles per hour, and it was zooming towards us. It was like the ball was destined to end up in my grasp. To make a long story short, I caught the ball. It didn't even hurt my hand at all. It was a miracle. The ball just ended up in my hand. Everyone around me was cheering as the usher came down and said, "Are you alright?" I said, "I'm fine" as the wife and I giggled like little children. So much for being inconspicuous! An inning later, the people who were supposed to be sitting in our seats arrived at the game, and we had to move over. It was a little embarrassing, but there were plenty of open seats. It wasn't like the Angels were playing the Yankees or something. That's the end of my story. The ball is now sitting on a pedestal in my room, and I fulfilled a life long dream to catch a foul ball at a Major League Baseball game.

38 Scratching the Itch 5/17/10-5/29/10

In many ways, I find Las Vegas to be the PG version of adult entertainment. It's like watching soft porn. You don't really get to see everything. Of course, if you have a heavy wallet, you can get anything, yet I've never been part of the privileged elite. I've always been a middle-class American. Statistically, it appears I am now upper middle class, but spending $300 dollars on a hooker doesn't make sense to me. I'd rather get several lap dances, a deep tissue massage, and leave the jerking off to me. This way I won't catch a sexually transmitted disease and screw up my marriage again.

Vegas itself has changed. The decline is obvious, and it will only be a matter of time before the extravagance turns to poverty. The common folk will not be able to survive there at these high-end prices. During this trip I spent a lot of money, and I was being prudent by gambling scarcely. My drug intake was about the same as any other Vegas trip. But honestly, the whole desert excursion didn't have the same edge it once held for me. Sure the experience was fun at times, but the payback was not worth the investment. You and I are both better off by not drinking, not smoking, or doing drugs. And I'm an expert on this subject, so here's some advice from someone who has been down that road. Don't do drugs! Remember Snoop Dogg once said, "Getting faded is a basic human drive like food and water and sex and sleep." So if you got that itch for the vices, you're going to scratch that itch; and once you've scratched it, you're going to be back for more. So that's the lesson to be learned. Don't start because once you've tasted the euphoric feeling, you'll probably be back for another hit. I've been back many times. Have you? Only the Lord has kept me free from those obsessive addictions. I may be a "normy" by the AA people's standards, but when you add up all the numbers, it comes down to the grace of the Lord. He has been my protector. He is my sense and sensibility.

39 Here's the Rope… Now Swing Away 5/30/10-6/14/10

According to the scriptures, true wisdom comes from the Lord and hearing His Word. (Prov.1:7; Rom.10:17) But if you have not taught your children about God, how strong is their education? And if you don't have a personal relationship with God yourself, how can you teach them? How will they ever come to the knowledge of the truth? I suppose God could reach them through some other means, but you are taking a giant risk with the ones you love the most.

Many parents have also asked me this question. "Will my children go to heaven if they die?" According to Paul's teachings, the children of believers are covered by the Lord, but it doesn't say anything about the children of unbelievers. (1Cor.7:14) Does that mean God will not grant them entrance into heaven if they die? I'm not sure. The *Bible* is silent on the subject. Paul does not mention the children of unbelievers, but if you or your spouse is a believer, you could rest assured at night that your children will enter into the Kingdom of God if tragedy befalls them.

Does that mean parents should send their children to a religious institution to teach their kids about God? Yes and no. There are some fine Christian schools out there, but most of them are fallen establishments that teach tradition rather than His holy Word. You'd be better off reading a children's *Bible* to your kids at night and let God reach them through His Word.

As a teacher of the *Bible* myself, I leave the dirty work up to Him. I simply teach the *Bible* like any other great work of literature. In class we read it, study it, and analyze it from as many perspectives as possible. If the text truly is inspired by God, which I believe it is, God will reach them through His Word. I leave their salvation in His hands.

So how does this entry apply to you? It means that I'm holding you accountable to reach out to your children before it's too late. It seems foolish to leave your pride and joy in the hands of fate when you can simply reach out to your children on your own. You're the best teacher of your kids, not me or anyone else. But how can you teach your children if you don't have the knowledge yourself? Well, you'll need to educate yourself first, and there's no time like the present. Set aside some time each night and read the Word on your own. If you're not a great reader, listen to the *Bible* on CD or MP3s. For beginners, I'd suggest to first read the *New Testament* in its entirety then go back and read the *Old Testament* after that. It might be wise to find a good teacher or book to help you through the text, but don't fret. God is the best teacher of all. And once you've been enlightened, you'll be able to pass down this knowledge to your kids.

To close, I'm sorry for the heavy exhortation, but I thought I'd lay into you a little because I know how important your kids are to you. I'd hate to see them miss out on the plans God has for them because of your blunders. And if I haven't told you already, it's going to be difficult to have children during the Tribulation Period because they will be an extra burden and one more mouth to feed. Then again, their resilience might come in handy and save you from calamity. But don't worry; it's going to be alright. You're going to pull through. The future is going to be glorious. What awaits us is beyond words. It's unimaginable. So I'll depart on this note, *"I'm no dope. I give you hope. Here's the rope… here's the rope… now swing away…" Wire by U2*

40 Mercy 6/15/10-6/29/10

Last night I had a dream about the Angel of Death. He was coming to destroy us, but I asked him to give us a chance to repent, and he relented. He came back shortly after and found that we had at least made an attempt to change our ways, and he did not destroy us. We were safe for the time being.

Later that morning, I was reading the story of Jonah and the Whale and how God spared Nineveh after the people put on sackcloth and repented. It made me realize that God does want to show us mercy and compassion, and that He is not all about fire and brimstone. I think a lot of people have been shown a poor representation of God in their upbringing, and that is why so many people are turned off by the Judeo-Christian God. We must remember that the *Torah* infers that God gave Noah's generation 100 years to repent before he brought the flood. I believe He is giving us the same chance this time around. We simply have to turn from our sin. It won't be easy, but it can be done if we trust in the grace of the Lord. God's willing to help us if we reach out to Him. This generation can still be saved. I know many of you are tired of this scene. I feel the same way at times, but we must remember that the younger generation has just begun. Their eyes have just been opened. They don't hold onto our pessimism. They see a future. They see hope. The Messiah's return may not be for many generations to come, so we must fight on a little longer and not throw in the towel. Past generations have reformed in the past, and we can too. We can still save the planet. We can bring back justice and righteousness. We can show mercy to our enemies and walk humbly with our God.

Chapter 2:
40 Days & 40 Nights in Europe

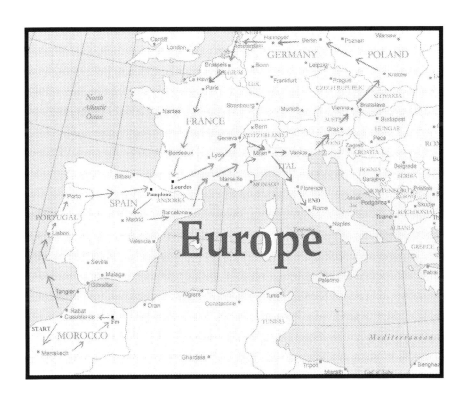

Day 01 Lost Luggage 6/30/10

After seventeen hours on several flights, I arrived in Casablanca with Kiana. We were tired, jetlag, and I smelled pretty bad. After going through customs, I went down to pick up my luggage, and it wasn't there. Kiana's luggage had arrived, but mine was either lost, stolen, or being detained. Regardless, it was missing. I was screwed. I had no change of clothes, so all I could do was rot in my stinky, filthy sweat. Remember, Morocco is in Africa, and it felt like it was in the 90's.

After filling out all the paperwork for my lost luggage, we took a 3-hour train ride to Marrakesh. In Marrakesh, we checked into our hotel and instantly went shopping because I needed to change into something. I ended up buying some cheesy Moroccan clothes to get through the coming days. I looked like a cheap imitation of a European model with my tight T-shirts and short shorts. Oh well, what can you do?

To sum up, the first day was a nightmare. Losing your luggage completely puts a damper on everything. I was pissed off, uncomfortable, and without some valuable items in my bag. For instance, if my bag doesn't show up, I stand to lose my 24-year-old traveling Bible that contains all my notes and cross-references. Maybe this book is the reason my luggage had suddenly gone missing. Morocco is a Muslim country so who knows? I'm sure I'll find out in the coming days, but right now I'm tired and stressed out. I'm going to try and get some sleep.

Note: I do realize Morocco is not in Europe, but the country is so close to Spain I couldn't resist including the country on this journey.

Day 02 The Veil 7/1/10

My luggage didn't turn up. Instead, I listened to more BS from the baggage claim department in Casablanca. After speaking on the phone for over an hour, Kiana and I went to Djema al-fna in Marrakesh. It's a bizarre outdoor spectacle with snake charmers, charlatans, annoying businessmen, and women with those funky veils that cover their entire bodies. Those poor women! But it's not as bad as other places in the Middle East I've seen like Egypt and Jordan. At least in Morocco the dress code seems to be more liberal. Some women wear the veil that covers their whole body. Others wear the veil with the slit cut out for their eyes. Some wear the veil over their head, and the rest of the Moroccan women dress like Western women. In the hotels, French tourists wear bikinis and some hang out topless by the pool. See, there is a reason to come to Morocco after all gentlemen!!!

As for equal rights, I do hope one day all women will be liberated, but with the spread of Islam, I don't see it happening anytime soon. Islam is an oppressive religion, but Judaism and Christianity aren't exempt either. Eve took the brunt of the judgment from God in the Garden of Eden, and Paul makes it quite clear that women are second-class citizens. So what am I trying to say? Nothing…I'm just stating the facts. As John Lennon once sung, "Women are the nigger of the world."

Everything else is going fine over here except for the luggage headache. We're taking a train ride to Fez tomorrow. It's known as the oldest town in Morocco. It's supposedly the artistic, intellectual, and spiritual helm of the nation. I guess I'll find out if it's true when I get there. Au Revoir! *By the way everyone speaks French over here not Arabic.*

Day 03 The Moroccans 7/2/10

Still luggageless but at least I'm not like my father who is now legless, so I might as well count my blessings and say it could be much worse. As for Day 3, not much happened. It was a travel day. We took an 8-hour train ride from Marrakesh to Fez. We went 1st class, but the AC wasn't working, so it was about 100 degrees inside our caboose. We met some cool people though, and by the time we left the train, Kiana had befriended everybody, and we had to give sorrowful kisses goodbye (one kiss on the right cheek and one on the left) to our new Moroccan friends.

As for the people in Morocco, their skin is brown, but only a few have the really dark skin like our African Americans. Their features look like a cross between a Frenchman, an African, and an indigenous people. Most of the locals are friendly. They speak loud, laugh, and are a bit in your face like the Israelis and Turks. It's too bad those two countries can't get along anymore. Keep your eyes open because a new prophecy is about to be fulfilled. A northern alliance is about to invade Israel from the north and a lot of theologians believe Turkey is part of this axis. They will be joined by Persia (Iran) and Gog/Magog (Russia). It will appear Israel will be overrun, but God will destroy the invaders, and Yahweh's name will get all praise and glory for the victory. Read Ezekiel 38-39 if you want to read the prophecy from the original source. This prophecy should be all the evidence you will need to prove that the God of the Bible is the only true God. Watch and see!!!

Kiana and I are taking it easy tonight. We ate at the hotel, rested, and plan on cruising through the ancient City of Fez tomorrow morning.

Day 04 Fez, Morocco 7/3/10

Today we cruised around the oldest town in Morocco called Fez al-Jdid. It's a chaotic walled-in city where people sell donkey heads, carpets are weaved, and leather is made at a tannery. You cruise around a town that dates back to the 9th Century and you brush up against other Moroccans in thin tunnels where the people live, sell, and do business. By western standards, the people are still living in the Dark Ages, but it appears the people are doing alright for themselves.

Due to the fact the tunnels are like a labyrinth, it's recommended for tourists to have a guide when going into this old city, so we hired one to lead us around for a few hours. Our guide did show us a lot of cool sites, but he was as crooked as a car salesman. Of course, at the end of the tour the fee for his guidance went up, and he was shouting and yelling like a madman because he wanted us to pay him more. In the end, we paid the senile bastard to calm him down. It was only about ten dollars more, and I cursed his name in Spanish and English to amuse myself in the back seat as we drove back to our hotel. Kiana and I were laughing, but I do hope this man's bad Karma comes back to bite him.

After roaming around the city, we hung out by the pool. I did as many laps as possible to get some exercise in. It rained later in the evening. Thunder and lightning pounded us like we were in the Serengeti as a Muslim mosque echoed out its praise to Allah in the background.
Disclaimer: Not all car salesmen are crooked. I put that in for a friend of mine, but aren't we all a little bit crooked too?

Day 05 1992 Vs 2010 7/4/10

We arrived in Lisbon, Portugal today. A sigh of relief crossed both our faces as the plane landed. Prior to leaving the airport, I went over to the baggage claim area and spoke to TAP Air about my missing luggage. They were very helpful but nothing turned up. I put a forwarding address to my parent's house just in case my luggage is found.

In Lisboa (that's how you really say it) we walked around the Bairro Alto. It's a hilly area like San Francisco that has thin cobblestone streets, but practically the whole place was closed because it was Sunday. In the evening, we went to Baixa (the touristy area) and had a bite to eat at the Hard Rock Cafe. Afterwards, we went back to the Sofitel Hotel, relaxed for a while, then I typed up these journal entries.

It's funny this time around I'm staying at 4 or 5 star hotels. Back in 1992 when I first went to Europe I stayed in hostels where you had to share a room with ten other people. It was fun at the time, but I'm not straight out of college anymore. I want clean sheets, a hot shower, and air conditioning. I know some of you will say, "I've sold out. That's not what a true artist would do." Well, I have only one response to your protests, "Screw you!" Whoever said writers and artists have to live like vagabonds for their craft? Most Europeans are middle class anyway, so I'm simply living at their comfort level while I'm over here.

As you can see, I do go off on tangents from time to time, so if you're okay with that, keep reading. If not, no worries, but isn't this far better than a picture show? There's no supplement for the written word, and now you truly know what's spinning through this head of mine.

Happy 4th of July everybody. Long live the United States of America! Fuck yeah!!!

Day 06 The Thrill is Gone 7/5/10

Yippee!!! I got to go shopping again??? Three hours later, I had a new pair of shoes, decent clothes, and I was on my way. I'm still upset about the loss of my personal stuff, but it's time to move on. I'll try not to bring it up any longer.

Right now I'm sitting on my bed getting ready to tackle the nightlife of Lisbon, but to be honest, I'm just moving from town to town because I'm hoping to see or experience something new. I want to be enlightened and say, "Holy shit, look at that poor blind beggar singing songs on the subway!" like the one I saw earlier today. Why did God curse him with such a fate? Did he deserve it? Was it because of something he did? God only knows. I do have to admit I'm getting pretty burned out of living in this fallen world though. As B.B. King once sang, "The thrill is gone," and now I'm trying to keep myself entertained from day to day. Wouldn't it be nice to go back and be a kid again where everything is new and exciting? You couldn't wait to get up and see the morning. Then somewhere along the line, life became stagnant and dull. Do you feel me? Am I bringing you down? Sorry, I'm just trying to be true to my feelings. And don't give me any of your psychological B.S. I'm not depressed. I'm not suicidal. At times, I just wish life had a little bit more to offer. I groan for something better. I'm waiting for the Millennial Reign. I want to feel that spark of love again. I want to have my eyes re-opened. I want my spirit to be reborn and rise above the ashes!

We're back from Baixa. We saw lots of people and tourists walking about and eating at outside cafés. There were many homeless people, street musicians, and artists. One artist drew this superb picture of the suffering Jesus in chalk. It was intricately done. It looked like he had spent all day working on it. On that thought, I hope you all remember what Jesus did for you on the cross. Sometimes I forget too. He died to save us. It would be like going to war and taking a bullet for one of your buddies. Now imagine the Creator of the universe taking a bullet for you. Pretty amazing!!! Adeus (goodbye)

Day 07 Lisboa 7/6/10

Cruise around the city. See another site. Gawk at all the misfits. Drink into the night. Lisbon's just another city. There's graffiti on the signs. It looks like Buenos Aires or Frisco with a trolley ride. There's cafés on the sidewalks. There's musicians on the streets. There's artwork on the fringes and homeless begging freaks. Yes, this is Lisboa. It's where I am right now. Tomorrow, I'll be off to Porto and begin the endless cycle. Maybe I'll swim in the Atlantic or walk around the park. I'll sample Porto's vino and say, "Isn't this just fine?" Yet I feel there's something missing. It comes from deep inside. This hotel vagabond living becomes bitter like red wine. I could go back to Cali and lounge down at the beach or head up to Big Bear and wakeboard on the Lake. Yes, this is the life of leisure. I'm not working 9 to 5. It's as if I am retired, but it feels like I'm doing time. There are no bars upon these windows. There's no terror in the night, but if you had my visions, you'd say, "Prison is alright." I have dreams of Armageddon. I feel it in my spine. This era's coming to a close. Lisboa will burn with fire.

Day 08 Welcome to the Machine 7/7/10

I woke up and ate breakfast at the hotel after spending numerous hours on the Internet last night booking hotels for the upcoming cities. I feel like the manager for a traveling band, only there are no groupies or orgies after the show as a reward for all my hard work. Instead, I'm another no name artist who plays to empty barrooms and half lit concert halls. Every now and then someone buys a CD or picks up a book, but my works aren't moving off the shelves. In reality, I'd be lucky to find them on the shelves at all. It's disappointing, but it is what it is. I've never had that big break, and I feel like a door-to-door salesman when I try to promote my books or music.

Right now, the wife and I are on the train from Lisbon to Porto. It's beautiful out here, and it sort of reminds me of the ride from Santa

Barbara to Monterey. There are wineries and trees and crops and small towns. It's nice and all, but I don't know if I could live out my days in a small town community. There's too much accountability, and everyone else knows what everyone else is doing. It might keep me honest, but it would probably bore me to death.

After arriving in Porto, we had our laundry done. We paid five Euro per kilogram. I thought this meant five Euro per load. The lady tallied it up and it was forty-five Euros for two loads. That's like paying $50 dollars for two loads of laundry. I just about shit my pants, but we were out of clean clothes, so we had to pay the price. It's impossible to find a laundromat in Portugal. Afterwards, we went and had dinner at an outside cafe and ate a full chicken ourselves. *Let's Go* (a travel book) recommended this place, and we feasted like kings for twenty Euro. The World Cup was also on at the time, and we watched Spain beat Germany. I was on the edge of my seat the whole match, and I can't wait until Spain plays the Netherlands??? Is my sarcasm coming through? One cool thing though, we will be in Spain when the final match is played, and it will be interesting to see how the Europeans react during their Superbowl or World Series.

Day 09 Purgatory 7/8/10

The wife and I cruised around Porto, a port city of Portugal. The weather felt about the same as any beach city of L.A. or Orange County; however, the views excel anything we have in our area. As for Porto itself, I liked it better than Lisbon. It was calmer and more relaxed than Lisbon. The traffic is bad though because the city center has such small streets, and the area is pretty rundown. By American standards, I'd say most people are living at poor/middle class levels. I felt quite safe in this city and would highly recommend it to anyone. The people are friendly, helpful, and respectful.

Earlier today, Kiana and I visited this church called Igreja De Sao San Francisco. Inside this church there is over 400 to 600 Kg. of gold, and it has this family tree tracing Christ's lineage all the way back to Jesse (King David's father). All the gold was donated by rich people who tried to buy their way out of purgatory and into heaven. This is a false doctrine that the Catholic Church has been spreading for hundreds of years. Sorry, but the *Bible* teaches there is no purgatory. You can't buy yourself or your loved ones out of this place because it doesn't exist. Purgatory was a scam to make money by the church. After death, you either go to heaven or hell. Then, at the Great White Throne Judgment in the *Book of Revelation* (Rev.20:11-15) those people who are in hell are cast into the Lake of Fire. So who are the people who go to heaven? It's those people who have put their faith in Christ before they die. This means you can't get to heaven based on being a good person or doing the right thing. According to the scriptures, the only way into heaven is by repenting of your sin and believing in Jesus. I know. I can hear your protests already! I have problems with the justice in this doctrine too, but that's what the *Bible* teaches. But be sure of this, there is no purgatory! There is/was a place called Abraham's bosom, but that's a whole other conversation altogether.

Day 10 Church 7/9/10

Kiana went to church this morning, but I skipped out. I've always found it hard to go through the religious rigmarole, but she seems to love it. To each his own. After breakfast, we milled around Porto and left our luggage at the hotel. At sundown, we have a night train to Madrid. It's about a 10-hour train ride, and this way we don't have to pay for a hotel. It's a trick low budget travelers use, and back in 1992 when I lived in Europe, I would even sleep at train stations to save cash.

Church was brought up, so I think I should address the issue. In Europe and abroad, we have these grandiose churches. They're magnificent feats of architecture, but most of these churches are dead now. These places have become ruins, and I doubt God still resides there. The church was never meant to be a building. It's supposed to be the body of believers. The church is wherever Christians meet. It could be at the beach. It could be at a tent, and it could be in a building. It doesn't really matter. As long as two, three, or more are gathered together, it's considered a church meeting. Personally, I should be meeting with believers more often than I have in the past, but being brought up Catholic has left a bitter taste in my mouth when it comes to church. I hated going to church on Sunday, and I still do today. I do enjoy going to *Bible* studies every now and then, but the church service is a major turnoff. How many times do I have to hear those same old prayers? Why don't we make a new prayer, a real prayer from the heart? And over the last decade or so, I don't even go to *Bible* studies anymore. I listen on the radio to Chuck Smith and other Calvary Chapel ministers, but I don't usually go to the meetings. According to the scriptures, I'm not supposed to "forsake the assembling of ourselves together," (Heb.10:25) but I still don't go. I do teach the *Bible* to 35 students each day at school, but I don't know if that counts because technically it's just another course of English literature. Anyway, that's enough talk about church. It's not one of my favorite topics because I stand condemned on the issue. Other people seem to really enjoy it. For example, Kiana loves it. But for me, going to church is as hard as trying to piss inside a beer bottle.

Day 11 Highlights 7/10/10

1. We almost missed our connecting train from Porto to Spain, but luckily a guardian angel was looking out for us and we found our way. Ten hours later, we arrived in Madrid. We were both exhausted. Riding 2nd class on one of those trains is almost as bad as flying. Most of the time we've been riding 1st class, but this train was full, so we had to ride 2nd class. When we arrived at our hotel we conked out and slept for a couple hours before hitting the streets.

2. We visited el Museo Del Prado. This was one of the best museums I've ever seen. I especially liked the works of Goya. His art is like viewing life through the eyes of a demented psycho-maniac. I also found El Greco's works to be breathtaking. Overall, I enjoyed the religious art best, even though many of the artists have not accurately portrayed what is historically written in the Gospels.

3. Travelers note: If you ever plan on going somewhere new, I'd highly recommend using the *Lonely Planet* travel guides. They've been lifesavers on many occasions for me. *Let's Go* is also a solid source, but it's more geared towards the low budget/student traveler.

4. Europeans and their smoking habits are driving me nuts. It seems like everyone smokes, and they light up right in front of you. They don't even care if there are children around. It's like living in the 1970's all over again. Today, I even saw a vending machine selling cigarettes right out in the open. And I thought Europeans were educated. They must know the dangers??? Maybe they think banning smoking to certain designated areas will hurt their outside cafe lifestyle. I'm not sure, but I'm sick of sucking in their secondhand smoke.

5. Spanish women are beautiful! I know some of you have a taste for Latina women. If that's the case, you might want to travel over to Spain.

6. On Montera Rd., there were a bunch of hookers hanging out right in the open. No one seemed to care. Is prostitution legal in Espana?

7. I've witnessed a lot of people smoking pot, especially by the young, but it appears to be mixed with tobacco. In Ireland the stoners mix hash (resin from cannabis) with tobacco and smoke it. Neither way appealed to me. I always ended up coughing up part of my lungs. Smoking pot has never been good for asthma despite what Peter Tosh may have claimed in his song "Legalize it."

Day 12 Espana, World Cup Champions! 7/11/10

Shouting, screaming, singing, dancing... Worrying, waiting, watching, celebrating. Over 50,000 of us cheered for Espana in the Plaza de Colon. In mass the crowd roared out, *"A por ellos oh eh. A por ellos oh eh. A por ellos oh eh. A por ellos eh oh eh…"* Over and over again the song rang out as the bucelas belched out their bugle call.

After the goal went in the net, I witnessed mass hysteria by the people of Madrid. People were jumping on cars, shooting off fireworks, and parading down the streets. It looked like downtown L.A. after the Lakers won the NBA championship only this was different. The Spaniards' passion for their country goes down to the marrow of their bones. The goal set off a sigh of relief, an exaltation of joy like when Darin Erstad of the Angels caught the final out in Game 7 of the 2002 World Series.

On the streets almost everyone wore red shirts as Spanish flags flew proudly in the air. As an outsider, you couldn't help getting swept up in the frenzy, and before we knew it, we were laughing and cheering like two school kids who had just won the local championship.

In the end, the euphoria lasted throughout the night. When we headed down to Sol's metro to catch our next train to Pamplona in the morning, people were still scuffling about in the streets. There were drunkards mumbling to themselves, gangs of looters meandering about, and broken bottles everywhere. Kiana and I passed right through them as we rolled our luggage behind us and hopped on the subway train out of there.

Day 13 Grapevine 7/12/10

I heard through the grapevine my luggage has been found!!! Oh, I do hope everything is still there. Tomorrow I'll be running with the bulls. If I'm gorged to death, I'll see you in the next life! I love you all!
God bless!!!
Enoch

Day 14 Running with the Bulls 7/13/10

A skyrocket explodes in the distance. Suddenly you see a mass of people fleeing for their lives followed by a group of angry bulls behind them. So you turn, run, and join the confusion. In seconds the weighted mass of animals are upon you. You feel like prey being hunted in the forest, so you dodge to the right or to the left to escape being trampled or bludgeoned to death by the torros.

This is Pamplona, Spain; the running of the bulls made famous in Ernest Hemmingway's book *The Sun Also Rises*. It's a two-week festival known as San Fermin, and everyday at 8:00 A.M. the bulls are made to run. Today the festival has been transformed into a tourist gathering where men (some women too) can show off how "machismo" they are by running with the bulls. I was part of the event this morning, and it was an exhilarating adrenaline rush. Obviously, I did not die or get run over by bulls, but I did see over thirty people get bull-dozed or thrown by mid-sized bulls after the run was completed.

The run takes about five minutes and ends inside a bullring. The people who finished the race are now fed one bull at a time in the arena. It's sort of like being fed to the lions in ancient Rome as a full stadium of people cheer on the violence. Most of the runners get out of the way and stand on the fringes as I did, but some fools taunted the bulls, ran around with them in the ring, and many people got hurt. It was interesting to say the least, but I'm getting too old to be partaking in that part of the event, so I watched by the inside wall as people were thrown, drilled into the ground, and trampled.

Overall, running with the bulls may have been life threatening, but if you have some common sense when you're out there, you probably won't get hurt. Most people walked away unscathed as I did. It was only the fools who pushed their luck in the arena that took a genuine beating. Sure some individuals may have been able to leap over a charging bull untouched, but many others were not so graceful.
Note: There was a rumor someone died yesterday, but I later heard he survived the injuries.

Day 15 Come on Down & Make the Stand 7/14/10

We watched a bullfight last night. We saw about seven bulls come to an untimely death. It was a gory event, but I have to admit I was rooting for the bulls. First, they are bled from the back before they actually face the matador, so the odds are stacked against the bulls. Shame...

shame... The whole sporting event is a bit archaic, and by the third fight my mind began to wander. I kept hoping the bull would get one of those bastards, flip one of them in the air, and gouge him in the ribs, but it didn't happen. One matador, El Fandi, was quite entertaining, but the others didn't keep my interest. I'm still waiting for the time when they bring back the gladiators to the Colosseum. Now that would be entertainment! Who knows maybe they'll throw the Christians to the lions during the Tribulation Period in the future??? That would be a true test of faith. The only problem is I don't see how people think they'll be willing to die for their faith when they're not willing to take a stand during times of peace. I have tried to hold up the truth, and it's brought me a lot of grief. I do hope I'll have the balls to make a stand when the shit truly hits the fan. For decades now, I've been mocked, laughed at, and criticized by unbelievers, but am I willing to die for my faith? I hope so. In the end, it will all be worth it. And believe me, I do know my testimony has not been white as snow, but I have stayed consistent on these points: Jesus Christ is the Messiah. He is my God, and one day He's coming back to set up His righteous kingdom.

Yes, my friends, the time is now to make a choice. You're not guaranteed tomorrow. Who knows you might get in a car wreck and die unexpectanly? So I'll make it simple for you. Make an honest prayer to God, and see if He responds. Truly cry out to God, and find out if He's real or not. I guarantee you He'll make His presence known in some way, shape, or form.

The wife and I are currently on a train to Barcelona after being swept away in the madness of San Fermin. We need a break away from the insanity, so we'll probably hang by the hotel pool or go to one of Barcelona's beaches to chill out for a day or two.

Day 16 Sabbath 7/15/10

After two weeks of travel, our bodies finally reached the breaking point, so we checked into a nice hotel in Barcelona and took a day of rest. I must have slept over ten hours last night, and today I've done very little; I worked out at the hotel gym and hung by the pool. Whew, I needed that!

I think all of us need to take more time off, but some of us are on the run 24/7. It's too bad. Some people just don't know how to relax. I've heard in Europe that most companies give their employees over a month off. Wouldn't that be nice in the U.S.A? How about we make it a mandatory rule that companies give full-time employees at least four weeks off or even better three months off like I do as a teacher? Well, it's a nice thought anyway. In a capitalist economy, it's all about work...work...work, so I don't know if that will fly. Would it be considered socialist? By the conservative base, absolutely. We are working ourselves to death though. Many of us are not able to take that much time off because we have bills to pay and kids to feed. I understand the dilemma. It's hard to take that much time off. FYI: Most teachers do not get paid during the summer, but many of us stretch out our paychecks through the credit union, so we can survive the long dry spell.

Biblically, the Sabbath was one of the 10 Commandments. The Sabbath was handed down by God to Moses, so the people would have a day of rest. The Jews celebrate the Sabbath on Saturday, and most Christians have made Sunday their day off. I think it would be helpful to our nation if the stores would close again on Sundays. The problem is we've become too work oriented and have forgotten our values. Others have Type A personalities, and they need to learn how to relax. And some Americans have become sloths over the years. These people aren't helping the problem either. Well, I don't have all the solutions, and I'm too corrupted to run for office, but I do know one thing, when I take a day off, the next day I feel more rejuvenated.

Day 17 Fade Away 7/16/10

Life has its own way of kicking sand in your face, and I'm trying to see through my blurred vision. Sometimes I come across like I have all the answers, but I'm really sleeping in the sty with everyone else. I don't know about love because I've fucked up every relationship I've ever been in. I've driven others away and made a lot of poor decisions. I've gone out to bring freedom to all, but all I've left behind me is division and rubble. I'm like the American Empire. Everything I've built is starting to fall apart, and I'm trying to keep it all together. Everyone is going on and doing their own thing, while I'm writing these lonely letters that are discarded and rejected. I could always go into the studio and make a new album, but my best songs are now behind me. I'm simply plucking at the same old chords. There's no passion. There's no creativity. I'm trying to reinvent myself, so I have a reason to keep on ticking. Even these entries sound like a repeat to me. It's Friday the 13th, Pts. 4, 5, & 6. I'm not living on the edge. I'm just living. I wish I could say I've fulfilled my dreams, but none of them turned out as I expected. There was always a fork in the road that led me down the wrong path. It's called the path of least resistance. Yes, I've fought and won some battles, but most of the time I've been shrouded in mediocrity. I'm like you. You're like me. And we're on this lonely road together. We're trying to figure it all out, but as the years pass by, the confusion only grows deeper. We feel the Grim Reaper breathing down our necks, and we know we can't live forever. We're both waiting for our turns like all the other blokes in the assembly line. We have our tickets in our hands. We're milling around at the train station, but the train is late. We always thought we'd go out in a blaze of glory, but it's looking more like we're going to fade and fizzle out.

Day 18 Hangover 7/17/10

Right now my nose is running. I'm tired, unshaven, and I feel like I'm waking up from a binge in Vegas. After the World Cup party in Madrid and running with the bulls in Pamplona, I crashed hard. I've been here in Barcelona three days, and most of it's been spent on my hotel room bed. Sure, I've seen a few sites and roamed around parts of the city, but at this moment, I wish I was home. Barcelona has been the lull of the journey. I thought about heading over to the Island of Ibiza for a day, but I'm so burnt out, I can't see the light of day. Ibiza's a party town anyway, and I can't see myself hanging out with a bunch of twenty-year-olds, drinking absinthe, and dancing at a club into the early morning hours. I've been there and done that already. It's fun for a spell, but the exhilaration turns bitter as wormwood.

Most of the time I'm a recluse anyway. I hang at my house and rarely go out. I schedule my day around Angel's baseball or whatever sporting event is on at the time. The other hours are spent in front of the computer. I'll watch repeats of Star Trek, and sometimes play my left-handed guitar. But over here, I'm on the move everyday. I'm going from city to city like a band on the run, and I'm expending all my energy on the stage at night. It's a love/hate relationship, but at least I'm halfway through the tour. I'll get my second wind soon enough, and I'll be feeling alright again. But as the years pass by, it's getting harder to roll out of bed each day. My spark is fading. I'm no longer in the prime of my life. I'm on the slow train heading west. I've fallen from the heavens like Lucifer and his angels, but I'm raising cane before I'm stomped out at the funeral pyre.

Day 19 For Freedom 7/18/10

At this moment I'm lying on a cot that's heading to Milano. It's 10:15 P.M., and I'm reflecting on my last day of Spain. It was a grand adventure, and I hope I'll be able to come back some day.

Now I'm off to the land of my ancestors, Italia. Actually I'm Sicilian/Irish, but I'm really just a Norte Americano. Over here I'm a representative from the States, and I'm not going to be a pussy and say I'm from Canada, so I don't get targeted by a terrorist organization. Screw that! If you're coming for me, well bring it on! "I got my Bible, and I got my handgun." (D.O.A.) There's nothing like those civil liberties back home.

That's enough of my patriotic babble. I did see a lot of patriotism on the part of the Spanish people though, and it made me realize other countries have as much nationalistic pride as we do. There's nothing wrong with that, but when people start marching in step and yelling, "Hail Obama!" or whoever is in charge at the time, that's where I draw the line. The only problem is I do see the U.S. becoming more fascist and socialist at the same time. Big Brother lurks on every corner, and our freedoms are slowly slipping away one by one. It's a sad state of affairs. I'm not blaming either party either. They're both guilty. I suppose I'm looking for a democratic government beyond the two-party system. I'm searching for truth, justice, and the American way, but the problem is Superman died long ago and left us with a corrupt government. In my opinion, America needs to move forward without going backwards, but we also need to remember our past if we have any chance in the future. Yes, I believe there's hope for our country. I've seen it in the eyes of every graduating class over the last sixteen years. But if we don't act quickly, there might not be anything left of our country that's worth fighting for. In that case, we'll have to pull the plug and start all over again. *"Meet the new boss, same as the old boss!" (The Who)*

Day 20 Love Your Neighbor as Yourself 7/19/10

It had been over 24 hours and neither one of us had showered. We stunk. We were sweating, and we couldn't wait to get to our hotel room to clean up. When we arrived there was a problem with our confirmation number, and the shower didn't drain properly. Also, the AC wasn't working. I suppose this is what happens when you book a two-star hotel in Venice. And this place was costing me over $100 bucks a night??? They sure do know how to gouge the tourists for every Euro they have.

It's sickening how corrupt our society has become. It's dog eat dog out here, and too many people are willing to take advantage of other human beings. For instance, earlier today in Milan, two people cut right in front us when we were trying to buy tickets to Venice. The rest of the time, we have to watch our luggage like hawks and wear our stone cold faces 24/7 so no crooks try to pull a fast one on us. It's not just Italy, either. This disease has spread to every corner of the globe, and that's one of the reasons why God needs to wipe the slate clean and start all over again. We're not fair dealing with one another anymore, and many people are only looking out for their own interest. Everyone needs to be more like Kiana who saw a hurt girl who was bleeding and offered her a hand and a band-aide. Everyone was staring at the girl like it was a picture show. It's too bad. I'm not innocent either. I've had my fair share of looking the other way, but I do try to be honest and straightforward with my fellowman. If we all followed the 2nd greatest commandment, "To love your neighbor as yourself," we wouldn't be in the conundrum we are in today. We could leave our doors unlocked. We could give our children a longer leash and not worry about kidnappings and killings. It is possible to change our ways, but I tend to wonder if we've gone beyond the point of no return. If that's the case, there's no hope for tomorrow. Please tell me there's hope for the next generation. Better yet, why don't you show me!

Footnote: When you type on foreign computers, the letters aren't always in the right place. This computer has the Y & Z in the wrong places, so I have to re-type all of them. A simple paragraph can sometimes take twice as long.

Day 21 The Venetians 7/20/10

I've lived outside the country for six months before, but I couldn't imagine what it would be like to live in a foreign land for eight years. Trying to effectively communicate the language alone would be enough to drive me crazy, but this is what my cousin and her family have done for the last eight years. First, they lived in Rome for four years, and they are about to finish four more years in Venice. Now they're finally coming home. Let's all welcome them back to the land of milk and honey, or should I say the land of normal water pressure and air conditioning. Their children, however, seem to be prospering in Italy. The two girls speak Italian fluently and walk around the canals of Venice like they own the place. They've become true Venetians. The youngest, on the other hand, is getting there, but he's only two. He quite an entertaining child, and my cousin says he reminds her of her father. As for her husband, he's working over 80 hours a week and still has not lost his sanity. And my cousin appears to be doing quite well despite all the trials and tribulations she has endured over the years...

I didn't finish this entry. I fell asleep on the train, and right now I feel like seeing the City of Vienna before I head off to Krakow, Poland.

Day 22 Post Austria 7/21/10

It's been two days without a shower because I've been sleeping on trains the last couple of nights. Oh, I smell charming! Splash a little water on my face, and I'm on my way. Next stop Krakow, Poland after visiting Vienna. I'm heading to Auschwitz on the death machine. I'm going to relive the past of some of Europe's most memorable history.

Currently, I'm on another train without AC, and I'm sweating up a storm. The humidity is killing me. Moments like this are when I realize how lucky I am to be living in Southern California near the beach. To me, it feels like Bangkok where you walk around with that sticky feeling all day.

As for everything else, no real tragedies have occurred except the pulley on my cheap Portuguese luggage broke, so it looks like I'm going to have to buy luggage for a third time. Yes, it's getting tiresome. Someone must have put a curse on my baggage this trip. I don't believe in curses, but my mother is highly superstitious, so I grew up believing all sorts of stupid things like knocking on wood, Saint Christopher, going out a different door than the one you came in as a sin against God and a zillion others.

Smack! Yes!!! I just killed a mosquito with the back of this journal. Die motherfucker die! I hate mosquitoes. Why would God create something as annoying as gnats and mosquitoes? I suppose it has to do with the fall of man. Maybe before Adam and Eve bit into the apple there were no mosquitoes. By the way, it probably wasn't an apple at all. It was more likely a vine of fruit as mentioned in the *Book of Enoch*. Then again, who knows, so don't quote me on it.

I'm signing off. I'm going to try and get some sleep. Right now I'm going about 70 miles per hour with the window open. I can't hear anything. Then again, I can't hear Kiana going on about this and that, so maybe this is a blessing in disguise.

Day 23 Krakow, Poland 7/22/10

It's a bright and sunny day in Poland. I'm still on the train. We're two hours late. I asked the conductor why, and he said with a smile, "It's Poland!"

Right now I have to take a dump, but I'm holding it in. I'm trying to make it to the hotel because the train toilet looks like one of those porta-potties. There's piss everywhere and no toilet paper. Luckily, we booked two nights at a Holiday Inn in Krakow. It's supposed to be a five-star hotel, but it will probably end up being like any other Holiday Inn back in the States. It can't be worse than that shithole we stayed in at Venice. I just want to shower and be clean again. Kiana's dancing in the train corridor to some dance my cousin's kids showed her back in Venice while I'm moping around disgruntled because I had very little sleep, and I need to make some bowel movements.

We arrived, showered, then took a long nap before walking into the Old City of Krakow. Its cobblestone streets have a bunch of restaurants, bars, entertainers, retail stores, and all the amenities we have in the West. There's a blend of old and new in this little town, and I felt completely comfortable walking around here. Overall, there weren't too many tourists like Venice but just enough. In ten years I could see this place being overrun with visitors. Presently, Krakow has a quaint Polish feel to it. I'd highly recommend it to others.

Tomorrow we're heading off to Oswiecim, the city that holds the Auschwitz concentration camp. It's about an hour away from Krakow. It should be an educational experience.

Day 24 The Holocaust 7/23/10

It is written in the *Book of Revelation* that there will be a "multitude which no man can number" (Rev.7:9-14) that will oppose the Antichrist and die for their faith. During this time this Man of Lawlessness will overrun the Nation of Israel, and a great genocide will occur amongst the Jews. It happened before during WWII, and it will happen again during WWIII.

Today at Auschwitz, I witnessed the first genocide of the Jews, Poles, and other gentile nations. I walked through the camp that murdered over a million people. I saw the guard towers and electrified barbed-wired fences. I saw human hair, baggage, shoes, combs, and an actual furnace that burned the bodies of those who had been killed. It's a horrific site but an eye-opener for the tourists who flock to the camp each day.

The troubling thing about Auschwitz is that someone actually carried out these orders. Who in their right mind would buy into this way of thinking? Apparently many Nazi soldiers did, and there were nations of people who marched in step with them. It's a scary thought, isn't it? Guess what, it's going to happen again. Only this time, the death count will be magnified a hundredfold. Everyone will "be given a mark on their right hand or forehead" (Rev.13:16-18) if they want to live and survive. What would you do? Where would you stand?

Yes, it's easy to say you will oppose this system, this Führer, this ultimate solution, but I don't think it's going to be that easy. How will you feed your kids if you don't get the Number of the Beast? You won't be able to go down to the market and buy groceries. Do you plan to hunt game or store up food to survive this Tribulation on earth? I hope you make it. If not, please go out valiantly and make a stand for the Lord. But whatever happens, do not get the Mark of the Beast. If you do, you will suffer eternal consequences. No matter what, you've heard the Word. You are now going to be held accountable if it takes place in your lifetime.

The Mark of the Beast makes sense. In this global economy, it would solve so many problems. Everyone would be marked like the Jews and Poles of Auschwitz, but only this time around, all who are marked will do it voluntarily, and they will be sent to the Lake of Fire for complying.

Day 25 Eating, Drinking, & Screwing 7/24/10

I'm waiting at the train station again. I truly feel like the traveling circus. Stop for a few days in one town and move onto the next. After a while, everything looks the same. The only difference is the women and the people. As for the Poles, I did notice a lot of beautiful looking women. I think a western man could have a lot of success out here if he was looking to score pussy. Actually, I think any traveler can be successful with women in foreign lands because they stick out to the locals and are seen as being unique and different. But isn't there more to life than our instinctual drives? If Darwin's right, there really is no purpose to life. It's all about spreading your seed to as many women as possible before you kick the bucket. Your legacy might live on for a few generations, but eventually your family lineage will die out like the dinosaurs. You eat. You drink. You fuck. You die. It's a sad way to walk through life. This teaching leaves everyone without hope and a purpose to their existence, but this is what's being taught in our public schools today. Science classes teach that we evolved from apes, and that there is no god. Personally, I don't buy into this theory. I think it takes more faith to believe in this teaching than it does to believe that God is the Creator of the universe. He is the prime mover.

Stop!!! There I go off on another tangent when I'm supposed to be telling you about my journey. It's going well, but at times I wonder if I'm too old for this. I know some people think they're going to do all their traveling when they retire. I truly hope disease and age don't take that away from you. Maybe you'll make it to Paris in the long run, but if I were you, I'd travel now while you're young and strong, and you can climb those steps to the great cathedrals.

Day 26 Give Peace a Chance 7/25/10

Back in 1992, I cruised around the City of Prague with a beautiful blonde from Canada. We met at the train station that was heading to the Czech Republic, so we decided to see the sites together. In the evening we went to my first and last opera. We were both bored out of our minds, so we left early and got drunk at a Prague brewery. A day later, we were off to Berlin. We shared a room together for a couple of days before she flew home.

This time around I saw the City of Prague with my wife. It wasn't as wild and crazy as the days when I had long hair and carried a guitar with me, but I think I'm able to appreciate the culture better now that I'm wiser than I once was.

One of the sites I found intriguing in Prague was the John Lennon Wall. It's this giant wall of graffiti near Charles Bridge. On the wall are a bunch of sayings by John Lennon like "Give peace a chance" and "All you need is love." I have to admit John Lennon did have some revolutionary ideas, but I'm not a disciple of his teachings. Personally, I don't believe we'll ever have peace in this era. War will always be with us because greed and desire are in the hearts of all humanity. That is why I don't think world peace is possible the way things are today. As Bob Dylan once wrote on one of his Christian albums, "There will be no peace. The world won't cease until He returns." Yes ladies and gentlemen, one day we will have world peace, but not until we have a just king ruling the planet. His name is Jesus Christ, the Counselor, and we will have peace for 1,000 years. This is what the *Bible* teaches, and I'm waiting expectantly for "Thy kingdom come, Thy will be done on earth as it is in heaven."

Kiana and I are jumping onto another train. This time we're heading to Berlin after spending a day walking around Prague. It amazes me that we are able to travel to these cities at all after living through the Cold War. Is the war really over? If I were an advisor to the President, I'd say, "No way in hell." The threat has only grown greater. More nations have the bomb, and it appears a storm is rising against us. The Black Market sends shivers down my spine, and our unprotected ports are a ticking time bomb. As for Russia, I'd keep shaking hands with them, but I wouldn't take my eyes off them for a second.

Day 27 Berlin, Germany 7/26/10

As I stood outside the U.S. Embassy near where the Berlin Wall fell, I realized how far we've come in the last twenty years. The fall of the East has brought freedom and prosperity to a multitude of countries. The fear that Stalin is going to take you away at any moment is gone, and the people can rest in their beds at night. Yet I don't feel at ease. I don't feel at rest. There's still that threat of nuclear annihilation hanging on my shoulders. Is the press to blame, or is my American paranoia justified? I believe there is a reason to be afraid, but it appears to me the rest of the world has been lulled into a false sense of security. Nations like Germany and Poland are rebuilding. People are getting married and celebrating. Everyone seems to have forgotten about the troubles of the world. It's just as the Bible said it would be. It would be like the Days of Noah when suddenly the Flood came upon them and washed them all away. Only this time the world will be destroyed by fire. Yes, my friends, it is my duty to warn you about the coming apocalypse. If I don't, your blood will be on my hands. You may ask, "What am I supposed to do in the meantime?" I doubt you'll be able to change the greater outcome, but you may be able to get right with God before it's too late. Then try to live a good and honorable life the rest of your days.

As for the European journey, Kiana and I spent a couple of days in Berlin. We meandered around the city and saw some of the famous sites. Remnants of the Berlin Wall by the Sony Center were the most significant, but I wish they would have preserved more of the Wall as a memorial. Zoo Station was also interesting, but the walk through the park was the most refreshing. It allowed us to forget about the madness of the city for a spell. No major events took place in Germany like they did in the Czech Republic. In Prague, Kiana was almost arrested for not having a subway ticket. They made her pay a fine of 700 koruna ($35 dollars) on the spot. Luckily we had enough Czech money. If not, they would have taken her down to the station for interrogation, and she might still be locked away behind bars.

Day 28 Legalization of Pot 7/27/10

We arrived in the multicultural city of Amsterdam. As soon as we got off the train, we reserved another train to Paris in a couple of days, so we'd get out of here on time. I figured this was wise considering I met several people eighteen years ago who hung around this place too long. Some acquired jobs working at coffee shops, and some just milled around the city so they could get high everyday. Yes, it's true; marijuana and prostitution are legal here. They have these cafes that look like coffee shops, and you can order an ounce or more of weed like you would order a latte or a burger. It's very odd, but it's probably the direction California is heading. As for prostitution, everyone knows it exists under the radar, but I don't see it becoming legal anytime soon back in the United States. Then again, who knows? It's already legal in Nevada.

Personally, I think marijuana should be legalized for a variety of reasons. First, hemp can be made into many products. For example, we could make paper out of it like our Founding Fathers did, and we would no longer have to cut down our rain forests to supply our voracious appetite for paper. It would be beneficial to the environment. Second, we could tax the product like cigarettes and boost our failing economy. Who knows, this might be the product that lifts the country out of debt? Third, there are some medicinal benefits to marijuana. They say it eases pain and gives the user a greater appetite. This could help people who have cancer and are going through Chemo like my uncle did before he passed away. It could also help people with AIDS who have significant weight loss. Eating or smoking marijuana might give them more of an appetite and they might live longer.

Now I know many people are against the legalization of pot because it is a drug. Yes, it can be psychologically addicting and a real danger if people are smoking it while they are driving a car or doing something that involves a lot of concentration. But this applies to any drug. All drugs can be potentially dangerous if they are not used in a safe environment. As for alcohol and nicotine, they are already legal drugs, and I believe marijuana falls into the same category as these two. Hence, I think we need to make it a vice that's available to adults only, tax the hell out of it, and teach our children about the dangers of using it. No matter what, prohibition does not work. Users of marijuana will get the drug regardless if it's legal or not, so we might as well make some money on it and help the environment in the process.

Day 29 Vices 7/28/10

I got stoned for a second time in Amsterdam. It's a vice that I partake in a few times a year to take off the edge and let myself go. Sometimes I want to check out and not worry about the state of the world for a spell. I know it's considered wrong by the Christian community, but I figured I might as well tell the truth and be upfront about it. Is it acceptable with God? I don't know, but I am honest with the Lord when I smoke the peace pipe. I don't go into denial with Him when I'm smoking. I always try to keep an open heart with God and leave nothing hidden. God is my friend, my Father, and my Counselor, and He knows me better than my wife and mother. Yes, I do look to God for advice at times, but He's really my trusted friend that I communicate with on a daily/hourly basis. Yes, I know it sounds strange to an unbeliever, but my spirit is alive when I speak with Him, and His Holy Spirit resides within my soul.

As for marijuana, I think God understands I need an outlet a few times a year to deal with stress and other troubles on my mind. I suppose I use it every now and then because I don't really have many vices except my addiction to sports and Internet porn. I drink very little. I don't smoke cigarettes. I do drink tea in the morning, but it's decaffeinated, and I have about one Coke a day. Beyond a few joints a year, that's it. I'm clean. It's usually a couple of times during summer, once during Christmas Break, and once during Spring Break. Notice I never use it when I'm on the job. I need to focus and be sharp at all times when I'm dealing with rebellious teenagers. Well, there it is. I hope my impure testimony does not turn you away from believing in God.

Kiana and I walked around and saw a few sites in the city. We were going to see a live sex show to spark up the marriage, but there was too much testosterone in the line, so we skipped it. Instead we quickly browsed through the Red Light District and gawked at all the prostitutes in the windows wearing lingerie. Of course, I could have stayed longer, but it wouldn't have been appropriate, so we moved on and will be heading to Paris tomorrow.

Day 30 Unlike Paul 7/29/10

The haze is clearing. My lungs are burning. My nose is dripping. It's cold outside. Summer in the Netherlands is similar to summer in San Francisco. I don't like it much. I want the sun to shine more often, and its heat to warm my bones.

Right now I'm on a speed train to Paris. The ride's a little over three hours, so I'll be there in the blink of an eye. Last night I found it quite interesting to be able to buy pot legally in a coffee shop and smoke it on the premises. The shop was very busy and people were coming and going the whole time I was there. I suppose that's how it will be if pot becomes legal in California. On the whole, I have mixed emotions on the issue. I am for legalization, but I wonder if more people will start using the drug when they can buy it at their local 7-11 store. In some ways it doesn't sit well with me because I know many people are uneducated on the subject and will abuse the drug. In my case, I do have some regrets about smoking pot. First of all, I have asthma, so it makes it more difficult for me to breathe afterwards. A better option for me would be to eat brownies or not smoke at all. Second, some people will stumble over this because I'm giving a poor Christian testimony. In Europe some people think drinking caffeine is a bad testimony. In some parts of the world, eating meat is frowned upon. And back in the States, drinking alcohol and smoking pot is seen as a deviation from conservative Christian values. I understand their point. I must be "all things to all men," (1Cor.9:23) but if I take Paul's point to its extremity, I might as well become a monk and live in a monastery the rest of my days to please everyone. Still, if smoking pot a few times a year is a stumbling block for you, I might need to change my behavior. I don't want others to turn away from God because I eat marijuana cookies. Believe me, I've done far more evil deeds over the past two decades that would make you say, "I thought you said Enoch was a Christian." I know. I'm guilty. There are a lot of sins I've done over the years that are far worse than smoking ganja. Just know I'm not perfect. I'm being reformed. I make mistakes, sometimes big mistakes. The only difference with a non-believer and me is that Jesus' blood covers my sin. Does this give me free reign to sin and do as I please? Absolutely not! I should be an example to others and live by a higher standard. I know all this. I'm trying. But in the end, I'm as flawed as everyone else, and I don't see myself being perfected until the day I die.

Day 31 Hail Mary... Hell No 7/30/10

We're in Paris. We just spent a day visiting the Louvre Museum. It is by far the best museum in the world. The paintings are magnificent, and there are antiquities from the Egyptian, Greek, and Roman eras. Of course, there's tons of religious art and more statues of Jesus and Mary. Almost every one of the major museums I've gone to in Europe has an over-abundance of art dedicated to Jesus and Mary. The ones dedicated to Jesus I can understand, but what's this fascination we have with Mary? Yes, she was blessed. Yes, she bore the Son of God, but she was not a perpetual virgin, nor did she live a sinless life. After 2,000 years it's time to put the Mary issue to rest despite what the Catholic Church teaches. Jesus had brothers and sisters. It's mentioned in the Gospels several times, so it means Mary was not a virgin. She was most likely a virgin up to the birth of Jesus, but after that, she did have sexual intercourse. (Mt.1:25; Mt.12:46; Mt.13:55; Mk.3:31-32; Mk.6:3) As for Mary living a sinless life, the idea is preposterous! If Mary did live a sinless life then what was the purpose of Jesus dying on the cross? Jesus died on the cross for "all" the sins of man/woman and that includes Mother Mary. It's true. Mary was blessed. She deserves honor; however, she should not be worshipped, and it's idolatry to pray to her. She is not God. There is only "one mediator between God and man" (1Tim.2:5) and His name is Jesus of Nazareth. That means we need to dump the prayer dedicated to her. "Hail Mary!" Hell no! There's only one person we should hail and that's God, not Caesar, not Hitler, not Napoleon, and not Mary.

Whew! That was a load off my chest. Now back to Paris. It's the same as I remember it twenty years ago. The people are friendly and will try to help you out as long as you try to speak some French to them. I usually say something like this when I address someone in France. "Excusez-moi, parlez-vous anglais?" (Excuse me, do you speak English?) If they say no, I respond by saying "merci" (thank you) and head on my way. If they say "oui" (yes) then I continue by speaking in English. In general, I've noticed this simple courtesy makes them smile and more willing to help me. A lot of the French get upset when you start speaking to them in English right off. It would be like someone coming up to you and speaking to you in Japanese and expecting you to understand them. In other areas, the French love their outside cafes and appear to be more open about their sexuality.

Day 32 Ménage à Trois 7/31/10

Last night we were sitting at a crowded French cafe, and we were sharing a table with this exotic looking French woman. We ended up getting into a pretty intimate conversation with her, and before we knew it, we were taking her back to our hotel. Yes, ménage à trois, I was in French heaven! We rock and rolled all night, and I was able to live out one of my childhood fantasies. The next morning was even crazier. The maid came in unannounced and abruptly opened the door. She was wearing one of those French-maid outfits that you see the girls wear on Halloween, and I almost orgasmed on the spot. The maid said, "excusez-moi," and was about to leave, but our new friend invited her to join us, and she did. Before I knew it, I was sleeping with three women at the same time. It was a wild orgy in my hotel room. I was in ecstasy. It was the best day of my life...

As most of you can tell, I'm bullshitting you, but I thought I might let you know what I hoped Paris would be. Of course, reality never lives up to our fantasies, but this is what I was dreaming about this morning before Kiana's alarm clock went off.

Later in the day, we went and saw Jim Morrison's grave. I was unimpressed. It was this little gravesite with barely any graffiti on it or anything. Oscar Wilde's grave was far more impressive. It's at the same cemetery. We then went and saw a couple of the sites, and we plan to go and see the Eiffel Tower later in the evening. Yes, I'd prefer the French-maid scenario too, but I might not be able to live out that fantasy until I'm dead and residing in heaven. Then again, I might be in hell. Either way, I hope my fantasy comes true someday.

Well, it's time to hit the road. I'll speak with you all soon. Bon jour!

Day 33 Finding Solace 8/1/10

I have no idea how those bands go on tour for years or months at a time because I'm wearing out. I think forty days is a bit too long for a trip. A month is pushing it, but I think three weeks is just about right. From now on I believe I'm going to condense my trips down to shorter ventures.

Today we saw the Eiffel Tower and headed out of there as soon as possible because the place was crawling with tourists. We then cruised around the Red Light District. It's nothing to write home about, gentlemen, and it sort of reminds me of Downtown Vegas with all the strip joints and sex shops. Afterwards, we went and saw the Hollywood movie *Inception*. I liked the concept behind the movie, but it lacked the tension of a high quality thriller. In any case, it was nice to checkout for a while and get lost in the story.

Right now, I'm on a night train to Lourdes with Kiana. We're sharing a compartment with another girl. She's pretty quiet and is keeping to herself. Thank God for the quiet people of the world. They're like a running stream during times of chaos.

Today was uneventful. I'm going to get some sleep. I'll speak with you all tomorrow.

Day 34 Lourdes, France 8/2/10

Our train arrived early in the morning, so we had time to kill before we were able to check into our hotel. Therefore, we went to an outside coffee shop and had breakfast. Before we knew it, there were hordes of people passing by us like they were making a pilgrimage to the top of Mount Sinai. Only these people were in wheelchairs and gurneys. I would estimate that over 300 handicapped or infirmed people passed us by as we ate our breakfast and sipped our tea. You may ask, "Enoch, where were they going?" They were heading to these pools of sacred water where two people supposedly were healed long ago.

Back in 1858, there was a girl named Bernadette who saw apparitions of Mary. The apparition told Bernadette to "Go and drink from the spring and wash herself in it". A few months later, two people were healed by having contact with the water from this spring. The result of this miracle now brings over 400,000 people a year to be dipped into the pools of water. Everyone is hoping to be healed, and the Catholic Church has confirmed that over sixty-seven people have been healed since Bernadette first saw the apparitions.

Is the water holy? I doubt it. I think people believe the water is holy, and that allows them to release their faith as they're being dipped into the water. I think some people are so thoroughly convinced that the water will heal them that they get healed. It's mind over matter, I suppose. But do real miracles of healing occur today? Yes, I believe they do, but they're probably few and far between. Personally, I think Lourdes is a con. It's just another scam like the healings you see on Christian television stations. "Be healed in the name of the Lord Jesus!" Yes, I do believe God can do miracles today, but why are the donation booths on every corner? It's because the church knows they can make a lot of money promoting these miracles. Every now and then, someone really does get healed because they believe God will heal them. It has nothing to do with their smoke and mirrors.

Am I a skeptic? Yes I am! I'm sick of people getting ripped off by these conmen. They wear funny hats, and they walk around in holy robes. They do a trick or two, and before you know it, you've handed over your life savings to them. These are the corrupted clergy, and it's my duty to call them out. They call themselves priests. They call themselves prophets. But really they're false teachers who are leading the flock to hell.

Day 35 On the Train to Switzerland Thinking 8/3/10

1. Traveling is all about taking shits in public bathrooms. It's about sleeping on beds that are too hard, too soft, or infested with bed bugs. It's about getting lost, looking at maps, and trying to communicate you want a burger cooked medium rare with fries on the side.
2. Now that I've bitten into the fruit, and I've traveled the lands, is there anything else to taste or see?
3. When you started out, did you think you'd end up working behind a desk day in and day out? Did you think you'd end up with someone else? Yeah, I know we all have regrets, but if you had the chance, wouldn't you do a few things differently?
4. We're heading to Switzerland on a train. I saw a beautiful Swiss girl. She made me think of Swiss chocolate and Swiss tits at the same time. Mmmm...yummy.
5. Sinead O Connor once sang, "These are dangerous days to say what you feel is to make your own grave." I don't know if she said it first, but she's probably right. I am digging my own grave. If I dig deep enough, will I reach hell?
6. I just listened to a duet by Joe Strummer and Johnny Cash singing "Redemption Song" by Bob Marley. Wow, all three of my heroes are dead now, but their music will live forever...

Day 36 Neutrality Won't Save You 8/4/10

We spent two nights in Geneva, Switzerland. We didn't do too much. We ate. We slept. We saw a few sites, but neither of us felt like climbing the hill to see the rest of them, so we hung out by Lake Geneva. The place reminds me of Tahoe. There are majestic mountains, rivers, waterfalls, and a giant lake. It's tranquil here. As for this train ride, it stinks. There's a family of tourists sitting a row ahead of us and for some reason they must shout as loud as possible to the person sitting right next to them when they want to say something. It's annoying. They're obnoxious. It's like one of my neighbors back home. They have parties every other night. They block our driveway with their cars, and they leave their trash everywhere when they're done. They have no respect or civility. At times I feel like standing on my balcony and opening fire on everyone of those motherfuckers. Instead I play nice, hold my anger inside, and hope their house goes into foreclosure.

I don't understand people today. Has it always been this way? It appears like no one gives a damn about anyone but themselves. People graffiti private property, throw trash into rivers and streams, and pollute the atmosphere with their loud music and boisterous play. At times like these I want to light a match, watch it burn, and laugh at the assholes screaming.

As for Switzerland, I think I understand why they don't take sides. They keep the madness out with their mountains of snow and watch the world burn around them. In the next world war, neutrality won't save them. Their refuge might spare them for a spell, but by the time it's over, they'll reap the whirlwind like everybody else.

Day 37 Modern Conveniences 8/5/10

We arrived in Florence, Italy with rain showers and lightning, so we decided to catch up on our laundry, which was way overdue. Fortunately, there was a laundromat right across the street from our hotel. This is the first time we've been blessed with this holy site. On this trip it's been difficult to get our clothes cleaned. Either we can't find a self-service laundromat close by, or they charge an arm and a leg to dry-clean your clothes. Thus, we've been washing our clothes in the sink and hang drying them in our hotel rooms. The clothes come out stretched and wrinkled, but it's better than walking around in a dirty pair of socks.

I must say modern amenities are the holiest sites I've seen on this trip. Sure the churches were beautiful, but finding an Internet cafe and a laundromat was far more impressive. Yes, we are lucky to be living in the 21st Century. We have running water, toilets, refrigerators, stoves, microwaves, computers, electricity, and much more. There are so many conveniences we take for granted. I wonder how we'd survive without them. And if our supermarkets stopped stocking food, how would we put food on our tables? I suppose we'd have to hunt rodents and dogs to get by.

Well, I hate to be the bearer of bad news, but our civilization has just about reached its pinnacle. A new Dark Ages is coming. Soon it's going to be all about who has the most ammo and canned goods. And don't forget about water. Our water supply is already polluted, and it's getting worse with each passing decade. Now try to imagine if a terrorist poisoned our water supply. It might be easier than a walk through the park. Just take out the Colorado and the Mississippi, and the U.S. would be at a standstill.

Like I said before, these are unstable times, and all it takes is one major disaster to pull it all apart.

For the sake of the young, I hope God will give us more time to repent. Maybe if we change our ways and live righteous lives, God will spare our homelands. Maybe if we set things right and put things back in order, the apocalypse won't come for many generations in the future. God has spared scores of generations in the past. He might spare this one too. But if you read the stories of the Hebrew people, they never learned their lesson and neither do we. They constantly went back to the idols that angered God and brought His wrath down upon them. Look around you. There might not be any statues of Mary or Zeus hanging on your walls, but how many TV's do you have in your house? How many hours do you sit in front of her? Now tell me, who is your god?

Day 38 The Meaning of Life 8/6/10

Going downhill now. Tomorrow, we're leaving Florence and heading to Rome. It's our last city. Thank God! I'm tired and missing all the familiar things back home. In general, it feels like my life is going downhill now too. When you're younger, you're always trying to achieve something and reach those lofty ideals, but somewhere in your thirties or forties, you get comfortable. Many of us know our lot in life and have come to accept who we are by then. We've reached many of the goals we set out to achieve, even though some of them have fallen by the wayside. I am satisfied with how my life has turned out so far. Sure, I have a lot of regrets like everyone else, but I've learned a lot through my failures. Isn't life all about trial and error anyway? Yes or no, I'm pretty comfortable in my skin nowadays. I know who I am, and I know where I'm going. I doubt I could say that back in my teens or my twenties, but now that my hair is getting gray, and I've been around the block a few times, I can tell which way is east. Sure, I still make mistakes, but I'm wiser than I once was. Imagine how knowledgeable we'll be when we are in our seventies or eighties, if we make it that far? Our grandparents must be geniuses by now! It's a shame our bodies have to decay right when we're at the peak of our intelligence. The thing I do find perplexing about some of our most brilliant citizens, however, is that many of them never find God. They know physics. They know astronomy, and they've read thousands of books on a variety of topics, but they still wander in the wilderness lost. The *Bible* says, "The fear (reverence) of the Lord is the beginning of knowledge," (Prov.1:7) not going to school and earning your Masters Degree or Ph.D. Yes, these people have reached great achievements, but so many of them walk through life never having a personal relationship with God. That's not what life's supposed to be about. It has nothing to do with money, status, fame, power, and all the other bullshit we've been brainwashed with since our childhoods. Life's supposed to be about walking with God and sharing our joys and tears with Him. Yes, family and friends are important, but if our relationship with God is not on the top of our list, we really haven't lived at all.

Day 39 Caesar's Rome 8/7/10

Italy is remnants of an empire that slowly broke apart. There's the Colosseum, the Pantheon, and the Baths of Caracalla. They're all ruins now. Someday tourists will come to America and say the same thing. "Here's what's left of the Golden Gate Bridge. This is where the White House once stood. In the distance is the Manhattan skyline..." I don't like the sound of it either, but all empires come to a close eventually. Is America on the verge of going down in history? I can't be for sure. The United States is not mentioned in end time's prophecy. Does that mean we will vanish from the scene or become part of the revived Roman Empire? Either way, Rome's reign won't last long. Their revival is a short stint before the final apocalypse. Interpreting Daniel's prophecies and figuring out John's *Revelation* has confounded theologians for years, so I'm not going to say I completely understand the visions. Even the dreams I've been given sometimes become cloudy streams of consciousness, so I'll wait and see like everyone else.

As for the Caesars of yesterday, it's amazing how quickly their names are forgotten. All that's left of them are heads of marble. All that will be left of us is a gravestone in some cemetery. We will return to dust and be remembered no more. One in a billion might make it into a history book, and a few people will be remembered for their contribution to society, but for the rest of us, our deeds will be long forgotten. Only in heaven will we be known as we are known. For those cast into hell, I suppose they will dwell in outer darkness. It makes one realize that our lives are passing. We are like the flowers of the field. We bloom in the spring and die in the fall. In the blink of an eye, our lives are over. Hence, we need to love one another and capture every moment before death comes for us and our epitaph is written.

Day 40 Forty Day Fast 8/8/10

Twenty-six train rides. Eight overnights. Seventeen hotels. Six plane flights. We've been all over Europe. We've been here and there. We crossed into Africa and got caught in a snare. It's been quite a journey. We've seen tons of sites. We got chased by bulls and lost several times.

We've seen parts of Morocco, Portugal, and Spain. We cruised through Vienna, Prague, and Germany. We saw Switzerland, the Netherlands, and Italy. We dined with the French, and saw Krakow's Polish streets.

It's been forty days without the comforts of home. Forty days without American sports. Forty days without driving a car. Forty days without my TV shows. It's been forty days without looking at Internet crap. Forty days without my family or friends.

Yes, there are a lot of things that we can go without. These needs and addictions don't define who we are. We've just become spoiled, gluttons, and fiends. Most of us are walking around like zombies. We need to fast from all our hang-ups and let them go, so we can see clearly and not stray from the fold. There will be plenty of detours because nothing goes as planned. You have to take it like a woman or take it like a man. So let's rise above the ashes. Let's live an honorable life. Let's be true to our country and true to the Lord. Let's help out the widows, the downtrodden, and the poor. Let's give of ourselves and slowly change the world!

Chapter 3:
Visions of the Absurd

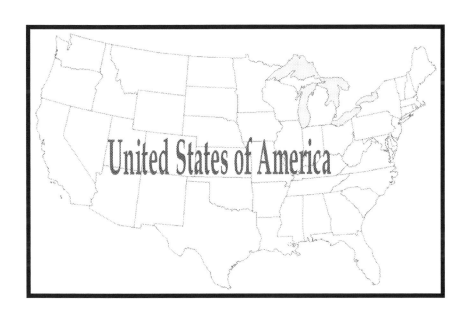

01 The Clock is Ticking 8/9/10-8/30/10

I'm home again. It didn't take long to get back into the routine of things. My European trip is already slipping back into the recesses of my mind. Now what? I suppose I have a few more chapters to write until my time is up. That means I have about 472 days left of my life. According to the prophecy when my testimony is completed the Beast will overcome me, and I'll be put to death. Am I afraid? Hell yes! Who is not afraid of death? Yes, I have faith that I'll join the Lord in heaven, but I still have doubts like everyone else. I'm like the father in the Gospel of Mark who said, "Help my unbelief" (Mk.9:24) when he wanted an unclean spirit cast out of his son. I'm another Doubting Thomas. I don't have the faith to move mountains, but if I did I'd walk on water and perform many miracles in the Lord's name.

I tend to wonder if my 1,260 day testimony is another fleeting dream that one day is here and the next is gone. Either way, I'm going to lay it on the line whether anyone's listening or not. Maybe someone out there will relate to my tale, and there will be some fruit from these confessions. If not, I'll go back to what I was doing before. I'll dig a hole and put my head in the sand. Maybe I'll head out on the road again and try to make a difference somewhere else. Then again, maybe I'll rot in hell. I could spend all eternity reliving my glory days when I was younger or spend eternity watching reruns of *I Love Lucy* and *The Twilight Zone*.

Ah hell! It feels like everything is such a waste of time, and I'm banging my head against the wall. At least the pain lets me know that I'm still alive because sometimes I feel like I'm comfortably numb. I'm sure there's someone out there saying, "Quit your moping and blow your brains out already!" If I had the cojones, I'd play Russian Roulette, but I would never take my own life. I'd love to see the other side and head out on the next trip because this one's kind of getting dull and boring. There's got to be something more to life. Do we simply fade and fizzle out? I hope not. There have been some great times down here on earth. I just wish the good times would be more frequent and last a little longer.

02 Bearing False Witness 8/31/10-9/7/10

A week ago I was informed that they cut my *Bible as Literature* class from the curriculum. Why did this happen? The principal dodged the issue when I asked her, but I'm sure it has to do with that lawyer who came in last spring arguing that the *Bible* can't be taught in a public school. That's all it takes these days to eliminate one of the best classes I have ever taught in my tenure. One lawyer threatens to sue the district, so the district gets nervous and cancels the class. This sort of thing has been happening for decades now because we have too many lawyers and judges deciding the fate of our nation. Yes, it's time to get rid of all the litigation and start all over again. These bastards have too much power, and they're completely undermining the democratic process. The populace has become "sue" happy too, and everyone's running around with their tails between their legs because we're afraid we'll get sued. People don't even care if it's right or wrong anymore. It's all about how much money one can get out of the company/person they're trying to screw over. It's a shame. It's a damn shame.

Our judicial system has been corrupted as well. If you have enough money, you'll probably walk free through some loophole. People are bearing false witness against one another and bribes are taking place behind closed doors. Who can you trust nowadays? Who can you believe? Can you believe the newspapers or what's being seen on television? I honestly can't tell fact from fiction anymore. Sure, making a profit is important, but what happened to the integrity of our news media? How can I learn about what's really going on in the world when all I hear about is Hollywood crap? It's hard enough to see through all the propaganda dished out on the airwaves, but it's even more difficult to focus on the story when I'm staring at the weather girl's tits and ass. Yes, I am distracted. TV has numbed my senses. Law and order has made me senseless, and the press is being taken over by Big Business and special interest groups.

03 Written in Stone 9/8/10-9/14/10

Ahab was an evil king who reigned in Israel long ago; therefore, God pronounced a strong judgment against Ahab because he followed the advice of his wicked wife, Jezebel. When Ahab heard the news from the prophet Elijah that he and his wife were going to die, he humbled himself before God, so the Lord decided to spare Ahab from immediate destruction. This made me realize that even though you and I have done wrong, there is still a chance for us to repent and change our ways before it's too late. Sure we could wallow in our misery and accept our evil fate, but why don't we change our fate instead? It's not written in stone. And even if it is, we can break that stone and start all over again. I don't want my epitaph to say, "Enoch was an evil prophet who did not follow after the Lord." And the same goes for your final words. Maybe our epitaphs could read this way instead: "Enoch had his shortcomings and failures, but overall, he did right by the Lord." Now just change the name from Enoch to your name, and we'll be on the same page. It can be done. We can be overcomers. Instead of being remembered as evildoers, lets be remembered as the just and honorable ones. We can change our fate like Ebenezer Scrooge did and turn our life around before it's too late. How are we going to accomplish this task? There are many ways, but I believe if we focus on doing more good deeds and helping others, we won't have time to indulge in our sins. Of course, we'll also need to humble ourselves before God like King Ahab did, and let Him guide our footsteps. Each of us has been blessed with a gift. Now we need to use that gift for good instead of evil.

04 Absurdity 9/15/10-9/20/10

The more I think about it, the more absurd the Gospel becomes to me. Death, hell, fire, and brimstone. Sin, sacrifice, and staying holy. Good, evil, the Devil, God??? It leaves me with one giant question mark, and I ask myself, "Why?" There's so much I don't understand. The closer I get to God, the further I realize I've come. Our relationship is a paradox beyond comprehension. As for God Himself, I feel sort of sorry for Him. To have always been. To always be. To be nothing. To be something. To create. To uncreate. To destroy. To build again. Everything that we have done, even our greatest achievements is like a 5-year-old's drawing with crayons. Shakespeare, Beethoven, and Da Vinci's greatest works of art are all posted on the refrigerator with a magnet. We're clearly little children to God. We fight. We compete. And we pray for God's help. I'm tired of playing this game. I'm tired of following the rules. I don't want to make any more petitions. I won't throw another sacrifice on the altar. God does not require our sacrifices, our blood and tears, our great works. He requires nothing. He is God, life is life, and that's it. At times I feel so used by Him like we're on the stage, and He's out there in the audience watching. He already knows the outcome because He's seen this scene before. He probably quotes our greatest moments and laughs at our funniest lines. Oh God, trying to understand you is beyond comprehension! All I want to know is why? Why the Garden? Why the Tree? Why did you come here at all? What does it all mean? The Word of God doesn't answer all my questions. It leaves me half full and hungering for more. It makes me put faith in the unseen. It pigeonholes me into a corner saying, "This is right and this is wrong." Well, I don't want to play the game anymore. I won't be your cheap entertainment. I won't be your hot date on a Friday night that gets all hot and horny, loses her virginity, and feels remorse afterwards. I don't want to feel guilty. I don't want to be tamed. I want to break out from the status quo and start a revolution. God, you'll always be my God, but at times I get frustrated with your Law and order. I want to rebel against your authority like a teenager and drive my car 100 miles per hour into a wall.

05 Was Jesus a Murderer or a Maniac? 9/21/10-9/25/10

Every Christmas time I hear those jingle bells about Jesus, the Messiah, born in Bethlehem. Over and over those songs are played and played as I cruise through the mall buying gifts. Now over the years, I've heard the sleigh bell ring, but I started thinking about Jesus, not old Saint Nick. Was Jesus the Messiah, God in the flesh, or was He just another lunatic without a gun?

So I went home and searched the source. They say He performed miracles and healed the sick. They say He was crucified and died for our sins. They say over 500 saw Him rise from the dead. But I just laughed and said, "This can't be. Why would God care for a suicidal race?" In fact, if there's a God, I think He'd agree. But it got me to thinking, so I went ahead and asked, "Was Jesus a murderer or a maniac?"

Now some time has passed, I've sought and found. I've read the pros and cons and been tossed around. Ancient prophecies bewilder and confound. The coincidences are beyond belief. Now I've come to the conclusion though some may disagree. You might call me a fool or a Jesus freak. But I don't care because I believe. Jesus is the Messiah, not a lunatic. Jesus wasn't a murderer or a maniac.

06 Death, Rebellion, & the Unknown Soldiers 9/26/10-10/3/10

Death is a cruel companion. He lurks in the shadows then sneaks up on you and robs you of those closest to you. This week he took the mother of my wife, so there's been a lot of weeping at my house. Yes, she was old. The Alzheimer's had already started to kick in, and she'll be better off up in heaven, but death is still an uninvited guest. I wish death did not exist. Why did God create sin and death in the first place? Yes, I know the Tree of Good and Evil was placed in the Garden to test our loyalty, but I believe God could have played the game of man with a different set of rules. In the end, I'm sure our suffering on earth won't compare with the glory in heaven, but from my angle it appears there's a bit too much suffering going on around here.

On another track, I've been back to school for a month, and sometimes I wonder why the hell I went into teaching. My classes are a bit unruly this year, and it feels like I'm spending too much time on discipline than education. It's wearing me out a bit, but eventually the kids will come around, and they won't see me as a ruthless dictator. They'll remember me as one of the better teachers they've had, but for right now they're feeling the wrath of their disobedient behavior. I suppose God has to do the same thing with His children from time to time. I've been a rebellious student like many of my kids, and some of you are the jokers, the hecklers, and apathetic youth too. We need God's discipline and order. Without it, we would never find the straight and narrow path. We'd wander lost in the wilderness for decades and even generations.

My generation is one of the lost ones. It's like we've been repeating the story in Hemingway's book, *The Sun Also Rises,* over and over again. At the end of the day or at the end of the decade, we ask ourselves, "Where did the time go? There's got to be something more to this picture show." Instead, we go from place to place or never go anywhere at all. We're either Hemingway or Steinbeck and some of us are unknown soldiers fighting battles and doing time down here on earth.

07 Fall of the White House 10/4/10-10/9/10

At 2:00 A.M. this morning, October 9th, I awoke from a prophetic dream of the Lord. I was in the White House when I received the vision. He said, "No room in this house will be left standing." Immediately after I heard the word, my heart sunk in my chest like hearing the news that someone close to you just died. So I headed out of there as fast as possible and sought cover from the coming storm.

After I woke, the Spirit confirmed that this was a true vision given from the Lord. I was not given the interpretation, but I think it could mean either three things. First, it could mean that just the White House will be destroyed. Second, it could mean that the capital of the United States will be destroyed. Third, it could be interpreted that the fall of the White House as a symbol of the fall of my country. Maybe it means that the entire country will be destroyed. I hope the Lord will give me understanding later, and I can tell you the interpretation. All I know is that this prophecy is not good for the United States of America. It speaks of gloom and misery for my homeland.

(Here is another dream I had six months later 4/2)

In my dream I was looking back at history. There was a terrible force unleashed upon the earth. It brought humanity almost to the point of extinction. At first the poison had a quick effect upon all flesh and killed them. The force of the impact then turned the bodies to ash, and they melted away. I saw this transpire in my dream. I was watching a replay of history, but I was there. I was caught inside some vehicle like a bus, but I managed to get away. I was spared somehow. I ran as far away from the destructive force as possible. Was it a nuke? Maybe. It was something similar to one. At first the bodies froze, then disintegrated. Could it have been chemical warfare? It's possible. One thing for sure, its results were overpowering, and it brought much death upon the earth.

"I will pour out My Spirit on all mankind, and your sons and daughters will prophesy, your old men will dream dreams, your young men will see visions." (Joel 2:28)

08 My Only Friend…The End 10/10/10-10/23/10

I wish I had better news, but I don't. "This is the end, my only friend, the end." (Jim Morrison) Until the fall, I'm waiting around for the inevitable. I'm going about my business. I'm working my job. I'm doing my time. In December of 2011, I'll head off to Jerusalem to fulfill what must be, what shall be, and what has always been. At last my calling will be complete, and I'll be with the Lord again. I'll be going back home. A smile comes to my face in expectation. Despite all my failures and shortcomings, the Lord will meet me in the clouds. Liberty at last! No more running this way and that. Peace and tranquility awaits me. I will be one who's in tune with the orchestra and flow to the sea like river water. I will join my ancestors. I will eat from the Tree of Life and live on forever and ever. Won't you join me? Will you partake? Come with me. Eat the bread and drink the wine. Join the wedding feast. Become the bridegroom. Be one of the Lord's many wives.

09 Liberty & Anarchy 10/24/10-10/31/10

At the end of the day, I really don't give a damn about sin. I don't care about your gluttonous behavior. I don't give a shit about lust and sensuality. It doesn't bother me if you get high every night or do vile deeds on the side. If you want to feed your flesh with whatever turns you on, it's not going to affect me at all. I'm so tired of hiding our true natures. I'm sick of all the rules and regulations and people telling me what's wrong or right. To me, it all seems like a piece of propaganda that we've believed all our lives. I want to let it all go. I'm tired of the guilt. I don't need to make amends because it's part of our natural inclination. Some call it evil. Some call it wrong. But after awhile, we become numb. I'm numb and apathetic. Ever since my eyes were opened I've been living with this Christian guilt, but I don't want to be ashamed of thinking radical ideas anymore. Liberty and anarchy are my only friends, but I have Big Brother looking over my shoulder. I only want to go play in the sandbox. I want to play doctor and tie me up without thinking about the ramifications, but I'm locked down in marriage. I'm a slave to the Law. Moses and Paul are calling all the shots, and the legislators are driving me nuts. O Lord, you're lording over me, and I'm tired of being your submissive servant. It's not that I want to be God. It's not that I want to be in control. I just want to let it all go. I want to be free like a bird sailing in the wind. Take me wind where you want me to go. Drop me off on some remote island where there's no worries, and I can strum my chords. Let me be free from all this anxiety. Give me a hit of that blissful drug, so I can forget about tomorrow.

10 The Quest 11/1/10-11/12/10

I went searching a long time ago upon a weary quest. To find out why I'm in confusion, why I can't find rest. When I came across a wise old man who saw the world upside down. He said, "Our world's in confusion. It's inside out and upside down. The planets aren't aligned. Fates can be turned around." So I continued on my journey, and one professor did agree. He said, "Disorder is the order. Fact and fiction are the same. Good is bad, and black is white. Right is left, and left is right." As I departed I passed a maid who answered my questions in dismay. She said, "Love is war, and I need more like an addict dry and broke." After her, I met a monk who baffled me with a paradox. He said, "If one man kills, then he must die. It's called an eye for an eye." Then again, he said, "To turn the other cheek." It doesn't make much sense at all to me. Thus, I headed home confused in doubt and concluded I was lost, not found. Not knowing left from right or truth from lies or black from white. Cause the answers are all censored, and what's wrong is what's right.

11 Repentance 11/13/10-11/23/10

Hours earlier I had returned from a Vegas trip. Of course, I was up to my old tricks. I don't need to explain because you already know. However, my sin did make me feel guilty, so I decided to meditate on the Word of the Lord. After reading the Good Book, it made me realize I need to turn from my sin and start again. Can it be done? Can I give up everything and begin a new leaf in my life? The path I've been on has turned sour. I can't continue any longer on this road of indulgences, this nightmare adventure into the depths of apostasy. Long ago, I set out on this path to understand it, to become one with it, to know as Solomon had known. And now I know. But maybe it's time for me to be like the Great Buddha, Siddhartha, and make a transition in my life. I have learned love and lust from Kamala. I have learned much from the great merchants of the world and have indulged in every sin known to man, but now it's time to leave this life of fornication and gluttony and return to prayer and fasting. Is it possible for me to make this about face? Can I really start again? Can I be reborn into the faith, be baptized in that holy water, and come out clean? Yes, I can make this change. All I have to do is walk away and leave it all behind. On the side of the road, I've set down my obsession with television, movies, and sports. On the side of the road, I'm going to leave the Internet behind and no longer feed my addictions. I cannot flirt with disaster any longer. Eventually my card will come up. I must be ready. Therefore, I've confessed my sins, and I'm going to start anew. Someone must be out there praying for me. Someone must be out there watching my back. And someone has been my true and faithful friend. Thank you all. Now that I have repented, I will need to return to the deeds I did at first and be a true and faithful servant once more. I honestly don't know how I'm going to overcome my flesh, but I'm putting my faith in the Lord. He has overcome, so I can overcome too. He is my Rock. He is my shelter from the storm.

12 Holy Bible Atomic Hell Fire Heat 11/24/10-11/29/10

If I was a card carrying member of the NRA or a rolling racketeer carrying heat, I would barge on through those closed doors and shoot Elohim into thee. But I ain't no pusher, and I bear no badge. I'm a vigilante without a plan. My pen's my sword. I'm a piper's son. I'm a rattling, rumbling reed. I'm a Holy Bible atomic hell fire heat.

Holy Bible atomic hell fire heat. Holy Bible atomic hell fire heat. I see the pearly gates, the eternal flame. Gotta get myself back on the beat. To the Holy Bible atomic hell fire heat.

A Raven perched itself on my back door. She brought me bread and sang to me this song. About the times ahead and what's to come. About a butterfly that once was a slug. About the Holy Bible atomic hell fire heat.

Holy Bible atomic hell fire heat. Holy Bible atomic hell fire heat. I see the pearly gates, the eternal flame. Gotta get myself back on the beat. To the Holy Bible atomic hell fire heat.

Now there ain't no future, and there's no turning back. But there's a narrow path off the barren track. Take a left on 4th and head up Main. Push the gas until the tank is empty. You'll be a Holy Bible atomic hell fire heat.

13 If I had One Year to Live… 11/30/10-12/5/10

During the year, I ask my students what they would do if they had only one year left to live. I suppose I should ask myself the same question, because according to the scriptures my time is almost up. Idealistically, I should use up all my sick days, quit my job, charge up my credit cards, and stop paying my bills, but in the back of my mind, I'm not sure my end will come when my testimony is over. I'm like a cancer patient, and the doctor estimated that I have one year left to live. At least I don't have to go through all the pain and misery that they must endure. In reality, I haven't changed my normal routine. I am trying to right my ways and live more honorably, so when I go, I'll have a clean slate. The only problem is I've accumulated a lot of bad habits over the years, and they're not as easy to kick as I thought they'd be. I do want to let everyone know who is close to me that I love them and that I'm truly thankful to have shared our lives, our dreams, our thoughts, and so many other intimate moments together. These times were the best part of my life. I'd also like to say I'm sorry to anyone I may have wronged. If you find it in your heart to forgive me someday, I would be much obliged. I know this all sounds like a deathbed confession, but it's important to say these things from time to time. I think the lyrics to the song "The Final Message" by the Faithful Church pretty much sums up my final words. Still, if I really have only one year to live, I would like to see as much of the world as I can. I'd like to see the Caribbean and Africa and Russia and China and India and Japan and the Philippines and so many other places, but I'm not sure if time will permit this. So I'll have to see the places I can in the time I have. Meanwhile, I'm going to head back on the path and meander home. I'm in no rush, and if I'm blessed with more time, then so be it. If not, I thank the Lord for the time I've had. Sure, sometimes I've grumbled, and I've been down'n'out, but when I look back at the years, I laugh, not pout. Life has been a bizarre, tragic trip. I've walked with my mind wide open, seeking out the subtle, dissecting what is rich, tasting what is sweet, and knowing bitterness.

14 Passing 12/6/10-12/11/10

If I had my way, I'd have a different woman every night. Instead I have one woman, and she's my wife. If I was a rich man, I'd have a house in Newport Beach and all the finest things. I'd watch the sun go down and take walks upon the beach, but I live in a suburban community. My house is small, and I squeeze by each week. My paycheck comes in increments, and I'm working all the time. Yes, I know I should be satisfied with what I have. I should thank the Lord for this and that, but it feels like my needs and wants are never satisfied. "Not my will but Thy will be done." (Mt.26:39) I've heard these words so many times before. I still find myself in yearning. I find myself in lust. I reminisce about old lovers and hope their doing fine. It would be fun to roll the dice one more time. Presently, my love is stagnant. I'm in the quagmire. My passion has been blunted. I've lost that childhood fire. There's no skip in my step, not even them walking blues. I'm in the middle class, mundane, murky waters. There's a lot of road ahead. There's a lot of road behind. I can't see the finish line. If I could, I'd sprint to the end. I'd read the final page. I'd put an end to it. But my legs have lost a step or two, and my soul's been tossed and soiled. I don't have many tender thoughts, and sometimes I don't care at all. My skin is calloused to the sun. My beauty's gone. My strength is lost. There's still a sense of vanity that says, "I would, I know I could," but this is not the movie screen. This is my life passing in front of me.

15 Drought 12/12/10-12/22/10

A monsoon like storm is passing through California. I haven't seen this much rain come down in a long time. It's refreshing. I like it. It feels like I'm in Thailand again. I do wonder, however, if it's a prelude to another long drought. Back in the Days of Joseph, they had seven years of plenty, then seven years of drought. They also say that the two prophets spoken of in the *Book of Revelation* will have the power to shut up the sky at will. Do you think it will make anyone repent and listen? Maybe a few. Most people will curse God's name and react with more violence and hatred. In the Third World, another long drought would be devastating. As for America, we'd turn into a dust bowl. I think we could survive a drought but for how long? Much of the West is like Australia's Outback. During the Tribulation, there will be one absolute truth. It will be about water and who has access to it. At first one-third of the springs will turn bitter then the scorching heat will come. By the end of the seven-year period, the springs and rivers will turn to blood. I'm not bullshitting here either. All you have to do is read John's *Revelation* to find out where we'll be tomorrow. I don't know when it's all going to kick into gear, but it's on the horizon. It's "minutes to midnight" as the Oils used to sing, and I'm trying to forewarn you about the coming plagues. When it comes to pass, don't say you haven't heard the Word. In retrospect, people will think I wrote this after the fact. That's what some critics are saying about the *Book of Daniel* today. "It's too accurate. It's too precise. There's no way this could be written hundreds of years before." Oh I'm so sick of these critics that have their heads up their asses. It merely proves that the *Bible* is the inspired Word of God. It's true I've come across some errors and discrepancies over the years, but it's still God's holy Word. Some would say that we should discount the entire text because there are a few flaws. I think that perspective is hogwash. And others try to prove apologetically that the *Bible* is 100% infallible. C'mon, give me a break! Don't be so narrow-minded. The *Bible* is still the Word of God. The prophecies are relevant. The history is accurate, and archaeology holds up the stories told.

16 Retirement 12/23/10-1/12/11

At the rate I'm going, it will probably take me another twenty years to retire. In the meantime, it's another day of fighting the morning traffic, dealing with rebellious teenagers, and going through the same old rigmarole day in and day out. Is this it? I thought life would have more adventures and challenges, but it turned out to be one long day shift at the factory. The thought of continuing down this path for another two decades makes me want to vomit. Being old and retired sounds even worse. Envisioning myself old and decrepit with a cane in my hand or slumped over an armchair watching television doesn't sound too appealing either. Better the miscarriage than this fate! I'd rather go out with a bang and die young than have to suffer through this misery. Sure, I'm only focusing on the negative, but isn't this an accurate description of our futures? Maybe I'll still be able to get it up with Viagra and have some young tart sucking on my tool when I'm retired. Maybe she'll stick around long enough to inherit my possessions and take care of me while I wet the bed and shit my pants. Then again, maybe I'll get lucky and she'll grow tired of my complaining and poison me to death. This way I won't have to suffer through more years inside this decrepit cell of mine. Yes, it's a grim outlook, but it's looking more like my future as I watch my parents' generation grows old and dies off one by one.

17 Alternate Realities 1/13/11-1/17/11

It's quite possible that our realties as human beings are transient. I believe there are alternate realities out there and sometimes we tap into them during our dream visions. When we pass from this world unto the next, we will realize that this life was a mere breathe. We'll look back at our time on earth and remember it as a dream. Death will wake us to a new existence, which is greater than or less than to the one we currently know. For instance, the other night I had a dream. I walked through a door into an alternate world. In this world everything was left-handed. People wrote with their left hand, threw with their left hand, and favored their left hand in almost every situation. People who were inclined towards the right were frowned upon and shunned. These people were forced to do things the left-handed way or they were ostracized from society. Even parents would painstakingly take steps to make sure that their children did things the normal way.

This is only one example of how realities could change. The Apostle Paul described the heavenly realm as being "inexpressible." (2Cor.12:4) In the *Book of Enoch*, the prophet said heaven "excelled in splendor and magnificence that he could not describe it to us." (1 Enoch 14:16) Our next reality will be beyond what we can "see, hear, or feel." (1Cor.2:9) It might be similar or twisted in baffling ways. When we enter the next realm, it will seem as if we had just entered or left the *Twilight Zone*. Either way, we'll be perplexed or feel that everything finally makes sense. Some of us will reunite with our loved ones and others will enter into a nightmare scenario.

18 Gadulsay 1/18/11-1/23/11

It's something that you can't describe. It's a feeling you can't pin. It's something that you cannot hear. It's a place you have not been. It's a question without answer. It's a black hole out in space. An equation you can't figure. A thought that's gone astray.

No mind has imagined. No eye has ever seen. It has not crossed the heart of man. Ears cannot perceive.

No philosophy will describe it. No theology makes sense. There's no word in the language. No translation's adequate. It's hidden deep within your soul in the recess of your heart. It's found within the depths of hell in the corner of your mind.

No mind has imagined. No eye has ever seen. It has not crossed the heart of man. Ears cannot perceive.

It's a dream I can't remember. It happened as a kid. I was frightened but excited. Now it's lost in oblivion. Vague pictures I remember. Fractured images. There was demon on a bicycle. I was Toto with the witch.

No mind has imagined. No eye has ever seen. It has not crossed the heart of man. Ears cannot perceive.

19 Sick until Summer 1/24/11-1/31/11

I'm sick again. It seems to happen more often than not these days. Back in my teens and twenties I could stay out all night and bounce back in the morning with grace and ease. Now, I'm limping along nursing old sports injuries and fighting off another bout with the flu. As the Stones used to sing, "What a drag it is getting old." I agree. I could probably last hundreds of years on earth if I didn't have to fight for survival everyday of my life. Each year there seems to be a new thorn in my side, a new addiction, a new god, a new angle taken by Satan and his minions to destroy me. They work 24/7, and they're doing all they can to destroy you too. Only by God's grace will we be free. Only by His mercy will we break the bonds of slavery. Without a fight, we go into captivity. Willingly, we are put in chains and controlled by our fleshly whims and desires. Yes, the flesh is weak and lately, my vices have been controlling me. Have they been controlling you too?

This summer, I'm planning on heading out of town again. I'm thinking of going to the Philippines to get my TEFL certificate. It's a 4-week course overseas that will allow me to teach English to second language learners. This will open up doors of employment abroad if I lose my job or find myself in dire straits for employment somewhere down the line. Of course, this will all be irrelevant if the Lord decides to take me up into the heavens when my 1,260 day testimony is over. If it doesn't happen, this certificate will give me a chance to see foreign lands from the inside out and experience exotic places during my summer breaks. It will also give me something to write about because right now I'm as dry as Death Valley. There's no milk and honey flowing from my pen. There's no vision from God. There's no comfort and edification being written down because when I'm back home in California, I'm occupied with mundane affairs and worry more about the outcomes of sporting events than I do about God. However, when I'm abroad I seem to be more focused and inspired. Being in a foreign land exposes me to new and shocking impressions that will give me something enlightening to write about. For now, I'm going back to the plow. The game on the TV starts in about an hour. So until the sun reaches its highest point in the sky, you can expect more of these everyday thoughts being typed up on this screen to be scorned and mocked at later.

20 Famine 2/1/11-2/7/11

All the days of my life, I've gone without hunger or thirst, yet there will come a time when even the wealthiest countries will feel the pinch of not being able to fill their bellies. After the third seal is broken, the black horse will ride and bring famine upon the earth. Food prices will rise insurmountably, and to buy a quart of wheat, you'll have to work all day to pay the price. (Rev.6:5-6) The poor people of the world already know about these hunger pangs, and it will only get worse during the apocalypse. Even right now, there is a shortage of food in certain parts of the world. There is enough food to go around, but greed and hatred have prevented the food from reaching the people who are in the most need. It's a terrible misdeed on the part of humanity. Now imagine what it would be like if food became a scarcity. For example, let's pretend two-thirds of our food supply was destroyed by a series of calamities that struck the earth. Who would get the food? Who would pay the price? Most likely, the rich would survive, and the poor would starve. The price for wheat and barley would skyrocket in the marketplace. There would be long lines and violence. Riots would ensue and many people would die.

Yes, I know it sounds like another doomsday story made for Hollywood, but this is what the *Bible* predicts. At the end of this story, we don't get to lick the butter off our fingertips. In John's *Revelation*, we get to go home and explain to our wife and kids why there's no food on the table.

21 Vanilla Sex 2/8/11-2/13/11

I've been sick off and on all month. Every year it feels like these colds last longer, but I suppose it can't be as bad as living in other parts of the world. It's as if one of the Bowls of Wrath accidentally poured out upon the earth. Maybe it was an intentional spilling. I must say these are interesting times to be living. The Middle East is in an uproar, and the energy crisis is becoming burdensome once again. The economy is staggering along, and many people are struggling to find work and put food on their tables. Yes, it's dire times, but this is only the beginning of birth pangs. I hope it's a false alarm, and that everything will get better, but if the planet's water has broken, there is nothing we can do to stop the tide of judgment from overwhelming us.

As for everything else, I'm doing fairly well. I can't complain. I'm not exceptionally high or low. I'm just cruising along. But tell me, when did life get so ordinary? At what point did life become boring? Do your relationships still have that spark? Is love abounding? Or are you quietly hanging on because that's what you're supposed to do? I'm going through the motions over here. I wish I could say that I'm living on the edge, but I'm not. There are times when I'm pushing the pedal to the floor, but these moments are brief. The rest of the time I'm bored as hell. The sex is vanilla. The relationship has no spark, and at work I'm punching in the time clock. I guess that's why I like traveling abroad. It's almost always an adventure. Anything could be around the next corner. I hope all is well in your neck of the woods. I hope you're flying high like a soldier who just jumped out of an airplane. If not, I'm sure a change is gonna come around soon.

22 Dark Side of Love 2/14/11-2/28/11

Roses are red and violets are blue. They say love is special and it won't harm you. But within every rose bush, a thorn waits for you 'cause I've seen the dark side of love. There's sorrow and regret and plenty of tears. There's a lovesick feeling and depression. They say love endures and to always forgive, but this is the dark side of love. I've been thrown in the gutter. I've been left for dead. I've been cheated on, spat upon, and abandoned. I've been broken and beaten like an ox with a whip 'cause I've seen the dark side of love. The dark side of love, it does not seek its own. Instead of kindness, you'll suffer and groan. You'll hope and pray they'll come back some day. Yes, this is the dark side of love. They say love's not jealous. Love is not cruel. But after they're gone, you'll feel like a fool. The heartache, the loathing, the pain, and the grief. Yes, this is the dark side of love. You'll ask, "Is it over?" You'll ask, "What went wrong?" You'll blame yourself and count the cost. You'll dream about them and reminisce 'cause this is the dark side of love.

23 The Rebels 3/1/11-3/9/11

On Sunday I was reading the *Book of Hosea*, and it left me feeling like such a failure. I've had success in my life, but I feel like I've let my God down. I have so many shortcomings, and the minor prophet pointed them out to me. Honestly, I don't know how anyone makes the grade when it comes to measuring up with God and his Law. In a way, I feel like the criminal on the cross who said, "Jesus, remember me when You come into Your kingdom." (Lk.23:42) I hope He does not forget about me because I deserve to rot in hell. I deserve the abyss like every other sinner in the past, and I imagine you're walking in my shoes too. Sure, I wish there wasn't a place called Hades, but the Bible says there is. Who am I to go against scripture? Who are you to say God's rules are not fair? By grace the penalty was paid on the cross thousands of years ago. The scriptures say that He died for our sins. All we have to do is believe in Him and ask forgiveness, and we get to join Him in heaven. Well, I have believed, and I have asked forgiveness, yet I still find myself in bed with the Devil. I'm talking literally and figuratively here. I confess, but I still do the same old sins over and over again. I've been doing these sins for so long that I don't even feel remorse anymore. I can't seem to break the chains Satan has around my neck. I'm in bondage to the underworld. I'm a slave to sin. Father, is there room in heaven for a sinner like me? I know the rules. I know You. Yet I still choose the crooked path. I wish I could be like the church folk on Sunday, but I've been a "rebel from birth," (Isa.48:8) and a rebel I'll always be.

24 Roots, Radicals, Rockers, & Reggae 3/10/11-3/14/11

I've heard ministers go on and on about how we need to live lives that are free from sin, but rarely do I hear the pulpit speak of practical righteousness. I've heard a lot of hate directed at different groups and sly remarks made on the side by these so-called holy men, but it's time to let this go. Instead of telling us how we should live by a standard that no one can meet, we should focus on helping the poor and needy. Instead of telling us how we're all going to hell, we should feed the hungry. I know the Gospel is important, but it's hard for the poor to see God when their bellies are growling. It's hard for them to hear about mercy and justice when they're downtrodden and homeless. That means we need to help those who cannot help themselves. We cannot turn a blind eye to the suffering in the world.

I've heard a lot of preachers like myself go on about the Apocalypse and the Kingdom Age, but it's been 2,000 years now, and it's likely we'll have to wait even longer. Yes, I want to get out of this hell too, but while I'm waiting, I'm going to fight for equality. I'm going to sing out the words to "Roots, Radicals, Rockers, and Reggae" by S.L.F. and make a stand. *"We are all in a one and one in all, so throw away the guns and the war's all gone, throw away the hunger and the war's all gone, throw away the fighting and the war's all gone, throw away the grudges and the war's all gone."*

The band mentions this as a solution, and it can be that way right now if we merely reach out to our enemies, turn the other cheek, and forgive one another. I know a lot of us have been wounded. I know many of us have been hurt, but we can overcome this with God's help.

One day we will "hammer our swords into plowshares and our spears into pruning hooks." (Isa.2:4) At this moment, we need to "fight the good fight" (1Tim.6:12) and not add to the turmoil. That means within our neighborhoods we need to hit the streets. There are many people amongst us that need our helping hands. Yes, give all you can to organizations abroad, but the best place to start is within our own communities.

Now I know all this sounds idealistic, but I believe these are realistic goals. They are not as far-fetched as it seems. So I'll end this entry with another quote from S.L.F.'s song. *"You got to pass the bowl and make the food go round, 'cause that's the only way to trample crime to the ground. Equal rights and justice for one and all 'cause only through liberty freedom shall form. Don't fight against no color, class, or creed for on discrimination does violence breed. We are all in a one and one in all, so throw away the guns and the war's all gone…"*

25 Grandpa's Dying & It Won't Be Long 3/15/11-3/23/11

There's nothing whatever the matter with me. I'm as healthy as I can be. I'm not as strong as I was, you know. Whenever I sing, I sound like a crow. My breathing is tough, my hair is thin, but I'm awfully "well" for the shape I'm in.

All my muscles are out of whack. Got terrible pains all over my back. My legs feel like the stump of a tree. I act like a drunk on a ship at sea. My hearing is poor, my vision is dim, but I'm awfully "well" for the shape I'm in.

Grandpa's dying & it won't be long. Grandpa's dying & this is his song. Grandpa's dying there's not much time. Grandpa's dying so say your goodbyes.

Sleeplessness I have, night after night. In the morning, I'm just a sight. My memory is failing, my head's in a spin, but I'm awfully "well" for the shape I'm in. It's better to say, "I'm fine," with a grin than to let them know the shape I'm in.

Grandpa's dying & it won't be long. Grandpa's dying & this is his song. Grandpa's dying there's not much time. Grandpa's dying so say your goodbyes.

*Song based on the poem by Maurice Ingram

26 Environmental Damage: Hawaii 25 Years Later 3/24/11-3/27/11

The Hilton lifestyle has worn me down. I just need a hut as my beach house. Forget the tourist festival of Waikiki. Find me a secluded beach, and I'll have peace. Right now I'm feeling cooped up in this hotel room. This is not the Hawaii I envisioned in the Beach Boys' tune. So tomorrow I'm heading out to the North Shore. I'm going to find a place where no one's around. I'll hang out with the corral and the fish in the sea. They're the ones who know what paradise can be.

The last time I was in Hawaii I was eighteen-years-old, and I thought it was the most beautiful place in the world. Twenty-five years later, I'm not sure what to think. As I was snorkeling, I saw giant coral reefs without coral, scarce fish, and murky waters. The visibility was so bad that I thought I was swimming in a sewer. I'm sure once you get away from Waikiki the ecological damage is not as bad, but it was disturbing. Jacques Cousteau, the former oceanographer, said that he went to places he dove twenty years earlier, and he was astounded at the pollution and lack of life. He also said, "Water and air, the two essential fluids on which all life depends, have become global garbage cans." I've also read that even in the Polar Regions where mankind is scarce, there is human waste everywhere. I'm sure if I saw the giant rubbish dump in the Pacific Ocean, that's supposedly twice the size of the United States, I'd be even more disillusioned.

I did enjoy my time on Oahu, but I don't know if I'll go back there again unless someone guides me to the pristine spots. Oahu is too overrun by tourists and the Hilton lifestyle. Yes, it's true Honolulu does look more plush, but something is missing. Maybe it's the Hawaiian culture, the

Hawaiian music, or the native people that are disappearing. Maui and Kauai, please tell me you're not the same! If that's the case, I'm ashamed at what the American Empire has turned the islands into. In one century, we've managed to strip away hundreds of years of Hawaiian culture.

27 Forever & Ever 3/28/11-4/4/11

Sometimes it's hard to figure out which way to go in life. We travel down paths that are unfruitful, but after reading the *Book of Micah*, everything has become clearer. The Lord informs the prophet that we "need to do justice, to love kindness, and to walk humbly with Him." (Mic. 6:8) It's pretty basic, and it's the same way Jesus summed up the Law when He said, we need "to love our neighbor as ourselves." (Mt. 22:39) I know there's a lot of talk on the airwaves about all this other mumbo jumbo, but I've never been a follower of the rules. I prefer common sense and to let my conscience be my guide. Nevertheless, it's become apparent that some of my sins are incurable. I can't seem to overcome my lusts and desires. It's gotten to the point now where I've just given up resisting. It's been twenty-five years since I've been born again, and I've only become more wretched. I thought the Lord was going to perfect me, but I'm far from being perfected. Are you with me on this or have you been victorious? I'm guessing you've fallen short too. There may be nothing we can do about it. We'll just have to keep on confessing and hope God will have mercy on our aberrant souls.

The *Book of Micah* does give us hope though. The prophet writes about a time in the future when the Messiah will come to earth. During His reign "nation will not lift up sword against nation, and never again will we train for war." (Mic.4:3) God says He's going to take the lame and the outcasts and build a strong nation out of them. We are those chosen ones.

Imagine God restoring the earth to how it was in the beginning when Adam and Eve roamed the earth. He says He's going to do it, and we'll get to reign with Him for a thousand years. It's going to be amazing. We'll get to eat and drink with the Counselor and live in the Garden of Eden.

If we can keep our eyes focused on these hopes and dreams, maybe it will make it all better. Maybe we won't be so melancholy because we've fallen short of our expectations. Maybe we won't be so depressed when we see injustice everywhere and our loved ones falling by the wayside. We will know there is a bright future for them. We will know there is hope, even though the cynics and the scoffers and the forces of evil have tried to tear us down. We will overcome! We will make it in the long run! We will be one with our God and live on forever and ever!!!

28 The Jester 4/5/11-4/10/11

"When is a door not a door? When it's a jar!" I laughed and the crowd laughed out too.

"I have another. I have another. Can you figure me out? It once was great, but now it's not. It's used by fifty states and will soon be gone. Two pence, two shillings for the man who guesses right."

"The U.S. Dollar!" The Piper cried.

"Correct, my friend. Here's your reward. Buy yourself some pancakes or some wheat or ammo."

"If you take two apples from three apples, how many apples will you have? Hold your fingers in the air, if you think you know you're right. The answer is two, not one or three or five."

"A man left home and made three left turns. He met a man with a mask on. What was his career? The woman with the baby, what do you think? You're shaking your head. You haven't got a clue?"

"A baseball player!" hollered the man in blue.

"Stupendous, tremendous, a genius in our midst. Should I give him two pence or a whack over the head?"

"Ha, ha ha…what was I saying, my friends? Oh no, the Alzheimers is kicking in. Okay, this one is simple. It's an old one too. An oldie but a goody, oodie booty, moodie shoodie."

"Which creature in the morning goes on four feet, at noon on two, and in the evening upon three? My oh my, a lot of hands I see. How about you, young man, what do you think?"

"Man, Mr. Jester."

"He's right, my friends, let's give him a hand. In the morning he crawls as a baby. At noon he walks as an adult. In the evening he uses a cane when he's elderly."

"Now this one's difficult. Is it time to speak the truth? I'm tired of dodging shadows and drinking down brews. I'm in the house of mirrors, but this one's for you."

"His arm will be withered. His right eye blind. He'll reign for a time, a times, and half a time. He'll magnify himself and will destroy. And cause the rich and poor to be given a mark? Can anyone guess? Does anyone know? Daniel, is it 8:23? Is it time for us to go? Okay, one more before the circus hits the road."

"Hear ye, hear ye but understand not. See ye, see ye but perceive not. I'm just a watchman. I'm blowing my bugle. Yahweh is God. Yeshua is Messiah. No jivin' here, no Jah Rastafarin. Are these the last days? Are the plagues a coming? Run to the hills and duck for cover. Adios, Ciao, Sayonara. Hear the train choo choo. Yes, the train's a comin'."

29 Zephaniah 4/11/11-4/17/11

According to the prophet Zephaniah, his generation was so evil that God said He was going to remove man "from the face of the earth." (Zep.1:2) They were wicked so often that God brought a harsh judgment down upon them. Is our generation as bad? Are we deserving of the same wrath? Sure, I've met a lot of evil people that the world would be better off without, but I've met a lot of good people too. In fact, most of the people I know are upstanding citizens. It's true, everyone has their flaws, but is God so mad at us that He wants to destroy us completely? The God I know is not that vindictive. He does correct me on occasion like a father does with a son, but I think He's doing it for my best interest. I believe He's guiding your steps too.

Much of the *Book of Zephaniah* is about fire and brimstone, but it does offer hope. He even calls the prophets "reckless, treacherous men." (Zep.3:4) There's a lot of truth to that because I am much the same. The prophet informs us that if we will humble ourselves and "seek righteousness," perhaps the Lord's wrath will pass over us, and we will "be hidden in the day of the Lord's anger." (Zep.2:3) Maybe we need to try and do what's right more often than not. Maybe we need to be less proud and malicious. Zephaniah says that one day God is going to deal with "all our oppressors," and that He will "save the lame and gather the outcast." (Zep.3:19) I truly hope that one day God will turn "our shame into praise," (Zep.3:19) because right now, I know my thoughts are evil continually. I need mercy. I need forgiveness. And I need God's helping hand.

30 Israel, Israel, Israel 4/18/11-4/24/11

People always ask me about the end times and what's going to happen next. The answer is easy. You simply have to watch Israel. For instance, God made a promise that He would bring His people back into the land, and He did in 1948. For almost 2,000 years, the Jews were scattered abroad, but when Israel officially became a nation, all of that changed. A prophecy was fulfilled in the modern era. Read Ezekiel 34-37, if you don't believe me. Then read Ezekiel 38-39, if you're curious what prophecy is going to be fulfilled next.

Another prophecy, which will soon be fulfilled, is the rebuilding of the temple. Since 70 A.D. no temple has stood in Jerusalem, but another one will be built. In the *Book of Haggai*, the Lord cries out that He wants the temple rebuilt, and it will be in the near future. Zechariah makes the same proclamation. As for Jesus, He predicts the temple will be rebuilt in Matthew 24 when He's telling the disciples about the things to come. At that time, the Man of Lawlessness will step into the Lord's temple and proclaim himself as god. Most people will praise him as the savior of the world, and many will be killed if they do not. As for Israel, the true followers of YHWH will flee to the wilderness, and God will protect them from the holocaust upon the earth.

Most prophecy centers around Israel. I truly wish the prophets spoke about the United States of America, but it appears we're missing from the scene. Either we become part of the new confederacy that's opposed to God, or we become so insignificant that we're not a major player in the world. In my opinion, I think we are a figurative type of Babylon. If that's the case, we will be destroyed in "one hour on one day." (Rev.18) Believe me, I don't like that interpretation. If it's true, I shake my fist in anger at the decree. Even so, aren't we all to blame for our own bad Karma? I think man is to blame not God. We are the ones who didn't tend the Garden well. We've destroyed the environment. We've polluted and killed almost everything in the name of capitalism, in the name of God, in the name of some ideology. God is not going to destroy us. We are going to destroy ourselves. And Jesus is going to save us from complete extinction when He returns. If not, it would be the "end of the world as we know it," (R.E.M.) and man would be no more.

31 Zechariah, the Prophet 4/25/11-5/1/11

I don't know exactly how many times I've read the *Bible* from beginning to end, but there are certain books that I come back to more often than others. The *Gospels of Matthew, John*, and the *Book of Revelation* are my favorites in the *New Testament*; however, I have to admit I've spent more time in the *Old Testament* than the *New*. There are so many great stories like King David, Samson, Adam and Eve, and Joseph. My favorite books in the *Old Testament* consist of *Isaiah, Daniel, Ezekiel, Psalms, Proverbs, Ecclesiastes,* and *Zechariah*. I don't really have a favorite order. I just wish everyone knew how rich this literature is. This entry is going to be about the *Book of Zechariah.*

Zechariah was an *Old Testament* prophet who lived around 520 B.C. This date is widely disputed like many of the books in the *Bible*, but the early or latter dates do not change the Messianic references to Jesus. This book is broken down into fourteen chapters. The beginning starts off with these four horses that patrol the earth. They are probably the same ones mentioned in *Revelation* that bring about war, famine, and pestilence. There are also many Messianic references in *Zechariah*. For instance, there's a reference to the "Branch," (Zech.3:8) which is Jesus, Judas' future betrayal, (Zech.11:12,13) and Jesus' sacrifice on the cross. (Zech.12:10; 13:6) Remember these were all written hundreds of years before Jesus walked the earth. That is why they are so significant. Looking back at the *Old Testament* prophecies, I'm amazed that so many of the Hebrews missed His first coming. I think they were looking for the conquering king not the suffering servant. How were they supposed to know that there would be two comings of the Messiah? There really is no excuse for missing Him today. The prophecies clearly point to Jesus of Nazareth.

Zechariah also offers some glimpses into other intriguing prophecies. There is a worthless shepherd mentioned in one of the chapters. Some theologians believe this is a reference to the antichrist. It says that this shepherd will have an "arm withered" and his "right eye blind." (Zech.11:17) Some scholars believe this Man of Lawlessness will be "fatally wounded" (Rev.13:3) but brought back to life. Maybe he will be shot in the eye and he'll lose the function ability in one of his arms. It's not absolutely clear, but it is something to consider.

Jesus returning to the earth and setting up His kingdom is written about in the last chapter. It says, He will stand on the "Mount of Olives" and "bring His holy ones with Him." (Zech.14:4,5) In Revelation 20, it says He will reign for 1,000 years and much of Conte's fictional book, *Millennial Reign,* was based on this teaching in Zechariah's final chapter. It says, "It will come about that any who are left of all the nations that went against Jerusalem will go up from year to year to worship the King, the Lord of hosts, and to celebrate the Feast of Booths. It will be that whichever of the families of the earth does not go up to Jerusalem to worship the King, the Lord of Hosts, there will be no rain on them." (Zech.14:16,17)

To close, I hope you do get a chance to read the *Book of Zechariah* for yourself someday. I think it will convince you that Jesus really was the one spoken of by the *Old Testament* prophets. If Zechariah does not fully convince you, read Isaiah 53 and Psalm 22. These two references to Jesus on the cross made me believe wholeheartedly, and I believe it will persuade you too.

32 Malachi, Mischief, & my Nakedness 5/2/11-5/8/11

I just finished reading the *Old Testament* by reading the *Book of Malachi* today. The most quoted verse is about the coming of Elijah before the Day of the Lord. It reads, "Behold, I am going to send you Elijah the prophet before the great and terrible Day of the Lord." (Mal.4:5) He's one of the signs we've all been waiting for. You ask me why? Why am I looking forward to this? Believe me I'm not happy about the wrath coming down upon us, but I do know that once Elijah does come, the Messiah will soon follow. Once Jesus returns, He's going to make everything right again. That is one of the main reasons I'm so interested in end times prophecy.

One scripture does talk about a "messenger" who is going to "clear the way" for the Lord. (Mal.3:1) In the Christian community, we believe this man was John the Baptist. He was the one "crying in the wilderness and making straight the way of the Lord." (Jn.1:23) The Baptist was much like Elijah, but even he himself said, "I am not" (Jn.1:21) Elijah.

The rest of the book made me realize that I'm as guilty as the wicked priests who "do not listen or give honor to the Lord's name." (Mal.2:1) It is true. I have not honored the Lord, as I should have. I am constantly questioning Him, rebelling against Him, and being flippant with His teachings. I should be honoring my Father, but I've only brought Him shame. Instead of being a shining example to others, I've stumbled many. Instead of being salt that makes one thirsty, I've spoken with a forked tongue. I wish I could have lived a more honorable life and take back what I've said, but I can't change the past. I can't change the fact that I've "dealt treacherously with my wife" (Mal.3:14-15) by being unfaithful. Kiana has had to put up with my fornicating ways and my short temper for years. I don't need to be reminded about my inadequacies. In my heart, I do wish to be me more loving and patient, but I can see my own reflection. All I can do is try to be better and work harder to be a more righteous person. Yes, the *Book of Malachi* has exposed my nakedness. I can only pray for mercy when I'm deserving of His wrath.

33 Juvenile Delinquents 5/9/11-5/17/11

Looking back at the past, you remember it in a different light than it really was. Events that may have been minor disturbances on the timeline became defining moments in our lives. Events that seemed to hold great importance now have become afterthoughts that we can barely remember. This entry is about some of the events that took place on that timeline. Some were profound. Others were not. But many of the exploits that took place back in high school defined who we were and the people we'd become later in life.

To begin, I'm going to start with a urination story. Back when I was drunk at age seventeen, I went into a grocery store to use the restroom, but I could not find the facilities. I walked around to every corner of the store, but the restroom appeared to be invisible. Consequently, I did what any drunk would do. I whipped it out and pissed right where I was standing. I soaked the whole soup aisle with urine and spoiled all the food in the vicinity. After reliving myself, I stumbled out like a drunken sailor and felt proud of my late night endeavor. Back then I thought my act of rebellion was the pinnacle of juvenile delinquency only to be topped a few months later by my friend who worked at a pizza joint. He decided to pee in the pizza dough batter. I have no idea who ate those pizzas, but I'm sure they had a unique, bitter flavor.

Other friends did bizarre acts of pandemonium. One group would drive around and throw half-eaten burritos at moving cars. Just imagine a football lineman pulling up next to you at an intersection and chucking a bean burrito at your windshield, then driving off with his buddies who are screaming and yelling hysterically. This is what happened with that group on a daily basis after football practice that summer.

Another friend used to go around to suburban homes and punch in dining room windows late at night. Visualize yourself lying in bed at 2:00 A.M. when suddenly you awake to a crashing sound inside your house. Most likely you would jump out of bed, the wife would scream, and the kids would hover for cover under their sheets. This friend was lucky he was never shot by some armed homeowner thinking it was a perpetrator robbing his house, but I suppose this was his way of coping with all the angst spinning around his head as an adolescent.

I was never as extreme as that companion, but I did make it a regular habit to punch the door of my room when I was angry. I would leave huge dents in the door, and my knuckles would be left bleeding. Yes, it's true my hands hurt, but I still felt much better after releasing the tension. I think that's why my friends and I loved going to punk shows on a regular basis. We could dance, slam into one another, stage dive, and fight amongst the crowd. When the night was over, we were sore as hell, but we slept like babies in our cribs afterwards.

Driving in the car drunk, stoned, or high on coke was something we did almost every weekend. We would drive through alleys, side streets, and freeways listening to punk tunes and slamming into one another. The car would rock back and forth, and the driver would join in with the festivities. I am highly surprised none of us died in an accident. It was fun as hell though, and I'd give ten years of my life to be back in that crappy, piece of shit car howling like a wild maniac again.

Another friend had an obsession with starting fires. He was definitely out of control. We had to keep a close watch on him because anything was possible with that motherfucker. He lit fires in parks, parking lots, and even hotel rooms. Of course, we egged him on and danced around the flames with him, but sometimes the fire would get too big, and we had to snap out of our delirium. I know for sure we never caused any major fires in the area, but we were only a spark away from causing real mayhem.

To conclude, I wish I could tell you all the rest of the crazy stories, but this entry would go on forever. One thing for certain, we were living on the edge. We had no house payments, no kids, and no obligations. We were as free as the wind. We blew every which way, and sometimes, we swept through a place like a tornado and touched down causing chaos and turmoil.

34 Miracle Man 5/18/11-5/22/11

Over the years I've met many intriguing people with different ideas on the purpose of life, but no one has influenced me more than Jesus Christ. Every time I go back to the Gospels and read about the words He said and the acts He did, I am blown away by His deeds. No man in history was more profound than Jesus of Nazareth. Many times I can picture myself living back in the day when He walked the earth. I see myself working as a fisherman, a farmer, or even a tax-gatherer. I can picture Him coming up to me and asking me some obtuse question that would baffle me, and I would not be able to answer it. Or I would witness Him performing a heroic act of righteousness that would make everyone's jaw drop like the woman caught in adultery. As for the miracles He performed, I'm sure I'd be impressed, but I believe Jesus' words and subtle ways would have influenced me the greatest.

Looking back at history, there is no one who stands close to Jesus and His ideas. Not Socrates, not Gandhi, not Siddhartha, nor any other. Jesus is at the pinnacle of understanding and stands above all philosophers and writers. Although Jesus did not write His ideologies on paper, His stories and teachings are more memorable than the others. Jesus' humanity, His love, His simplicity, is still making waves across the universe. He truly was and is the Son of God.

Now I know many of you out there have their doubts about this Savior. What makes Jesus so special? The answer lies within the Gospels. All you have to do is read the first four books of the *New Testament* on your own and come to your own conclusion. If at the end of the day, you still don't believe the man from Galilee was the Messiah, at least you will have read His parables and been exposed to one of the greatest teachers in human history.

35 Restraint 5/23/11-5/31/11

As I watch the strong winds blow in Big Bear, I've come to the conclusion that we are a lost species. We are self-serving, territorial, and cruel. There are humane aspects about our character, but when push comes to shove; it's all about me, myself, and I. I will admit there are people out there who have come close to finding peace and happiness, but I believe no one has found inner bliss. I haven't. Have you? Do you know anyone that has reached Nirvana? I doubt it, but even if someone has come close, there is always someone or something that upsets our equilibrium. As an illustration, one might be having a wonderful time at an event or social gathering. They are smiling, feeling good about everyone and everything until that shadow descends upon them. All it takes is one stray bullet to turn the day into night. The problem is there are far too many loose cannons in the world today. They are upsetting everybody's peace of mind. They seek one goal and that is self-satisfaction, despite all the other people they cheat and use on the way. I despise these self-absorbed narcissists, and I know you do too. Respecting people's feelings, their freedoms, and their rights has become a bygone principle. Maybe this ideal never existed in the first place, but I do long for the day when people will come together and be fair and honorable with one another. Until that day, I'm going about my business trying to fly under the radar. Most of the time I get by without anyone hassling me, but every now and then, someone spits in my face and gives me hell. On most occasions, I'm able to turn the other cheek or look the other way, but sometimes I can be provoked or riled. These are the times when I have to restrain myself and hold back my anger. Sometimes it works and other times it lights a bomb in me that detonates. This is where our race stands today. We have been pressed. We have been shoved. Others have stepped on our toes, and right now we are on the verge of igniting. Even the planet itself has been pushed too far by our malcontent, and it's warning humanity with hot lava, hurricanes, earthquakes, and tornadoes. Can you feel those winds blow? Can you feel Mother Earth groan? She's weeping! She's roaring! She's howling, "I can't take it anymore!"

36 Politics 6/1/11-6/4/11

It's difficult for me to find a place on the political spectrum, but I am registered as a Democrat. I do like what the Libertarian and Green Party bring to the table, but everyone knows they can't win an election. So I usually tell people I'm a liberal/libertarian, but I'm pretty moderate when it comes to my voting. I vote with my money like most conservatives do, so that means I vote with the left because I'm part of the teacher's union. As for past presidents, I do admire Jefferson, Lincoln, Teddy Roosevelt, and F.D.R., but I don't really have any modern day heroes. I do like listening to the opinions of Jello Biafra, Bill Maher, Rich Marotta, Henry Rollins, Ron Paul, Dennis Miller, and Chuck Smith, but they're all a bit extreme. That's probably why I enjoy hearing their perspectives. It's outside the mainstream. One thing for sure though, I'm pretty damn sick of the Democrats and the Republicans. They both bow to special interests groups. Big Business has both parties by the balls, so that means the American public is the one taking it in the ass.

37 Rich Man's Blues 6/5/11-6/8/11

My rich uncle is in the hospital again. It looks bleak, but he might pull through. I'm amazed at what modern medicine can do. Still, I'm sure my uncle would trade all the money in his bank account to be young and healthy again. Sure, he can buy the best medical coverage out there, but there are some ailments the doctors can't fix. Ultimately my uncle will have to face the judgment seat like everyone else. The scriptures say, "It's easier for a camel to go through the eye of the needle than for a rich man to enter the Kingdom of Heaven." (Mt.19:24) I hope not, because I know a lot of people of means, and I'd hate to see them miss out on the glory of heaven because they were born with a silver spoon. Thus, my advice to the wealthy would be the same as it would be to the poor. Follow God's advice and let your conscience be your guide. I would also add, to live humbly, rule fairly, and to not give into the many temptations that come your way. As for my uncle, I hope the Lord has another mansion awaiting him in heaven, but I suppose that all comes down to whether he's repented and believed.

38 Witch Hunt 6/9/11-6/16/11

Another public figure was lynched by the media today just like yesterday and the day before that. The mob moves and takes action. There's no trial here. Justice is swift and quick, leaving another family utterly destroyed. *"The righteous rise with burning eyes of hatred and ill will. Madmen fed on fear and lies to beat and burn and kill." (Rush)*

I don't advocate immoral behavior, but instead of pointing the finger, I think we need to take a long look at ourselves. I see hypocrisy in those puritanical eyes, and it's leaving me with a bad taste in my mouth. Even if the claims might be true, I hate to see a person being brought down by vigilante reporting. From their angle, they think they are fighting a righteous cause, but these are the same people who picked up stones and were ready to throw them at the adulterous. They used to wear hoods on their heads and carry torchlights. Now they crucify you with their cameras. Jesus said, "He who is without sin, let him cast the first stone." (Jn. 8:7) It's time for us to stop prying into everyone else's affairs. Let's forget about all this mischief and go back to business. Aren't our sins dark enough already? Righteous indignation is unfitting. Forgetting and forbearing is forgiving.

39 Laughlin 6/17/11-6/19/11

This past weekend, I spent some time in Laughlin, Nevada. It's a place people go to hangout by the Colorado River in 100-degree heat. People party, drink all day, and gamble at night. It's a place one can checkout and get away from the rat race for awhile. Laughlin is much like Vegas and Lake Havasu and countless other places people go to have fun in the sun. I enjoyed myself and have no regrets about going, but I have to admit this party in the desert has lost a bit of its edge. When you're in your teens and 20's, you live and die for the party, but by the time you get into your 30's and 40's, it's kind of like watching a rerun on the television set for the 3rd, 4th, and 5th times. You still get a chuckle out of the funny lines, but when you wake up broke and hung-over, you ask yourself, "What the hell was I thinking?" Sure, when I look back at the photos in ten years, I'll say,

"Look at that young chump with a smile on his face." As of right now, I don't feel that well. I have a sore throat, and my body is dragging. I went to the gym to work off the chemicals, but I still feel like shit. As for my thesis on Laughlin, I don't really have one. I could tell you that drinking is bad, if you do it to excess, and being sober is much better, but you already know this. I could go on for hours telling you how sin and debauchery is the road to hell, but nothing I say is going to stop you. You're still going to reach for the bottle, smoke that cigarette, and gamble at the crap's table. It's the way we are. We are weak, and our vices control us.

40 Fading Vision 6/20/11-6/22/11

Ever since I was eighteen, I've stood on the watchtower. I've blown my bugle. I've played my guitar, but no one heard my warning cry. I've seen tons of visions, and dreamed many dreams, but I doubt if they have influenced change. I've preached from the pulpit. I've acted on stage, but will any of these performances alter our ways? I've played in many bands, and written many songs, but when the set was over, it seemed like a lost cause.

It's hard to admit that I've fallen on deaf ears, but maybe you were listening all these years. Maybe your cold exterior was a disguise. You've known all along the truth from the lies. Maybe you were tapping your foot to the beat, and behind closed doors you prayed beneath the sheets. So I'm holding out hope and not giving up yet. We can rise above and kill the devil in our midst. We can be one with our Lord Jesus Christ and shine brightly like the stars in the sky.

Chapter 4:
The Philippines

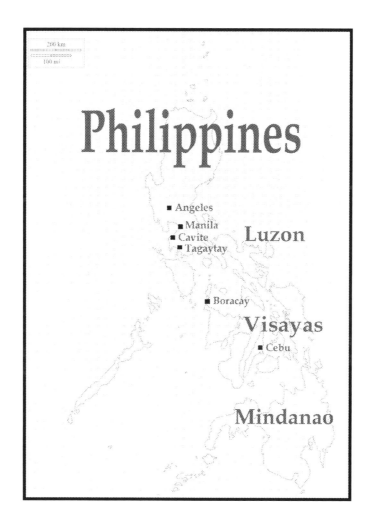

Day 01 Typhoon Landing 6/23/11

As the plane made its approach into Manila, it swayed back and forth like a feather being pushed by the wind. We sat strapped in our seats as the turbulence pushed us up and down, and I prayed that this wasn't the end. Time seemed to freeze for a moment as Kiana tightly grabbed my hand and looked at me with fright. I said, "Everything's going to be fine," as the plane descended closer to the earth. Inch by inch the altitude of the plane dropped, and the metal beast finally thudded down upon the runway. At first, no one made a sound then one man yelled out, "That's what I'm talking about!" and the rest of us smiled and clapped like little children.

This was how our trip to the Philippines began. We arrived in Manila at the same time a typhoon was passing through. In fact, we almost didn't make it here at all, but our pilots defied the odds by not refueling in Hawaii, and we made it here safe and sound. When we left, the airline told us we would be arriving early due to a light load, but I don't believe it. I think they were trying to beat out the storm, so they wouldn't have to cancel the flight. I don't know which tale is true or false, but I suppose it doesn't really matter now. All I know is that there were a whole bunch of other flights that were cancelled later in the day.

After exiting the plane and saying a quick prayer of thanksgiving, we flagged down a taxi and fought the wind and rain to our hotel. Amazingly, we made it there in no time at all, but we had to sit around for a few hours because our check-in time wasn't for another six hours. Luckily, Kiana seemed to hit it off with the hotel clerk, and she allowed us to check-in three hours early.

When we arrived at our room, we seemed to be blessed with a miracle because instead of getting a standard room, we must have been upgraded to an executive suite, and it's like we're staying at our own little apartment.

As for the rest of the day, we slept, ate, drank, and watched the storm from the 35th floor. It was quite amazing. I've never experienced hurricane weather before, but now I know what it's like to live in Florida. Apparently, that's what this storm was, but it's called a typhoon because it took place in the West Pacific Ocean.

Day 02 Disaster Delight 6/24/11

The brunt of the typhoon passed through Manila as we were sleeping in our hotel room. We were awakened by hammering winds and a deluge of water. I looked out the window and stood in reverence of God's power.

The wind and rain smacked hard against our windows, and I prayed that the storm was not going to bring down the building. I thought to myself, "This is amazing," but Kiana didn't share my excitement. She seemed more terrified, but I stood in awe and wonder at the great storm pounding the City of Manila.

By morning, the storm had passed through, and everything returned to normal. According to news reports, there was damage all over the city, but when we walked around the city in the morning, we didn't see anything. There was flooding everywhere, but I didn't witness any broken windows or blown out buildings.

In the afternoon, the two of us spent some time with Kiana's family. They said the typhoon that hit last night was nothing compared to the one that hit two years ago. Her family said that the Storm of 2009 left the city flooded for weeks, and they had to live upstairs in their two-story tenement because the entire first floor was flooded.

Looking at the world today, it does seem like these disasters are hitting the earth more frequently than in the past. Then again, maybe the Internet has allowed us to see these global disasters up close as compared to decades ago when our news resources were limited. Maybe this is the way the planet has always turned, and there is nothing abnormal about its churning. This is one theory, but I don't buy into it. I think these floods, earthquakes, fires, tornados, and typhoons are God's way of getting our attention, and I do believe they are happening more frequently due to the damage mankind has done to the planet. If we as a race would have respected Mother Earth and God's natural laws, we wouldn't be in the situation we are in today. We are merely reaping what we have sown as a species. It is true many innocent people have been hurt in the crossfire, but I'm not going to blame God for everything. God could have prevented these events from occurring, but if He did, it would take out the wildcard that makes life interesting. Without the joker, life would seem placid and predetermined. I suppose that's why Lucifer is still permitted to roam to and fro across the earth. He is still the great deceiver and destroyer, but through calamity our faiths can be put to the test, and sometimes we come out more enlightened and stronger from the experience.

Kiana and I hung out with her family the rest of the day. We ate. We laughed. We had communion. Although many Filipinos are poor financially, culturally they have deep family ties and a strong sense of community.

Day 03 Family, Family, Family 6/25/11

Coming from an Italian family, I understand the importance of family, but in the Philippines, it's at a whole new level. Family is everything. Even if you're not part of the family, they will make you feel welcome. They will cater to you. They will be one with you. They will treat you well. From an American perspective, it's a bit overwhelming, but for two days straight, I've experienced the tradition of the family kin. Believe me, I had a wonderful time, but being a red-blooded American, there's something within me that cries out in protest against these traditions. Is it my individuality? Is it my sense of independence? It could be both, but after two days of constant interaction, I needed to break away from the pack by barricading myself behind the pages of a good book.

Yesterday we traveled all over Cavite. It's southwest of Manila. A large group of us went to the small town of Ternate, the place where Kiana was born and raised. Getting there, you have to drive down a two-land road that's filled with jeepneys, a form of public transportation that looks like a cross between a jeep and a bus and can hold about twenty people. Also, there are motorbikes and tricycles everywhere, and they dodge in and out of traffic, brushing up against the shops and people that line the streets. I'm amazed that parents let their children roam free on the streets, because it's quite easy to be picked off by a passing vehicle. I'm sure it happens every now and then, but it doesn't appear to be a major concern amongst the locals. In the afternoon we visited a couple of old churches that looked like they were slapped together with bricks and cement after the war then all ten of us made our way in two cars to Tagaytay City. It's a beautiful destination that's highlighted by a volcano, a lake, and breathtaking views. As you make your way there, you see small farming communities that grow banana trees, pineapples, and other tropical vegetation. It looks a lot like the Hawaiian Islands to me. Afterwards, we made our way back to Quezon City and crashed hard on our hotel room bed.

Overall, I feel blessed that her family took the time to show us their native country. Her family didn't have to take time away from their busy day, but they did, so as a way of saying thank you, we splurged for their dinner. I believe Kiana and her American brothers and sisters also gave other gifts, but apparently that's part of the tradition. Those who have gone to live in America, bring back money and goods from Babylon.

Tomorrow is our last day in Manila. We plan on doing a few things within the city, but we'll probably take it slow and easy.

Day 04 Abraham Lives! 6/26/11

Abraham had been dead for many generations and so had his sons, Isaac and Jacob, when Moses walked the earth. That is important to know because when God spoke to Moses, He said, "I am the God of Abraham, Isaac, and Jacob." (Ex.3:6) He did not say, I "was" the God of Abraham, but He said, I "am" the God of Abraham. According to the Gospel of Mark, Jesus interpreted this as meaning that the God of the *Old Testament* is the "God of the living not the dead." (Mk.12:26-27) For us, this is significant because it means after we die on earth, we live again. Although our bodies may turn to dust, our spirits will live on eternally. Some of us will live forever in communion with God, and others will live forever apart from Him.

This is what I was reading this afternoon while Kiana went to visit an old church in Manila. To each his own, I suppose. I've never been much of a churchgoer, but I do like reading the scriptures. I try to set aside some time each week to read the Word, and I've almost completed the whole *Bible* again. Usually, it's only about an hour or so, but it does give an avenue for God to speak to me. Through the Word, the Lord can exhort, comfort, and edify me. I need to hear His voice because I go astray without it, and this is one of the ways my Father can instruct me.

I know; you weren't really expecting a sermon today, but that's what was happening today in the Philippines. Later, we plan to get dinner and hangout in the city. We'll take in the nightlife of the town before flying to Boracay Island tomorrow. Boracay is one of the top vacation resorts in the Philippines, but I don't know if we'll be spending much time in the sun because it's been overcast and rainy the whole time we've been here. It's a shame because summer is one of my favorite seasons. I suppose that's why I love living in Southern California. The sun shines almost all the time.

Well, that's all I have to write today. Tomorrow I'm sure something of interest will cross our way. I'll write it down, and you can experience the journey with us. Paalam! (Goodbye in Tagalog, the main language in the Philippines).

Day 05 From B.S. to a Boner 6/27/11

After the airline robbed me blind for checking in my luggage, I started mumbling and cussing like a madman as I made my way to the Air Philippines terminal. It cost me almost a $100 dollars because our luggage was over 15 kilos. One ticket for the flight cost about $150, so I was angry, and I let the airline know. Once again, I repeat, "Piss off, Air Philippines, for being crooks!" This is the sister company of Philippines Airlines, so you know they are in cahoots together. Although my flight over here on Philippine Airlines was fine, both companies can kiss my ass! Not only that, they moved our flight time up because they wanted to fill the earlier flight, and we agreed. As a result, we were late to the terminal because they moved up our departure time. So when we arrived at the terminal, the lady tells us, "You have to pay a fee because you were late." I was already furious, and this put me over the edge. At that moment, I completely lost it, and you would not believe all the obscenities that came out of my mouth. Everyone was looking at us, and Kiana was trying to calm me down. Eventually I paid the fee because our luggage was already being loaded on the plane. To make a long story short, never fly this airline. They conduct their business like loan sharks, and I hope everyone who reads this in the future will take their business elsewhere.

After getting on the plane at the last minute, I was fuming the whole way over. For one hour, Kiana and I sat next to each other, and we didn't say a single word to one another, but when we arrived at Boracay, all of that changed. Suddenly, we were on a small tropical island in the middle of the Pacific. The weather was perfect. The ocean was calm as glass, and the water was see-through. We were reaping the benefits of post typhoon weather, and it was like we had entered a picturesque postcard. We hung out at the beach all day, and watched the sunset. It was romantic. We held each other on the beach and watched the sun go down in the sky. At night we could see the stars in the heavens as we sipped our wine under candlelight. This is Boracay Island, and I would highly recommend it to anyone. It's remote, exclusive, and breathtaking.

Tomorrow I plan to go scuba diving since the Philippines is known as one of the best regions in the world to dive while Kiana gets a massage and goes shopping.

Day 06 Life of Leisure 6/28/11

I could get used to living the life of leisure-people waiting on me hand and foot, serving me, and taking care of me. On second thought, I'd probably get tired of this pampering after a few weeks, but right now it feels pretty damn good. I'm living like a king on Boracay Island. I'm spending all my savings. I'm burning up my wallet. I'm taking what I can, and I'm not looking back.

This is how our generation is living today. We're burning the fuse on both ends not thinking about tomorrow. We're eating all the big fish.

We're cutting down the trees. We're pissing on the Ritz. Yes, it's a hard reality check, but I don't see myself giving up my refrigerator or microwave oven anytime soon. We're like a heroin addict. We use. We shoot up. We live for the man. We then head to the tropics to get the monkey off our backs by building hybrids and solar panels only to be back at the needle and spoon a few months later. Then we do the cycle all over again.

Today, I'm in the Philippines drinking mango juice and eating guava. I'm diving offshore looking at the coral as I watch a diver pick up a sea star and put it in his bag. This is the type of behavior that drives a marine biologist mad. It's taken thousands of years to build these reefs then they're gone after the hotels have gone up. Presently, Boracay is still lovely and peaceful, but give it twenty more years and it will be run over with tourists. The sea life will be dead like Waikiki Beach and soon we'll be eating processed food at McDonalds.

You ask me, "Why are you so negative, Enoch? What's your problem? You're staying at a five star hotel. You're life's a contradiction." You're right... I am a hypocrite and so are you. I am you. You are me. Look at your reflection, motherfuckers!!! This is why we as a species are going to die!

Day 07 Sunshine, Rain, & in the Middle of Nowhere 6/29/11

It's another day in paradise, eating, drinking, and voyeuristically looking at all the cute girls in their bikinis. It's a tough life, but someone has to do it. I didn't see any missionaries on the corner evangelizing. Instead, I was propositioned by annoying vendors who are selling sunglasses, hats, mangos, and other crap. I suppose it's true that "the harvest is plentiful but the workers are few." (Lk.10:2) As for those who were working, they are now on the sidelines lazing in the sun. They used to be so gung ho for the Lord, but after some years past, they went back to their own ways. I'm a living example that "a fool will return to his own folly," and the rest of you are "dogs who are eating their own vomit." (Prov.26:11) Which is worse? I don't know, but I do find it ironic that the "last state has become worse than the first." (2 Pet.2:20) Long ago we said we were never coming back, but somewhere along the line we took that first sip, and now it's deluding our ambitions.

Am I making sense to anyone right now, or am I talking in circles? The scary thing about it is that some of you are following me. You understand what I'm saying. Are we over educated? Did we read too many books?

Maybe we've just seen too much and walked too many roads. It's obvious were not innocent and green anymore; we're feeling shades of winter.

Literally, I am witnessing winter right now because Boracay Island is being hit with thunder, lightning, and heavy rains. An hour ago, I was lounging on the beach with Kiana soaking in the sun. Now I'm wondering if we'll make it to the airport in the morning. My oh my, the tropics has bizarre weather. At one moment there's rain, and the next moment there's sunshine. Who knows what will come our way tomorrow?

Day 08 Tequila Bob & Risk Takers 6/30/11

One…two…three…ahhhhh!!! Splash!!! I sunk down to the bottom of the ocean floor then swam back to the surface. I made the leap from thirty meters up, and I checked off another feat on my bucket list. Before I made the highest leap from Aerial's Point, I jumped from the five-meter ledge then the ten-meter ledge to build up my courage. And finally after drinking down a San Miguel, I made a running leap from the highest point. Believe me I was scared as hell, but I knew if I didn't make the jump, I wouldn't be able to live with myself.

This leap was risqué for me, but it didn't compare with Tequila Bob who used to dive head first into the waiting arms of his compadres. Envision a teenage kid running full speed from a single family home into the arms of six young men with their arms locked together, and you'll have an idea what a real leap of faith looks like. I'm surprised he didn't kill himself or end up a cripple like that kid in my neighborhood who used to make back flips from a ten-foot wall. Now that kid's condemned to roll around in a wheelchair the rest of his life.

I don't know why some of us feel the need to engage in risk taking behavior, but it does make one feel alive at the time. I suppose that's why I need to push the envelope on occasion. For me, my risk taking is usually cold and calculating. I may drive 100 miles-per-hour dodging in and out of traffic on the 405 Freeway, but every one of my turns is done with the utmost precision. There's always the off chance that someone in front of me is going to do something stupid, but that's what makes driving like a maniac enthralling. Who knows, maybe Tequila Bob and I have a death wish? At least it's better than always worrying you're going to fall down a staircase or something. I have an aunt who won't even drive on the freeway anymore because she's terrified of all the crazy drivers on the road. I know another person who won't use elevators because they are afraid of getting trapped inside. I don't understand this behavior, but I'm not going to

115

condemn them for their actions. Maybe something traumatic happened to them when they were younger, and it's affected the man or woman they've become. Maybe my aunt was involved in a bad accident on the freeway or had a bad experience on the road. Hell, who knows? Still, I think many people are making too many excuses for not coming out of their holes. I do the same once in a while, but the time is now to break down those barriers and overcome our fears!

Day 09 A Cebu Story 7/1/11

There was a riot going on at the back of the bar. Two friends were fighting over a car. They were pushing and shoving until Pedro stepped in. He was trying to make peace of the situation. Yet when he arrived on the scene, it was at the wrong time because Frederico pulled his gun and shot Pedro dead. Minutes later, the police arrived. One of them said, "That's the Captain's little boy." Frederico was taken downtown and beaten up bad, but the Captain cried, "I want Frederico dead!" But his brother stepped in and said, "We got to do this right. We just can't take Frederico's life." So the Captain said, "Okay, let's let him go, instead we'll set a trap on the side of the road." Frederico walked home thinking, "I can't believe I'm free" just as two men knocked him off his feet. They threw him in the trunk and drove real far. The Captain said, "It's an eye for an eye." His brother said, "Okay, you do the deed," so the Captain put a bullet in Frederico's brain. They buried Frederico near a mango tree, and the Captain's brother said a eulogy. Ten years later the story leaked when the Captain was drunk during the Marcos' regime. They arrested the Captain's brother and took his land then built a golf course for the Japs. Marcos made out with millions and the Captain's brother died in a cold cell on the Fourth of July. No one said a word until Marcos was dethroned, but now that he's dead the story's well known. It's told around supper in a Cebu town, and the Captain's brother now wears a crown.

Day 10 Sad Day 7/2/11

It's a sad day today because Kiana is leaving. She has to go back to work after the 4th while I'm staying behind earning my TEFL Certificate. It's a four-week class that will permit me to teach English to foreign students. It will keep me busy, but it's not easy to be in a foreign land alone. There's no one here to watch my back, and sometimes it gets lonely, but I'm hoping I'll meet some cool people in the class, and I'll hang out with them. I've done solo trips to Europe and Australia in the past, so

I know what to expect, but I still wish she was here by my side. Kiana is a good traveling partner. She usually goes along with me on my odd adventures, even though she does have her red flags. On this trip she didn't want to snorkel, scuba dive, or leap from Aerial's Point, but she was willing to ride jeepneys, tricycles, and roam down uncharted streets. Most of all, she's able to deal with me and my odd idiosyncrasies. She has a few of her own, but there's no profit in mentioning them. Anyway, for the next month I'm on my own. I hope the Lord will watch my back, and I don't get into too much trouble. An adventure now and then gives me something to write about, but I don't particularly like putting my life in danger as some journalists do. The only problem is when you're a traveler you stick out to the crowd, and you attract every beggar, conman, and scam. It's annoying as hell, but I've been all over the world, and I'm an experienced traveler. I can usually read the signs in the streets whether it's the Middle East, South America, or Southeast Asia. In addition, I teach in a high poverty area that's overrun with gangs and violence. I will be alright, and I hope the rest of you will finish this journey with me, even though my better half has flown back to the States.

Day 11 The Beat on the Street 7/3/11

After getting my Masters Degree in Education, I swore I would never go back to school again, but here I am taking another class. I don't really need this international teaching certificate, but I figured it couldn't hurt if I wanted to retire early and teach abroad somewhere. Also, taking this class gives me a chance to experience another culture up close. So I'm in the Philippines playing the role of a student again. With certainty, I could be teaching this class myself, but I'm going to give this teacher a chance before I write her off. Hell, it's only two weeks of instruction anyway, and the rest is in the classroom, so I'll try to think positive.

I'm staying at a dump in the middle of Cebu City. Everything is old. There's no safe in the room, and I had no hot water last night. You don't really need hot water in the Philippines because it's so humid, but it would be nice to have. As for the beat on the streets, there are a lot of homeless people over here. It's depressing to see little children sleeping on the street or fishing in water that's as dirty as a sewer, but that's the way it is in this country. Down the road you have a five-star hotel and an immaculate mall, so the Philippines is the best of both worlds. The majority of the people are very poor though, and they live in shantytowns. By Western standards, everything is affordable here, but it's difficult to get a fair price because they always seem to raise the price for foreigners. As for the people, they are friendly, hardworking, and lovable. There are the less desirable too, but you could say the same thing about any nationality.

My stay in the Philippines has been enjoyable thus far, but my view might change in a couple of weeks. In Europe I was always on the run moving from place to place, so I could get out quickly if I was bored. Now I'm stuck in one country for an extended period of time. I hope the Philippines lives up to its reputation, and I'll have a story to tell.

I'm out of here. My first class starts shortly. At least the school is close by, and I can walk there. That's why I chose this hotel in the first place. I'll let you know how it goes soon. It's time for me to hit the streets. Hasta!

Day 12 The Class 7/4/11

It's the second day of school. There are seven students in my class. One is from Korea, another is from South Africa, one is Polish, one is Filipino, and there are three Americans. It's a good mix, and everyone seems to get along with each other. We've gone out to lunch as a group two days straight, and the four guys went out drinking last night. It was fun, but I was a bit burned out in the morning.

There are two main teachers of the class. One is very good. Even a veteran teacher like me is learning a few new tricks from her. A lot of the material is information I learned back in college, but I'm realizing now I needed a refresher course. It was similar to my diving experience in Boracay. I hadn't gone scuba diving since Australia, and I realized I needed to go over a few things.

I don't really have too many stories to tell at the moment, except for the people in the class. One of the Americans named Eastwood lives in Angeles City, which apparently has a big Red Light District. It's near Manila. He's an eccentric character. He reminds me of Dennis Hopper in Easy Rider, and his idiosyncrasies are amusing. Now he's living in a foreign land, and he plans to teach English in Saudi Arabia this September. The other American is a twenty-two-year-old Texan named Chuck who grew up a farmer. He has a Midwest feel to him, and he's easy to get along with. However, he still has that restless edge that many of us once had when we were in our early twenties. The last of the men is called Bong. He's a Filipino who married a Polish girl, and he now lives in Warsaw. He's amicable and serves as our interpreter when we're trying to find directions or can't explain what we mean in the local language.

The girl from South Africa is the most intriguing out of the women. Her name is Esmay. She's half English and half Afrikaner, so she's a native to both languages. I enjoy listening to her stories about her homeland because I've never been to South Africa before. It's a place high on my list of destinations I want to travel to. I hope I get there someday. Lyra is a local Filipina girl, and she is newly married. She's wonderfully nice and shy, but once she gets talking, there's no stopping her. The final woman is a Korean named Sun, but she's lived most of her life in the Philippines. She's the classic Asian woman. She's formal, speaks very little, and wants to do everything with perfection. I like her as with everyone else in the class, but at times I want her to loosen up and laugh a little.

There you have them; my new characters in the story. I will speak about them from time to time, and hopefully this introduction has given you some background information on them.

Day 13 Missing 7/5/11

Chuck, the twenty-two-year-old from Texas, went missing. Everyone was worried about him because he didn't show up to class. It's quite common for westerners to be mugged and taken advantage of in the Philippines, so everyone was concerned. Therefore, the school sent out a security force to look for him. By the grace of God, he didn't end up dead or in the hospital because he's still quite green to the traveling scene. What really happened is he met some guy smoking pot on the roof of his hotel that ended up being a drug dealer in the area. Chuck and him smoked a whole bunch of joints together then went out on the town. Luckily, the drug dealer was not trying to use Chuck because he could have easily done so if Chuck was completely stoned and out of his mind. Chuck went out with the drug dealer and went to a club. Later in a drunken, stoned stupor, Chuck made his way over to a strip bar and brought home one of the girls. Apparently it cost him around $50 to sleep with her, and that is why he went missing. He did show up later in the afternoon to the relief of everyone, and he and I went and bought cell phones that evening to make sure someone has tabs on where we are going. In a foreign land, it's always good to know someone has your back, and what Chuck did was dangerous; still, everything turned out alright. He ended up getting laid, and he had a big smile on his face when he showed up. Eastwood was making all sorts of jokes about it, and I was laughing my ass off.

I haven't been that drunk and stoned in a foreign land for a long time. Back when I was traveling around Ireland, I did go home with a Belfast girl, and I completely forgot where I was staying for the night. All my stuff was back at the bed and breakfast, and she and I drove around for hours in the morning trying to find the place. It was mere stupidity on my part, but sometimes that's what happens when you're in your twenties and your life experiences are minimal.

Day 14 Humidity 7/6/11

If you've ever been to the beach and wore suntan lotion all day and did a few errands afterwards then you would know what it's like to live in the Philippines everyday. As soon as you step outside, you get that sticking feeling all over your body. Then you start to perspire. The weather is almost identical to Thailand, but I know most of you have never been there, so my example isn't helping much, but if you've been to the South, you probably understand how bad the humidity is. Even a skinny guy like me starts to sweat. I went to the gym the other day, and I was dripping in perspiration. My whole shirt was soaked, and you would have thought I ran a marathon or something. And I'm a man who doesn't perspire all that much. Now imagine if you had a little weight on your body.

I don't have much to comment on today since I've been in school all week. The class is okay, and I've learned a few new teaching techniques. My fellow students make it fun, but this weekend should be far more interesting. I'm curious to see how crazy the nightlife is on the weekend. I'll let you all know soon enough. Later...

Day 15 Life in the Fast Lane 7/7/11

It's always around two weeks that I start to burn out, and right now I'm running on empty. There's still a little bit of fuel left in my tank though, so I think I'm going to drive this car as far as it will go until I need a tow. The only problem is I'm driving a beat up old truck, and I start shaking when I go over 65.

"Life in the fast lane. Surely make you lose your mind." (Eagles) And right now I'm in Cebu roaring down the highway. I'm screaming with my head out the window. I'm laughing like a deranged lunatic. I think I'm gonna die!

Day 16 Loss for Words 7/8/11

I have nothing to say today. Even if I did, I wouldn't say it...

Day 17 Snapped 7/9/11

I lost my temper this morning. I was out at a club all night and came in late, so I figured I'd sleep in this morning, but the hotel had other plans for me. At 8:00 A.M. I was awakened by construction right below me. They are renovating the room, so I've been hearing construction from about 8 to 5 everyday. The first five days I didn't mind too much because I wasn't there, but today I wanted to relax, sleep in, and read. So when I heard the guys working this morning, I packed up all my shit and gave the front desk hell. I demanded a refund and made a scene. I demanded, "I'm checking out early, and I want my money back!" At first they denied me the refund and said they'd move me to another room instead, but I wasn't willing to give in because I had already snapped. I was tired, irritable, and pissed off. I think I spoke to every damn person in that hotel as all the guests in the lobby watched silently. Eventually, they gave me my money and waved any charges I had accrued. Afterwards, I felt bad for losing it because Filipinos are usually so nice and accommodating, but wasn't I the one who was being violated??? The hotel is to blame, not me. They gave me a shitty room with minimal hot water, a leaky toilet, and a room built on a construction site. Now that I think about it, screw them! I don't feel bad at all, and why should I be sorry?

Day 18 Out of Gas 7/10/11

I ran out of gas last night at the gambling casino. My body finally said, "You have to slow down." I should have seen the signs and took a day of rest, but I went out anyway. Now I have a sore throat, and my nose is running.

The casino I went to wasn't very good. It reminded me of a rundown place in Downtown Vegas, but lots of people were playing. As for the games, there were a lot of different ones that I've never seen before. There was only one blackjack table, one craps table, and one roulette table. The rest were odd games I had never seen before except for Pai gow. There were slot machines, but I didn't see any video poker or receive free drinks. Once again, it wasn't that great of a casino, but I still lost about $50 playing roulette.

Now I'm back at my hotel room recovering. I turned the AC off even though it's hot and humid. I don't particularly like being in an AC room 24/7 because it messes with my sinuses, so I'm going to sweat this one out. That pretty much sums it up for the day. I'm having a hard time keeping up with these entries and writing at all. I'm in a black hole, and I'm exhausted.

Day 19 Hypocrites & Unbelievers 7/11/11

You don't need an alarm clock if you're living in the Philippines because it seems like everybody owns roosters. Then the dogs start barking, so you might as well wake up at the crack of dawn. Also, for those who've never been around roosters before, they cock-a-doodle-doo all day long. It's not just in the morning. Since you wake up before the sun comes up, you'll have plenty of time to count the number of mosquito bites that cover your body. I've been bitten at least one time everyday since I've been over here, and right now it looks like I have the chickenpox. I try not to scratch them, but it's difficult when there are so many.

Yesterday I was reading about a rooster that cooed twice. It happened just as Peter denied Christ three times. Peter wasn't the only one guilty. All the disciples fled for their lives. Judas' betrayal was the worst, but I sympathize more with Peter. I have not flatly denied Jesus as my Savior, but the way I've lived my life has been a denial in itself. So I don't know what's worse, someone who says they believe in Jesus and lives like a heathen or someone who flatly denies they believe in Christ at all. I guess it doesn't really matter. The hypocrites and the unbelievers will end up in the same place. If that's the case, I'm going to hell, and most of you are coming with me. The truth hurts sometimes, but the *Bible* is very clear about who will inherit the Kingdom of God and who will not. Believe me, I don't want to go to the Lake of Fire and burn for eternity, but that seems to be the place I'll be going. I can't get it right. I can't walk straight. I'm an evil man. I do wicked deeds. I'm one with the unbelievers.

Day 20 Under the Weather 7/12/11

Being sick abroad is never fun. At home you can always eat soup and drink hot tea, but when you're cooped up in a hotel room, you have to go out to get your dinner. What can you do? That's the price you pay when you're traveling. At least I only have a cold and don't have to see the doctor or need antibiotics. A few of us have gotten sick over here too. Eastwood has been throwing up and shitting diarrhea for the last three days, and Chuck was puking yesterday. Eastwood had food poisoning, but Chuck's was due to partying. His was a self-inflicted wound. My excuse is I have a weak immune system and need to eat right all the time. At least I'm not like my diabetic friends who can't even go out and drink one night without reaping the consequences. These are all the wonderful shortfalls of growing older. Our bodies break down much easier than they used to. Then again, being sick every now and then is far less painful than having asthma attacks every other week and being rushed down to the hospital so I can breathe again. It's funny. I hardly remember those days as a kid, but I can still see us flying down Harbor Blvd. in our station wagon and me sticking my head out the window so I can get air into my lungs. It must have been highly stressful on my parents. They dealt with it like all parents do when their kids have health problems. At least in the Millennial Reign we won't have to deal with this bullshit anymore. Everyone will be healthy, and no one will get sick. Imagine never getting sick or having to take pills or visit the doctor anymore. Wouldn't it be magnificent? I wonder if those in medicine will have to find a new profession. Will we even need doctors anymore???

Day 21 Gambling in the Backroom 7/13/11

Picture a small, dirty room with a card table in the center, a young Filipina showing cleavage and dealing hold-em, and eight men sitting around a table drinking, cursing, and smoking. Then you'll have a picture of where I was last night. It felt like I had entered the Filipino version of the Sopranos at a local card game in Cebu. There were some old guys, some young studs, and the two Americans carousing with them.

By Filipino standards, the stakes were high, so when a hand was lost, players would spit, throw down their cards, and have angry outbursts. Chuck and I would grin at one another as the onlookers pressed in against us. At one point, I thought one of the older guys was going to pull a knife on his opponent after he laid down the winning hand. Instead, he stared him down across the table as if he had been cheated, rose violently from his chair, and shouted something in Cebuano. Immediately after he left, another person took the seat and the game continued.

At 3:00 A.M in the morning, I finally went home. I was tired, drunk from drinking Red Horse, but satisfied that I broke even after hours of sitting at that table. Chuck lost a little bit, but he didn't seem concerned. One could easily blow three times that amount at one of the girly bars in town, so I imagine it was a light night for him.

Bong, the Filipino guy who now lives in Poland, didn't play with us. He went to the Waterfront Casino for the fourth night in a row. Of course, he lost again. He swears the roulette table is rigged, but he keeps going back. Explain the logic in that argument??? Bong thinks he can beat the eye in the sky, but I've grown to accept that when you're going to a casino, the odds are you will probably lose. Sure, there are times when I've paid for my trip to Vegas, but most of the time I've come back with an empty wallet. I do much better at a local game with the boys. There are a few friends I know who are very good card players, but the general public doesn't have a clue what they are doing.

I'm not suggesting that I'm an expert on the subject, but I do know the games that I play. Before I sit down at the blackjack table, I know the book like the back of my hand. Before I start throwing dice, I know what I'm doing and how much to bet. I would never throw money down on the craps table without reading several books on the subject and picking up as many tips as possible from trusted sources. I believe educating oneself on the games will help insurmountably. You may not come back a winner every time, but you will cut your losses in half.

Day 22 Teaching English Abroad 7/14/11

Today was a day of teaching, planning, and catching up on my sleep. Earlier, I tutored a Korean adolescent. He's a nice kid who is trying to learn English. Actually, there are tons of Korean people doing the same thing over here. They come to the Philippines to learn English because many Filipinos speak sound English, so they go to these Filipino schools to pick up the language. And if you're a native speaker from the UK, the States, or any other place where English is your first language, you are seen as an English teaching god, and they'll pay you lots of money to learn the language. This is taking place almost everywhere on the globe, so if you're really hard-up for work, you could easily find work in another country as an English teacher. Pick the place you want to go, look online for a job, and before you know it, you'll be a highly regarded teacher. People will look up to you, call you sir or ma'am, and pay you enough to get by.

I don't think people realize how coveted native speakers are abroad. It's a skill you acquired from your ma and pop. You know how to speak the words in the proper form and dialect. In addition, the American accent is more coveted than the British one. This is a bit ironic, but it's the truth. Apparently, our accent is easier to learn, and most of the business world and television shows have our unique twang. More power to the U.S.A., I suppose. I'm not complaining. If I actually live beyond my 1,260 day testimony, I'll probably retire early and teach abroad. It will be like having two incomes at once. Now you know why I'm getting my TEFL Certificate. It opens up many career opportunities.

TEFL (Teaching English as a Foreign Language)

Day 23 7/15/11 South African Robbery

Esmay was on the train returning from school late in the morning, and she was accosted by a gangster from Johannesburg. He sat next to her and said, "Give me your cell phone, or I'm going to kill you."

Esmay was reluctant to give up the phone. She said, "I'm not giving up the phone. It's old and out-dated anyway. Why would you want it?" and she showed him the phone.

The gangster looked at the phone and responded. "You are right. I don't want the phone, but you are a fool to be talking back to a man who's threatening your life."

"Maybe so," she answered, "but I don't want to lose all my contacts."

The gangster then warmed up to her and started telling Esmay his life story. Esmay was nervous, but she listened. He said he had just arrived in Cape Town, but he ran with gangsters back in Johannesburg. Eventually the gangster left, and Esmay was relieved. He went and threatened someone else on the train and was beaten up by three white men. As for Esmay, she couldn't move. She sat stationary in her seat. She missed her stop and ultimately had to call someone to help her get off the train.

Esmay says she's okay now, but it's a memory lodged deep within her mind. I imagine that's how my mother felt when the bank she worked at was robbed at gunpoint. She missed work for a week, but eventually she overcame her fears and went back to the teller line.

It's a shame people like this exist in our society, but I'm sure thieves and murderers have been with us since the beginning. I wish they would go away, so that we could live in peace. I suppose it's something that will be with us until the end of time. Maybe during the Reign of Christ, these evil men will be kept in check. I hope so. Until then, we'll have to learn how to protect ourselves and be as shrewd as serpents.

Esmay is the South African student from my class and this was her story.

Day 24 Kawasan Falls & Burning Charcoal 7/16/11

All seven students in the class took a 3-hour ride to Kawasan Falls. We endured public transportation that squeezes as many people as possible into a vehicle. Eastwood made a joke about it. He said, "How many people can you fit into a jeepney?" His answer, "One more." As a result, you have people hanging on the sides, the backs, and Eastwood said one time he rode on the top of a jeepney. It's very safe travel, and the fumes that come out of these little buses are as fresh as an ocean breeze??? Fortunately, we weren't taking one of these jeepneys but a real bus. They also squeeze as many people as possible into them, but it's not as bad. We were all laughing though when a big mamasan wanted to sit down, so I let her have the seat between Eastwood and me. Oh, it was painful, but she managed to squeeze in. The space is the size of a two-seater, but it has three little seats. It's like the seats were made for children. I sat next to the sweaty girl for an hour or so until I couldn't take it any longer. I stood up the rest of the way.

When we arrived in Kawasan Falls, we noticed that the bottom of the trail is at the ocean's edge, so we hung out for an hour at the beach, and the boys took a long swim. It was refreshing. Afterwards, we walked up the trail to breathtaking waterfalls. The first one is magnificent, so all the tourists stop there and usually don't go any higher. We stopped there for awhile and went swimming with all the Koreans and Filipinos wearing life vests. I'm amazed at how many people can't swim over here. It's embarrassing. You'd think if you lived on an island, you'd know how to swim, but that's not the case. After hanging out at the first falls, we went higher, and came across private coves and more intimate falls. We had stopped at each one, took pictures, and went swimming. All the men were jumping off rocks and bridges and acting like little boys showing off their prowess. It was an absolute blast. We were at the falls all day and didn't catch the return bus until the sun went down.

On the way home, there weren't as many people on the bus, so we had a little bit of legroom; however, the windows on the bus were all opened. That meant we had to breathe in the fumes from all the cars and the little fires burning on the side of the road. Most of the locals burn this charcoal to cook up their food, and it is terrible on the lungs. They also burn their trash, smoke, and are not environmentally conscious. It felt like I was in San Bernardino when all the fires were burning down Los Angeles a couple years ago. I was coughing the whole way back and was in desperate need of medicine for my lungs. I survived, but next time I take a bus, I'm taking the one with Air-con.

Day 25 Demon Possessed Boy 7/17/11

I was down at the SM Mall earlier when a prostitute harassed me. They flock to westerners because they think we're made of gold, but they usually leave you alone if you don't give them eye-contact. This one ladyboy, however, was exceedingly aggressive. As I was making my way down the street, she/he kept putting her hand in my pocket and grabbing my penis. She was also trying to grab my wallet, so I knocked her hand away and said, "I don't want any! Go away!" Immediately she withdrew her hand and went in the opposite direction. Ten minutes later by the taxi stand, she did the same thing. This time I raised my hand at her like I was going to slap her, but she laughed hysterically and walked away.

Later in the day, I heard some of the students in my class were going to barbeque down the street, so I joined them. We were all gathered around the barbeque area when suddenly a ten-year-old Filipino kid rushed up at us with a gun in his hand. He looked crazy, and his eyes were going this way and that. Instead of shooting us, he threw the loaded gun to the side of him, so I jumped at the weapon and pushed it away from the kid, but in the process, the gun went off. The bullet went screaming off in the distance but didn't hit anyone. Meanwhile, my buddy Chuck grabbed the gun as the kid looked in the direction where the bullet went and started screaming.

"It's starting a fire! It's starting a fire! My house is on fire! The village is on fire!"

One of the girls tried to console the lad. She said, "Everything's going to be alright, kid. There's no fire. No one was hurt," but the boy kept screaming like a madman. I had never seen a kid act so strangely before. His eyes were bloodshot red, and he was drooling all over himself. He was also punching himself all over and making odd body movements. At this point I thought the kid was either mad or demon possessed, so I attempted to cast the demon out of him. I said with authority, "Be gone in the name of the Lord Jesus! I command you out of him!" The boy froze like a statue, and the evil spirit left him. Afterwards, the boy started acting completely normal, so I went over to him and prayed. I touched him on the shoulder, closed my eyes, and quietly whispered, "Lord, free this boy from the evil spirit or spirits and make sure they never return."

The boy looked up at me and smiled. I didn't realize it, but everyone else was looking at me too. They were stunned by what had transpired. I felt a bit uncomfortable, but I proceeded to take the boy aside and said, "Is there a Bible in your house?"

He responded, "Yes," and shook his head.

I exhorted him, "I want you to read one chapter a day until you read the whole book. I don't want the evil spirit to come back and torment you. The Word will protect you. Do you understand?"

He shook his head yes, smiled, and walked away.

When I returned to the group, everyone was quiet at first. Finally, one of the Filipina girls asked, "What happened over there?"

I said, "The boy was demon possessed. This is the third time I've come across demon possession in my life, but I've never seen it like this before."

A few in the group looked at me like I was insane, but they couldn't deny what they had just witnessed. After that, one of the Filipina girls was afraid to speak to me. She looked upon me reverently, but I told her, "I didn't do anything. It was the power of God." She didn't see it that way though; it was like I had parted the Red Sea or something. As for the others, they got over it pretty quickly, and we went back to having our jovial time by the fire.

Day 26 Tale of a Working Girl 7/18/11

I was out at one of the strip clubs the other night, and I met a woman by the name of Jazzelle. She approached me after I had already brushed away the horde of women earlier. She asked, "Did you not like any of the girls?"

I responded, "No, that's not the problem. I just want to sit down, relax, and enjoy my beer for a spell."

She said, "Oh okay," and was about to get up.

I continued, "What I'm really looking for is a good story? Do you happen to have one for me?"

She laughed and said, "That's interesting. What kind of story are you looking for?"

"I don't know. How about your tale?"

She giggled, "You wouldn't be interested in my story. It's too dramatic."

"Actually, that's the sort of story I'm looking for," I said as I waved the waitress over and bought the woman a drink.

In the Philippines, it is customary to buy the working girls drinks if you're interested in them, so the woman scooted in closer and rested a hand on my knee.

I looked at her and smiled. "I'd love to hear your tale, but I only want the truth. First, tell me your real name."

She said, "My real name is Angelica Esperanza Santiago. I come from the province."

"Nice to meet you, Angelica. How long have you been in the city? Your English is flawless by the way."

"Thank you. It's been about seven years now."

"Well, tell me how you got here and where you're going?"

"When I was a child I was brought up in some of the finest schools. My father was a wealthy man; however, I was the product of one of his mistresses. He supported my mom and I until the day he died when I was age fifteen. Unfortunately, that's when the money ran out. We had no means of making a living, so we moved to the city looking for work."

I nodded and said, "Please continue."

"For a year or so, my mom and I survived washing clothes for this laundry man. My mom would sleep with him. In exchange, we would have food and sleeping quarters. Then one day the laundry man found me alone, and he raped me. That was how I lost my virginity. This went on for another six months until my mother passed away. God rest her soul."

"Tragic," I said, and she continued.

"At that point, I moved in with my friend who worked at one of these clubs. She helped me get this job, even though I was only seventeen at the time. The owner didn't seem to care that I was underage. He was more concerned about my looks and earning potential."

I asked, "So that's when you started working professionally?"

"Yes, it was, and I was one of the club's top earners until I became pregnant a few years ago."

"So you have a child?"

"Yes, her name is Melanie, and she's 2 ½ years old."

Angelica reached into her little bag and showed me a picture. She asked, "Isn't she beautiful?"

I looked at the picture of the two of them together and responded, "Yes, she is. So how are you doing financially?"

"Not as well as before, but we are surviving. My child is growing up strong. I'm saving all my pesos, so my daughter will get an education and not have to live the life that I have."

I shook my head as the waitress came up and asked, "Would you like to buy her another drink?"

I said, "Yes, and get me another San Miguel too."

The two of us sat there for another hour and had a wonderful conversation. Angelica told me how a dirty old European beat her up and how she had to go to the hospital. She showed me the scar. I asked her about her faith, and she told me she prays to God all the time. Angelica says she's sorry for what she's become, and she hopes God will forgive her. She says she's only going to stay in the business for as long as she has to. I hope's she's successful despite the odds being against her. When I left the club I said, "Thanks for the company and especially the story." I then flipped her a few hundred pesos and caught a taxi back to the hotel.

Day 27 Jeepney Accident 7/19/11

Esmay was hit by a jeepney last night. It's the equivalent of being hit by a minivan. She was jaywalking across the street and was hit by the left mirror of a jeepney. She fell to the concrete and was knocked unconscious, but fortunately someone stopped traffic in the other direction before she was run over and killed. Esmay was then rushed to the hospital and treated for her injuries. She suffered no brain trauma, but it looks like she just came out of a fight with Manny Pacquiao because she has bandages and bruises all over her face. The South African will be okay, but she has to stay in the hospital for a few days.

Esmay's accident shows you that you can't be too sure of the future. One moment you're alive, the next moment you're dead. For example, my friend lost his wife in a head on head collision with a truck. The truck driver was falling asleep at the wheel, and he veered into my friend's lane. She died. It was tragic. She was a wonderful person and loved by many, but now she's moved onto the next life. Another friend who I used to run track with died in a car crash in a drunk driving accident near San Diego. He was in his early twenties when he was killed. And another acquaintance died in a terrorist attack in the Gulf. All three were relatively young when they passed, so it proves that death could come at anytime, and there are no guarantees you'll wake up tomorrow. Anything is possible.

I suppose that's why Jesus said, "To be on the alert for you do not know the day nor the hour," (Mt.25:13) the Lord will return. He could come tomorrow or next week or sometime in the future, so we have to live in the present. If we did, I think we would have a much more enjoyable life. That doesn't mean we should go out and sell everything we have, but it does put things into perspective. For those false prophets who think they can predict the day Jesus is coming, don't believe any of them. The scriptures clearly state that "no one knows the day or the hour not even the angels of heaven." (Mt.24:36) We simply have to be ready all the time and not live depraved lives. Now if I only listened to my own advice. It's illogical for me to know the truth, but to keep living a carefree lifestyle. It simply demonstrates that I'm not prepared for the second coming. I am like the five virgins who did not have their flask of oil ready when the Lord came. They missed out on all the fun and were not permitted to join the wedding feast. And some of you are in the same position as me. That means we need to put our house in order and get ready for our untimely death or the Lord's return.

Day 28 Slow Day 7/20/11

Some days are slow. Some days are fast. Today is a slow day. I went to class. I bought some food at the market. I took a nap. I listened to the thunder and rain. I thought about people I care for and love. I thought about past relationships and old acquaintances. Some I miss. Some I don't. I thought about my country. I miss my homeland. I miss California. I miss familiar things. Right now I'm watching an old movie on television. I remember when that movie came out. It seems so long ago, but it feels like yesterday. In a month or so the Philippines will seem like a dream. It will feel like I was never here at all. My whole life is a mere breath. Breathe in, breathe out. Now it's gone.

Day 29 Eastwood's Tale 7/21/11

In life sometimes you come across people that knock you off your feet. Eastwood is one of those people. He's from California, but he's been living in Angeles City for twenty-one years. It's an hour outside Manila. It's where the old U.S. base was located. Eastwood once was a soldier, and he served some time in prison.

Eastwood's been a fisherman. He's hunted tuna. He's flown and worked on helicopters that spot the school of fish. One time he swam in shit when the boat was letting out the waste. Eastwood was hooked on opium until he got clean. He still drinks a lot of beer, but he misses marijuana the most.

Eastwood's been married three times. He has a daughter in her twenties. She's drop dead gorgeous. I saw the pictures. He hasn't had sex with his wife in over ten years. She's a fat Filipina woman. She's living in Guam. They rarely see each other, but they're still married.

Eastwood is fifty-three years old. He's heading to Saudi Arabia to teach in the fall. He needs the money. He hasn't worked in over three months. Eastwood's a bit sarcastic. He's funny as hell though. He's always telling a joke. I'm not good at jokes, so I admire people who can tell them. I like a good laugh. Eastwood can be an asshole at times, especially when he's drunk, but he's really a good guy. I've seen him giving money to the poor even though he's an atheist. He said, "If there's a god, he's a bastard. Look around you. There's too much evil in the world. There's no god. If there is, he's like Zeus taking what he wants and doing as he pleases."

Eastwood, I feel sorry for people like you. You believe in nothing, and you've never known God's Spirit moving through you. I saw you walking home last night to your hotel. You didn't see me standing in the shadows, but I saw the sad look on your face.

Eastwood was a boxer. He worked out at the same gym Manny Pacquiao once did. He still keeps in shape, but he says he's lost a lot of strength. Eastwood walks down the street with authority. People move out of his way. He won't budge when you're heading in his direction, but he will move a shoulder.

Eastwood can be a dirty old man. I've heard his stories and watched the way he grabs the club girls. He knows what he wants, and he refuses to pay extra. He says he doesn't tip, but I've seen him tip on several occasions. Sometimes Eastwood talks a big game, but I think he's soft in the middle. He's a fine gentleman. I'm glad I met him. Eastwood has flaws like everyone else, but his positives outweigh his negatives. Eastwood, I don't know your first name.

Day 30 Education & Vices 7/22/11

I taught yesterday at a university. The students were well behaved. When they answered a question, they stood up and gave their response. It was very formal. As I walked down the hall, they'd say, "Hello sir," and I was well respected. I could really get used to teaching over here. Back home, teacher's heads are on the chopping block. In my district alone, they fired 700 teachers last year. Who's going to fill the void? No one will fill it. Then you have the public complaining about low-test scores and how our educational system is failing. If we keep on the path we're going, you can only expect it to get worse. In truth, what I've seen of America's educational system is positive. Certainly, there are some flaws and bad teachers, but by tearing apart our unions, cutting our wages and benefits, and increasing our class sizes, you're going to get disillusioned teachers, and none of our brightest graduates will want to go into the field. Education is about teaching the next generation to think, read, and write. It's not about profits. So next time you vote against education and cutting programs, please reconsider your position.

Right now, I'm still in Cebu. The program is coming to a close in a week, and I'll be heading to Angeles City for a few days before I go home. Eastwood lives there, and Chuck is going to join us. Eastwood and I are flying, but Chuck is taking a ferry. He says he wants to experience the ferry ride, but I think he wants to bypass customs, so he can bring his marijuana with him. The truth hurts sometimes, and for Chuck, it's all about smoking the ganja right now.

Day 31 Ashen & Rashes 7/23/11

A day ago, my skin broke out in a rash. I don't know if it was an allergic reaction, bed bugs, or something else. Yesterday it wasn't too bad, but today it looks worse. Normally I would schedule an appointment with my doctor, but maybe a pharmacist can help me out. After finally getting well and feeling better again, I'm thrown back another two steps with this bullshit. There's always something on the road that makes being in a foreign land burdensome. Today, it's a rash. Tomorrow, it will be something else. Over here, they still have plagues that science eradicated many years ago. This is what happens when you're living in third world conditions where many people cannot afford to get their immunization shots.

I'm amazed a major plague hasn't struck the world in some time. I believe God is holding back on the ashen horse until the appointed time. It's true he's struck many times in the past, but I have a feeling the next plague is going to be a doozey. I'd much rather prefer living without another pandemic flu, but it is my job to warn you that another black death is coming. Johnny Cash even sung a song about it. He sang, "And I heard a voice in the midst of the four beasts. And I looked and behold a pale horse. And his name that sat on him was Death. And Hell followed with him." If you're interested in reading the actual prophecy, it's straight out of the *Book of Revelation.* (Rev.6:8) It basically says that this ashen (pale) horse will have the power to kill a fourth of mankind with sword, famine, and pestilence.

On a more positive note, I read an article that the people of the Philippines have a brighter outlook on the future than Americans and Europeans. Right now it feels like we're in an economic freefall, but over here in the Philippines, they appear to be untouched by our woes. It's obviously not true in a world economy, but if you really think about it, how much worse can it get if you're already at the bottom? It's only those who have something to lose that are feeling that bitter pill.

Day 32 Hash Run 7/24/11

Yesterday I was a virgin and participated in my first Hash Run. It's a group known all over the world that describes themselves as "a drinking club with a running problem." In short, a bunch of people get together and go for a run once a week. Alcohol is usually involved to make the run more enjoyable. Eastwood introduced Chuck and I to the group, and we went on a hike/run up in the hills of Cebu. It's not a cult or anything weird like that. It's merely a bunch of people getting together to drink beer and run. Most of the drinking takes place at the end of the run, but usually a beer or two is downed before heading out on the trail.

After the run was over, everyone gathered around in a circle and played drinking games. Songs were sung, and people were made fun of or put in the circle for doing odd things. For example, if you pissed during the run, you would be forced to go into the center and down a cup of beer. It was hilarious as hell, and I could easily see a lot of my friends joining a local chapter. If it involves beer, I'm sure my friends will be there.

Next week I may join the Hash chapter in Angeles City and see how their group does things. All in all, it's a great way to meet new people, exercise, and of course, drink until you can no longer see straight.

Day 33 Luke & the Lost 7/25/11

Currently, I'm reading the *Gospel of Luke*. The traditional view is that he was the same person who traveled around with Paul, the apostle. Luke didn't miss much in his retelling of the story, and I would surmise that Luke did a lot of research on Jesus before he actually wrote the Gospel down because he gave such a detailed account of the Man. I admire someone who actually takes the time to research a certain subject whether it is science, history, or any other field of study. I love it when people practice the scientific method and do not write their conclusions down until they've objectively completed their research. Lately, I've been coming across a lot of people today who speak out on subjects they have not researched or read any book on the topic. The *Bible* is one of those subjects. It seems like everybody has an opinion on it, but only a select few have actually read it from cover to cover.

Last night, Eastwood and I had a heated debate on the subject. He went off telling me that the *Bible* is a bunch of mumbo jumbo, and that Christianity and other religions are a way to keep the populace under control. I found it difficult to argue with Eastwood's second point because there is a lot of truth to what he is saying; nevertheless, I found out that Eastwood has never read the *Bible* himself. Immediately I threw out everything he had to say about the book. It would be like me telling you how to build an engine when I've never built an engine before. I'm not a mechanic, and I would have no clue where to start. As for the *Bible*, I've put in my twenty-five years of research, so I'm allowed to have an opinion on the subject. You may not agree with my conclusions, but I do think it's important to research the subject before you respond with a rebuttal. If not, you're only talking out of your ass, and there seems to be a lot of uninformed people sprouting off their opinions on the *Bible*.

To conclude, I hope more people will be as thorough as Luke. They will speak to eyewitness accounts. They will do their background information, and if they have a theory, they will follow every lead before they actually write down their findings. Once these steps are completed, I will listen and consider your opinions on the *Bible*. Until you read the text, it might be better to remain mute on the subject but feel free to ask questions as you go.

Day 34 The Prodigal Son 7/26/11

Chuck is the classic case of the prodigal son. He grew up on a farm in Texas. He was home-schooled. He comes from a small town. He's lived a relatively isolated life, and this is his first time outside of America. He stands about six-foot, Dutch built, blonde hair, and he walks with a limp because he had an accident with a horse when he was younger. Chuck's a friendly guy, and he gets along with everybody. Nonetheless, Chuck is a restless youth, and he has been partying pretty hard in the last year. In fact, the whole time he's been over here, I don't think he's gone a day without smoking or drinking. He's able to pull this off because he's only twenty-two. At the beginning, I tried to keep up with him, but I quickly fell by the wayside. My days of partying every night are long behind me. As for Chuck, he's still in his twilight years.

Chuck is also a Christian. He believes Jesus is the Messiah, and at some point he was born again. In laymen's terms, this means he made a conscious choice to believe in Jesus. Still, Chuck's lifestyle is inappropriate for a Christian. I should know because I'm in the same boat. There's no veil covering my eyes. I know full well what I'm doing. Chuck, on the other hand, may not. He does know that he is sinning, but I don't think he realizes how far he's fallen from the faith. Chuck is currently in the process of blowing all his money on loose women, marijuana, cigarettes, alcohol, and gambling. I have no idea why he's taking this training course. He doesn't want to be an English teacher. His life is on the farm, and that is all he ever talks about. Chuck really does know his stuff though, and it's like I'm getting a crash course in farming.

I believe one day, Chuck, will come to his senses and return to the straight and narrow path. It might take him a few years, but eventually I see him settling down with a foreign wife and living on a farm somewhere. At present, he's living on the edge. Sometimes I join him for a few hours, but staying up until the crack of dawn every night is out of my league. I might be a prodigal son as well, but there is a reason I am a reluctant prophet. I have been called to give you a living example of what it means to be a fallen brother or sister. I am your reflection. I am America, and this is why we are going to be judged so harshly for our crimes. As a Christian nation, we should know better, but we are living it up like there's no tomorrow. We are like the prodigal son. We are sleeping in the sty. We have spent everything we have, and we are now in debt. One day the creditors are going to ask us to pay up, and we as a nation and people are going to fall.

Day 35 Company, Culture, Food, & Language 7/27/11

Being in a foreign land can be a nightmare or an oasis depending on several factors. First, the company you spend your time with can make all the difference. When I made a journey to Australia and New Zealand back in 1996 I didn't make any real strong connections with anybody, so the trip felt lonelier. In the Philippines I've been blessed with a strong network of people to spend my time with, so I've felt somewhat satisfied. I've been able to share my experiences with others. In Australia and New Zealand, it was more of an introspective journey.

Second, the hotels and the food can make a trip more pleasant or miserable. In the Middle East I stayed in some dives and some nice hotels. Usually I had a more enjoyable time at the nicer places, but sometimes staying at a dive can immerse you into the culture more thoroughly. Usually dives are in the heart of the city, and it forces you to dine at a local restaurant where you can't even read the hieroglyphics. Sometimes your taste buds are exposed to delicious new fruits and vegetables. Other times, you sort of put the food down and hope you don't get sick. At the five-star hotels, you're usually pretty safe, but everything costs an arm and a leg, and you realize you could have bought the same food down the road for half the price. The food in the Philippines has been descent. I can't complain, but believe me when I get home, I'm going to gorge myself on real Mexican and Italian food.

Third, the culture usually has an impact on whether you will have fun or struggle on a day-to-day basis, and language is one of the most important factors. In Thailand, it was difficult to have a deep conversation with anybody or tell the taxi driver where you wanted to go because not many people have been educated in English. In the Philippines, it seems like everyone can speak Basic English, so it makes ordering a meal at a restaurant far simpler. Cultural differences can also be disturbing. For instance, European culture is quite similar to North American culture, so there's common ground between the Old and New Worlds. The Middle East and their customs can be a bit frustrating to say the least because everyone is so confrontational, but eventually you get used to it and become more aggressive too. As for the Philippines, most people are kind and will smile at you, but be aware a smile doesn't always mean everything's okay. Sometimes Filipinos hide behind their smiles even though they are angry, sad, or frustrated. At first you may not pick up on this, but after living with them, you'll be able to read between the lines and figure out if their smile is real or fake.

To finish up, I would suggest when you travel abroad to stay at both high end and low-end places. You might as well take in as much of the culture as possible at the time because it's likely you will never return there. You may not always be able to get your message across, but if your path entangles you with fellow travelers, journey forward with them and go places together. There's nothing like having a beer with an Aussie or Brit in Morocco and having no clue what you're going to see or do tomorrow.

Day 36 So Far Away 7/28/11

I'm sitting at a coffee shop bidding my time. I've got nothing to do and no place to be. It's unnerving to be alone. There are people all around me, but I'm off in my own dimension. I'm on the road in a far away land, but it doesn't matter if I'm here or there. At home I might have more distractions to keep me entertained, but I'm still living my life in solitary. It's these moments of isolation that I can really think about life and the greater picture. As for my thesis on the subject, I don't really have one. I simply have these sad words scribbled across the screen. What's next for me? What's next for you? I figure it doesn't really matter. Good times will come and good times will go, but most of the time, they're missing in action. A beautiful woman just walked into the shop. She sat nearby me, and I quickly forgot what I was thinking. She has dirty brown hair and dark skin. In my mind I see the two of us striking up a conversation, falling in love, and living happily ever after, but I learned long ago that reality is far from fantasy. Instead, I'll probably hide behind my laptop and miss out on another great opportunity. I'll head home to my domesticated life and wish I was far away from here.

Day 37 Certified & Saying Goodbye 7/29/11

It's the last day of class. Today I earned my TEFL Certificate. From now on I can teach English abroad and be a qualified professional. Yippee!?!? At least I'm done. A few more days, and I'll be out of this country altogether. I can exhale and return to the comforts of home. It will be nice to return to normal water pressure, recognizable food, and familiar streets. Believe me, I love exploring unfamiliar territory like any other ten-year-old kid, but when the sun goes down, I prefer being in the comfort of my own home. At times I get bored with the normal routine, but there's a sense of security within those city walls. Meanwhile, I have three more days to live it up in the Philippines. Tonight, I think everyone in the class is going to go out and have a few drinks. I don't know what will transpire the next couple of days, but I know by tomorrow night, I'll be in Angeles City. Chuck and I are heading that way because Eastwood lives there, and he promised to show us the town. It should be interesting, but I imagine the place can't be more shocking than Bangkok. The reason I say this is because Angeles has a reputation of being a den of iniquity. Eastwood says that it's a lot like Sodom and Gomorrah, so I have to visit the place before I head home. I plan on being more of an observer, but I promise I will give you a first hand account of all the exploits taking place in the town.

Day 38 Angeles City 7/30/11

As you walk down Fields Avenue in Angeles City, you see bar after bar of clubs that have women in front wearing skimpy clothes trying to draw you into their establishment. Each club has a unique theme, but usually it looks like any other strip club in the States except you'll have a horde of women standing on stage giving you the stink eye and trying to seduce you with their hips and breasts. At some places, a whole harem of women will flock around you trying to get your attention, so that you'll buy them a drink or take them home with you. They'll sit on your lap. They'll ride your legs. They'll even grab your pecker and start stroking it through your pants. For a man, it's like you've entered the Playboy Mansion, and all your wildest pornographic fantasies have become reality. It doesn't matter whether you are young, old, fat, or ugly. All that counts is whether you are willing to dish out the cash. If you buy them a drink, they'll sit at your side for hours because they get a cut out of every beverage you purchase for them. Then the girls or "mamasan" (supervisor of the girls) will try to manipulate you and say things like, "Do you want to take her home? Do you want to buy her another drink?" and it can become tiresome after a spell; however, if you are firm and wave them away, they will leave you alone. Others will come up and speak to you intermittently, but it's not as much of a nuisance.

Eastwood, Chuck, and I, hopped around to at least fifteen different bars last night. Some had gorgeous Filipina women and others weren't all that great. The two of them were getting quite drunk because they bought a beer at almost every club, but I was only drinking moderately. At the end of the night, Eastwood took us to a place called Blow Row. At these places, you can get a blowjob and not have to take the girl home with you. And there's also plenty of ladyboys out on the street that are willing to do the same deed for a discount. We walked around that area for about ten minutes, and Chuck was convinced he saw a cute one that would suck him off, but I saw the girl and she wasn't all that pretty. Eastwood and Chuck had serious beer goggles by this time, but I was able to convince them that we needed to get something to eat, and we did. After that, I grabbed a "trike" (motorcycle with a side seat) and went back to my hotel. The two of them said they were going to another club, but it was already 2:30 A.M. and most of the places were already closing. That was the moment I left them, but I'll call the guys tomorrow to see how the story really ended.

Tonight we are planning on hitting the clubs again. It should be fun, but right now it kind of feels like the second night in Vegas. I'm running on very little sleep. I'm somewhat hung-over, but I'm going to be a man and keep going. I don't plan on taking home any of the girls tonight, but they don't need to know that. I'll buy them drinks and give them tips, but that's it. I can always jerk off to relieve the tension between my legs later. I don't want to get herpes, warts, AIDS, or some other sexually transmitted disease by taking them home. I'm also trying to remain faithful this time around. It's not easy, but it can be done, if one remains sober and disciplined.

Note: I spoke to Eastwood and apparently he took home three girls from one of the clubs. I don't know if it's true or not, but Eastwood said he had them doing all sorts of lesbian acts as he traded off screwing each one of them. Chuck said he tried hard to take home one of the "cherry" girls (virgins), but the girl wouldn't let Chuck pop her cherry. She serviced him with a blowjob instead.

Day 39 Highway to Hell 7/31/11

I woke up around noon after partying for a second night in Angeles City. I ate brunch, took a swim, then went and had one final massage before heading back to Manila. Whew, I'm exhausted. At least I have a month to recover before I go back to work in September. It will be nice to get out of the rain and enjoy sunshine again because since I've been in Luzon, all I've seen is cloudy skies and rain.

It's hard to put my thumb on what I've learned from Angeles City. I wish I could say the Highway to Hell was a miserable experience, but it really wasn't. There were a lot of old men who looked like they had been in Angeles far too long. Maybe some of them were reliving their old Air Force days back when the U.S. military controlled the base. It's absolute that our presence is still lingering here. Imagine all the trouble a twenty-year-old kid could have gotten into if he was on leave and set free in Angeles City. That's exactly what happened for decades on the bases. Our Air Force may be gone now, but the nightclubs still remain.

Places like Angeles City and the people who come here will probably be judged harshly for participating in this lewd behavior, and it's hard for a Filipina girl to resist the sex industry when the poorer Filipinos are making around 200 pesos a day ($5 dollars). If the girl is good looking in Angeles City, she could make around 2000 pesos a day. The customers can also buy a hooker for a cheap price over here and live like a king. Consequently, I don't see places like Angeles City going away anytime soon. Right or wrong, this is the way the world is heading. Our purity is being lost. Our sense of morality is disappearing, and even people like me who know God's laws, are having a tough time resisting these temptations. Maybe it's always been this way, but what I've seen from my travels is that it's getting worse, not better. It's looking like the Days of Noah once again, and we all know what happened to that generation.

Day 40 Goodbye Emerald Islands 8/1/11

Another journey comes to a close. I'm one step closer to coming home. The Philippines gave me a new look at life. I've seen what it's like on the flip side. I've taken taxis and jeepneys and tricycle rides. I've gone here and there and put in my time. I've earned a certificate in teaching English, but the experience is worth more than paper and print. I've made new friends. I've partied hard. I lived the good life on Boracay. Most of my stay was in Cebu, but I enjoyed Manila and Angeles too. There are so many places I could have gone, but my Philippine trip is worth more than silver and gold. Now I'm heading back to the Land of the Free. There's no other place I'd rather be. The Philippines, you've earned a place in my heart. We are one with each other. It's a shame we must part. So farewell to the Isles of Fear and Hope. May God bless your country. May He watch o'er your shores.

Chapter 5:
The End

PART A: ANGER, ANALYSIS, & ANARCHY

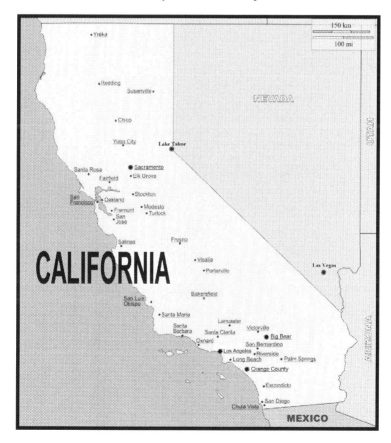

01 Post Travel Haze 8/2/11-8/5/11

I'm back in town, but I've lost my bearings. It's as if I've been spinning in circles, and I landed in Cali. I feel edgy. I can't sit still. I want to be on the move. I want to be somewhere else. I've been gone so long, I can see the cracks in the framework. The sun is bright, but there's a chill in my bones. I miss the Philippines, and all my friends on the road. I can't imagine going back to the same old job. Doing it year in and year out is getting old. So I've been looking for jobs in the world abroad. The pay's not good, but at least it's a fresh start. Yet I know that I'll go back to my 9 to 5 gig. The pay's too good to let this one slip. Maybe someday when I'm retired and old, I'll have a pension to support my exploits abroad. Until that day, I'll continue watching baseball on TV. Soon football will start, and I'll forget about these dreams. I'll be checking the scores and shuffling players. I'll be living through Sunday to deal with the frustration. This domesticated life is not my cup of tea. I like the people here, but I feel out of place. I feel like I'm fading and disappearing all the time. One moment I'm here, and the next moment I'm gone. Those that I've known will follow in step, a gravestone for each and everyone's head. I'm having withdrawals from my addictions. I can taste her on my lips, and I can smell her on my breath. To say someday is a deluding influence, and I can't go back to where I've been. It's probably better to forget about the past. I'm looking forward, but my heart is looking back.

02 Fickle, Cynical, & Frozen in Shape 8/6/11-8/12/11

My mother's in the hospital, but she'll be okay. My father's clock is ticking. He's slowly slipping away. My uncle has returned home, but he's living on the edge. My cousin, Mario, passed away, and now I've lost a friend. I don't really feel like writing about this life and death end game, but every corner that I turn, death's staring me in the face. I want to let it go and live an endless spring, but Adam and Eve ate of the fruit, and now this is our fate. Thank God, the Lord came down to earth to save us from our sin. I truly hope His death on the cross will be significant. 'Cause what I've seen of our hearts is wretched wickedness. Time and time and time again we repeat the same old sins. We might pray for forgiveness, but we are fickle in the end. As for me, I'm cynical. I'm frozen in shape. I long for the days when I was easy to mold, and the Lord had reign over me. Now I'm like a wild animal. I've lost my purity. All I think about is sex and sin. My lusts and passions rule my head. I'm afraid I've been exposed to too much. The Lord will have to reel me in.

03 The Bluffs 8/13/11-8/14/11

Back when I was a junior in high school, I was dating a senior girl who was a bit of a nymphomaniac. We would screw in the car, at the beach, and anywhere it looked like no one was around. Our favorite place was the bluffs behind our school. It was an Indian Reservation, so there was nothing built out there. It was a great place to go if you wanted to get stoned or get away from supervision. I knew one guy who used go out there to sleep or masturbate. He said that he was so disruptive in class that the teacher made a deal with him. The teacher offered, "If you don't come to my class, I'll pass you with a C." The kid agreed, and that was where he went during Period 4. The football coaches used to make us run out there too. There was this one hill called "Puke Hill" because so many guys would throw up their lunch trying to climb it. The bluffs were also a place where crooks hung out, and one night my friends were mugged in the brush. It really wasn't the safest place in the world, but it was a place I got laid numerous times during the fall of that year. At lunch, both of us would escape out the back gate, and I'd grab a giant blanket from my car and a couple of pillows. We then set out to the bluffs and had intercourse behind one of the hills. We went about our business quite fast because we were always worried someone was going to catch us, and we had to get back to class after lunch. One time an old lady walking the bluffs saw us, but she pretended like she didn't see us, so we kept screwing one another, and we both laughed in exhilaration. The sex wasn't that satisfying; it was a way for us to release built up tension, and I really didn't have a clue what I was doing. Honestly, I wasn't educated on sex until I was a freshman in college. It was then that I learned about all the things I was doing wrong sexually, but for a few months in high school, I was living the high life and scoring pussy a couple times a week. Sometimes we would come back to class late. We wrote fake passes to get back in, and the teachers never questioned us. As for the bluffs, they're still there. They've built a couple of parks on the land, but most of it still lies undeveloped in its natural setting.

04 Beyond Good and Evil 8/15/11-8/20/11

Escaping to the mountains is required every now and then. There's clean air, fresh water, and natural habitat everywhere. Instead of listening to construction, traffic, and unruly neighbors, one can see the stars at night and listen to all of God's creatures. It's a blessing to have this family cabin up in Big Bear. Many people are locked down in small apartments and shantytowns across the globe, but I have a second place that I can call home. It's something I do not take for granted.

When the Millennial Reign comes, I wonder if life will be similar to how it is up in the mountains. I wonder if we'll even need to wear clothes or work to put food on our tables. I truly hope it will be as pure and uncorrupted as it was in the beginning. In the interim, we'll have to make do. Even in a fallen state, life still has its magical mountains. It might be the day your son or daughter graduates from college or the day you get married. Life can be as sweet as the fruit on the vine, and at times, it gets even better. Remember falling in love? Remember that first kiss? Remember the intimacy before it all went sour? This is what life can be all about, but we must remember this even when the car breaks down and hardship comes. The good times will be back in bright spring colors.

05 Fresh Pussy 8/21/11-8/26/11

I'm on my mountain bike, and I'm coming down the mountain. Gravity is forcing me forward, and I'm riding uncontrollably towards the finish line. Even in the face of death, I'm disregarding God's laws and playing with fire. I can see the signs. I can see the outcome, yet I'm raising my middle finger flippantly to the heavens without the fear of God upon me. It's not that I don't give a damn. It's just that I've been waiting too long, and I'm starting to get antsy. "When's this God of ours going to show up? When's He going to put things right and fulfill His end of the deal?" I've read how the story ends so many times that I don't even pay attention anymore. It's become a religious experience to me. I mumble out the words without even thinking about what I'm saying. It's like my job. I've been doing it so long that I find myself sleepwalking through the curriculum. Sometimes there are brief moments that spark my interest, but most of the time, it's the same old rigmarole day in and day out. This is why I don't want to go back to working the plow. That fervent energy has been replaced with stagnant blood, and I'm like an old minister who's given that sermon one too many times before. I'm bored, and I need some fresh pussy to give me a hard-on again.

06 Exposed 8/27/11-8/28/11

At the end of the game, all of our hidden sins will be exposed. Sure, some of us have done a fine job of hiding them, but all has been seen by the Lord. He knows how wretched we really are. Yesterday, a lot of behind the scenes sins came to light in my family, and it left everyone stunned.

Many people, especially the kids, have been hurt, and it revolves around sexual immorality. I don't need to go into all the intricate details because I'm sure you can fill in the blanks with someone you know. But it does show how our lusts and passions can destroy those closest to us. I haven't been a saint either, so I can't stand on higher ground and point the finger. All I can do is write about it and inform you about the dangers of crossing that line. I do the same thing with my students at school. As an analogy, I teach my students about drugs. I inform them and tell them the dangers of using drugs, and hope that they'll heed the warning. I know many of them will go on and destroy their lives by smoking from the pipe, snorting lines, and shooting junk, but there's nothing I can do to change their fates. All I can say is that there's another path we can take. I have to admit it's not always the most pleasurable, but by saying no and not giving into our temptations, it will save us from a lot of misery. I should know because I'm one of the ones who's taken those pills and given into my lusts. It might have been fun at the time, but now I'm left with only regrets. I've hurt far too many people, and I know many of you have done the same. I suppose from now on we'll just have to do better. Some of us will have to make amends. Others will have to serve time, but whatever you and I do, I hope we make a turn for good in the end. God will forgive us even though some will not be able to forgive or forget. So since I have your attention now, I would like to say I'm sorry. I've done wrong. I'm guilty, and I hope someday you'll be able to forgive me too.

07 Writing Wall Memorial 8/29/11-9/2/11

I'm not really into cemeteries or gravesites, but since my time is almost up, I came up with an idea for a memorial site. In the middle of the desert, I want a giant wall built. It will be called the Writing Wall. On one side of the wall will be odd quotes I made up over the years (See the chapter titled "Proverbs" in the book *Disciplined Order Chaotic Lunacy*). Have these quotes engraved into the wall and others that seem appropriate. On the other side, people who visit the wall will write/graffiti something on the wall. If you visit the wall, try to make it something profound or funny, but if you can't think of any deep thoughts, write the first thing that comes to your mind. In addition, you are required to drink a bottle of beer or smoke a joint when you're there. The joint must be passed around from one person to another as a sign of unison. As for the empty bottle of beer, you must throw it against a small adjacent wall called the Breaking Wall as a sign of disarray. This will be the tradition whenever you visit the Writing

Wall. The Wall will be located off Zzyzx Road on the way to Las Vegas. The Wall will be built on a cheap piece of land in the middle of nowhere. As for my ashes, I would like them to be set free at the memorial site after the Writing Wall is completed.

*Note: Only the designated driver is exempt from drinking the beer or smoking the pot, but if you are strongly opposed to these mandates, you may rebel against them.

08 September 9/3/11-9/7/11

September has never been my favorite month because it means that summer is over. September means I have to go back to work. It equates with going back to school. It signifies the end of baseball and the start of football. It's the season when the leaves start to change and my allergies kick in. For me, September is an endless runny nose, and I can't tell if I'm sick or well. September is a month I don't care much for. I would rather be at the beach in mid-July or hitting the slopes in December. Instead I'm stuck in September, one of the worst months of the year. At least in October we have Halloween and November has Thanksgiving, but September equals nothing but the blues for me. I know some people who love the fall, but I'm not one of them. I'm a summer and winter person. As for spring, I love the fact that the birds are singing again, but the pollen count can make my life miserable, so it loses a few points on the Richter scale. Thus, the fall is the lowest of the four seasons, and September is at the bottom of the cesspool. So let's drink a toast to September, the most loathsome month of the year!

09 Deism 9/8/11-9/11/11

Many of America's founding fathers were deist. They believed in the existence of God, but they thought He was indifferent to His creation. They believed that God doesn't care whether we live or die and that He's unconcerned about our wars or welfare. My brother holds the deist belief and so do many of my friends. They don't believe in any god or religious institution, but they do believe a God created the universe. I understand why someone could hold this "Tom Sawyer" interpretation of God because it leaves the door open to many interpretations. Nevertheless, I disagree with it. There is one God, and Yahweh is His name. He is a triune God made up of the Father, the Son, and the Holy Spirit, and He cares deeply for His creation. He loved His creation so much that He came down from the heavens and lived amongst us. He even died upon a cross to save us from our sins, and He plans to return to the earth to set up His righteous kingdom.

Even as I write these words down, it sounds like a fairy tale made up by a creative writer. The whole concept sounds absurd, but it's the truth. I can see people objecting and holding up their hands in protest saying, "C'mon, don't give me that crap! God was a man? God walked amongst us? God is coming back to judge us?" Some deists believe there will be consequences for our actions, but others believe our fates are more anarchistic. If I was a deist, I would lean more towards the latter interpretation held by Thomas Jefferson and many others. After all, if God is indifferent, what makes you think He gives a damn about whether we live, breed, or go on a killing spree? I'm just taking the deist perspective to its extreme, but it is something worth considering. I am not a deist, but at least a deist does not disregard God altogether like so many atheists. I can grasp why someone could be a deist or even an agnostic, but to be a hard-core atheist seems so narrow minded and shuts down the door to too many possibilities. An atheist is so absolute about their disbelief in God that they come across as intolerant as Christians who believe there is only "one way" to enter into heaven.

10 Sickness Unto Death 9/12/11-9/17/11

It appears I am suffering from a sickness unto death because I keep stumbling over the same sins again and again. I can't seem to let them go. Now I know why Jesus said to forgive your brother 70 x 7 times because it's almost impossible to live a sanctified life. I do believe Jesus will forgive me because He always forgave sinners in the *New Testament*, but I wish I could be a more honorable individual. This morning I was reading the Word, and Jesus healed a man who had an infirmity for thirty-eight years. After He healed the sick man, He said, "Sin no more lest a worse thing come upon you." (Jn.5:14) When I read these words, my heart fell in my chest, and I was afraid. I don't want something worse to befall me because I've discovered there have been consequences for my wicked deeds, and it's brought me much pain. If I could have walked a holier path in the past, I could have saved myself from much misery, but I keep digging a deeper hole for myself. Jesus has lifted me out on many occasions, but after I get out of that hole, I start digging another. I truly hope my sins won't destroy my life, my career, and my hopes, but I know every action has a counter reaction.

11 Harvest Time 9/18/11-9/23/11

Everyday more and more people come to the faith by believing in Jesus Christ. However, I believe the ranks that are falling away greatly outnumber those new babes in Christ. This is why I believe the Christian Church is treading on water. We're spinning on a log, but most of us have fallen off. We are now swimming in the river and going downstream fast. This is because there are too many distractions in the technological world to bring about our fall. Our flesh is weak, and I don't think we can stand up much longer. Hence, I think it is time for the Lord to reap the harvest. If the Lord waits much longer, all that will be left is rotten fruit. Our works are decaying. They're becoming moldy, and if the Lord delays His coming further, there will be no church at the wedding feast. Almost all of us will have fallen by the wayside, and the reception hall will echo with silence. I entreat you Lord! O Lord Come! It's time. What are you waiting for? Let's kick start the Millennium. Let's live again in the Garden of Eden and bring the soldiers home.

12 Questioning the Omnipotent 9/24/11-9/28/11

Do you "remember how it all began, the apple and the fall of man?" (Natalie Merchant) The price we paid for rebelling that day. I wish there was no tree at all, then we wouldn't be stuck in this parking lot without no trees, breathing the smog-filled breeze. But that's the path that we have chosen. There's no going back. The Garden's lost. We'll have to work the plow until we're dead and gone. And God, you knew all along. You wrote the plot. You're a ruthless God. Yes, you came down and redeemed us, but I'm not sure what you thought it would get us. Instead we spit in your face and many have not believed. Oh how I hate this game of how can I be saved? Sometimes I feel like giving up. I don't like the rules at all. Let's play a different game. What do you say? I want communion with you God, but sometimes I ask, "What the fuck?" Give me a break. You've rigged the game. Most of my friends are going to hell. They can't believe in this fairy tale. I understand. I'm with you man. You say I speak the Devil's tongue. I can't deny I'm one of his sons. I'm a child of Cain. Enoch's my name. My God, I love you so much, but I still want to fuck that slut. I'd do that babe. I'd even pay. To wrap up this rebel's song, I throw up my arms. I've had enough!

13 Angry & Uninspired 9/29/11-10/2/11

My pen is dry. I'm uninspired. I keep trying to reword the text, but I'm fumbling over here. I spend hours looking at the same lines not realizing that I've lost the time. The rhythm is missing. There's nothing left for me to say. I feel like I've said it all before. I can't even finish the lines on this page. It's as if the Spirit has abandoned me. My callous heart, my wicked mind, I've given up on even trying. I've read all about the great works of the apostles, but I only see their shortcomings. Even today when I hear a preacher on the airwaves, I feel like punching him in the face. I can see through his lies. I know his evil deeds, but he still rattles on about truth and righteousness. Righteousness??? I have no idea how it feels to be that squeaky clean. Why don't you go fuck yourself, preacher man? At least then you'll have a few moments of clarity.

14 True Sounds of Liberty 10/3/11-10/7/11

Over the last month I've been reading *An American Demon* by Jack Grisham. It's an autobiography by the former punk singer of the bands T.S.O.L. and Vicious Circle. As I read his life story, I was amazed at all the cruelty and pain he brought to other people. Sure, he was abused as a child and had a rough upbringing, but that's no excuse for the evil actions he did to others. It's true I've done a lot of bad deeds too, but it doesn't compare with Jack's misadventures. I never went out to purposely hurt other human beings, but this is what Jack did. In my circle of friends, we always watched out for one another. We didn't steal from people we knew nor did we bully or torment others for the sake of entertainment. Jack literally lived like an anarchist and blames it on the fact that he had a demon within him. Maybe Jack was possessed, but I think he pushed the limits of what Punk Rock was trying to rebel against. He was downright malicious at times, and many of his exploits were counterproductive. As for "punk" I always thought it stood for truth and justice, and it meant you were willing to step outside the walls of conformity and look at life from a different perspective. It's true there were skinheads and all sorts of other screwed up individuals into the scene, but most of the kids I knew weren't there in the pit to punch in your teeth and kick in your ribs as Jack suggests. When you were knocked off your feet from slamming or stage diving, fellow punks would pick you off the ground and set you back on your feet. They wouldn't try to rob you or stomp on your face with their boots. I'll admit Jack wasn't completely evil. He did stand up for punks who were being picked on or mistreated, and I admired his bravado. With regards to his memoir, it was an engaging read, and I would recommend the book to anyone who experienced the scene; however, I was hoping that Jack would have some sort of epiphany and turn from his evil ways, but he just kept going down the same path until he was at the end of his rope. He was despicable, hopeless, and literally tried to hang himself unsuccessfully. In some ways, all of us are like Jack. We're hanging on by a thread. There are demons all around trying to destroy us, and God is waiting for us to call upon Him. Some of us finally reach the bottom of our well that we finally look up and ask for His assistance, but many of us are too stubborn or set in our ways that we're unable to see the light.

I heard through the grapevine that Jack finally did get clean and sober, and that he's helping others in need. It proves that even the most wretched individuals can reform their life and be a blessing to others. There is hope out there, but the first step to enlightenment is we need to repent and ask the Man upstairs for aide.

15 Sex, Marriage, & Multiple Relationships
10/8/11-10/11/11

At times I tend to question whether the institution of marriage is good for mankind. It does bring stability and accountability to a relationship, but is bondage to one man or woman the answer? Does it make sense that after we make those vows that we can never have sex with another person for the rest of our lives? To me, it seems a bit archaic. Wouldn't it be better if our relationships were more open-ended and marriage did not exist at all? It would eliminate all the cheating and lying that takes place in many marriages, and it would eradicate divorce all together.

Personally, I believe the institution of marriage needs to be reevaluated. Yes, I know my perspective is a bit liberal, but I believe one-day marriage will become obsolete. We will not marry or be given into marriage, but we will be like the "angels of heaven." (Mt. 22:30) We will be free to have sex with whomever we choose, and there will be no guilt afterwards. We will be like the Denobulan species on *Star Trek*. They had many wives and sexual encounters, and it was not considered sinful or immoral. Adultery would not exist nor would fornication be frowned upon by society. Some may suggest that my theories are evolutionary, but I consider my ideas to be liberating. It seems closer to our natural human instincts. In a world without sickness, there would be no need to protect ourselves from sexually transmitted diseases. We would not have to worry about the consequences of sex because there would be no fallout from intimate contact with others.

As for childbirth, modern science has already found a way to prevent unwanted pregnancies, but if two individuals wanted to have a child together, they could. They could make a commitment to raising that child together or the tribe that they are a part of could work as a whole to raise all their children together. There are endless possibilities, and that is why I'm presenting an old but new perspective on the issues of sex, marriage, and multiple relationships.

Part B: Broken & Parting

16 Running Death Dream 10/12/11-10/14/11

There was a woman. She was jogging. She was working up a sweat. Suddenly, she fell to the ground. She was having a heart attack. She felt her heart go into spasms. She thought, "Is this really happening to me?" She cried, "Oh Lord!" and died a few moments later. Her spirit quickly went up to heaven. She was recalling the days when she nursed her children. She was swinging a baby around in her arms. The woman had forgotten that she was dead. It all happened so fast. She barely even felt it. God then appeared to her in the form of a man. He said, "You're remembering the happiest days of your life, but it's time to go now." He took her away, and I awoke from my sleep.

17 Bailed Out 10/15/11-10/16/11

I was up to trouble again. I was about to go down a path that seemed okay in my eyes, but I prayed to God for guidance because I was unsure. I said, "If there is danger ahead, please send me a message so I can avoid the trouble." Later that night, the Lord came to me with a dream. I went down the road that I had chosen, and there was great danger down that path. There were evil people waiting to destroy me. They took advantage of me and bribed me for all I was worth. I was scared, and my situation looked hopeless. I then awoke from my dream and realized that the Lord had spoken to me in my night vision. He was warning me to stay away from this transaction, so I did. The next day I canceled my plans, and it saved me from much misery.

I am grateful that the Lord is looking out for me because I'm like a child at times, and I need discipline and guidance. I need someone to show me right from wrong and to look out for my best interests. On occasion, I want to do as I see fit, but many times I've learned that I am on the wrong path. I'm lucky to have God watching my back.

18 Freedom of Speech 10/17/11-10/19/11

One of the great aspects of being born in the United States is that we have freedom of speech. We can speak out against the president or the government at any time. Nowadays it's not always safe to speak your mind because we're living in a state of fear. And when people are afraid, they are quickly willing to give up their freedoms to live in a safe environment. It's a shame, but it's happened time and time again in history. Until it becomes too dangerous, I'm going to continue to speak out against the elements that I see as right or wrong. My pen has always been my sword, but if you don't agree with me, that's fine. My writings are not the Gospel. I'm not an Apostle of Christ. At times I have prophetic utterances, but essentially I'm trying to tell a good tale. Therefore, at any time you can turn the page if my opinions become too offensive. We don't have to agree on everything. In fact, I believe a dissenting opinion is a blessing not a curse. I've been a Devil's Advocate for most of my life, but I am patriotic as hell too. I would never turn my back on my country or my Creator. I'm not a Benedict Arnold nor am I willing to rise up against God like Satan did. It's true I disagree with God's laws now and again, but that doesn't mean I'm going to turn my back on Him either. I'm a follower of Jesus Christ even though Paul's words can sometimes send me into a tirade. I'm an American true and blue, and sometimes I get angry when I see our rights and liberties being stripped away from us one by one. In the future, I will be a part of God's country, but I have not forgotten my roots. My American brothers and sisters are always with me, and even if the United States is no more, it will live on within my blood forever. The flag will be raised high in my mind, and the ideals of liberty and justice will live on for eternity. As for the Kingdom, we will be even freer during that era, and like today, we will have the choice to either be His disciples or not.

19 Overcome 10/20/11-10/23/11

It is written that after my 3½-year testimony is over, the Devil will overcome me, and I will be laid to waste. The truth, however, is that I've already been overcome by my shortcomings. My eyes have been shrouded in darkness for so long that I can't see the evil that surrounds me. Long ago, I was baptized in water and came out clean, but somewhere along the line my defenses broke down, and I compromised. Now I'm dining with the swine and engaging in all sorts of immoral behavior. It's true the Lord set me back on my feet time and time again, but my days of grace are now numbered. Soon the Angel of Death will come for me and my deeds will be tested by fire. I hope some of my good deeds will remain because I've been selfish and ambitious. I've broken the Ten Commandments and have fallen from heaven with the Devil and his minions. Soon I will stand-alone without my friends, without my lovers, without my idols to face the Creator of the Universe. Unfortunately, I have no defense. I should be cast into the Lake of Fire with Hitler, Stalin, and all the other great transgressors of the past. My only hope will be that Jesus' blood will cover me. If it does, I will be one of the lucky ones who merely squeaks into heaven. I don't expect any reward or crown on my head because I have been a poor example. I was defeated long ago. I was overcome long before my testimony was over.

20 It's a Wonderful Life 10/24/11-10/28/11

As my testimonial is coming to a close, I'm realizing I have nothing else to give. There are no new songs within me, and even the ones I've written have fallen upon deaf ears. My stories have never reached the greater populace. Only a few friends opened up the books at all. They don't know that my heart and soul went into those writings. They don't understand that each lyric was written with blood and tears. This was all I knew. This was all I ever was. I thought about writing my will, but I looked around at my goods and realized I have very little to will away. It would be a short list, that's for sure. In some ways, I want to live longer, but I have nothing to live for. I could offer up a deathbed prayer like Hezekiah did, but if I'm granted more time, I'm only going to delve into more evil deeds. Maybe it's better if I go now before King Manasseh's seed is planted. Getting old is no cup of tea either. I look at my parents' generation, and they're falling apart. I'm already groaning in grief right now, so they must be suffering. What's the purpose of continuing on any longer? In some ways I feel like George Bailey in *It's a Wonderful Life*, but the truth is the future's not that wonderful for me. It might be bright for you, but there's nothing else for me to do down here on earth. I'd almost rather check out of this place and see what's beyond the horizon. Then again, maybe there's something more around the next corner. I'll have to wait and see. Maybe God has something else in store for me???

21 Halloween 10/29/11-10/31/11

Halloween is a fun holiday every year because people get to dress up and be whatever they want to be. The children get to put on costumes too and go door-to-door trick or treating. Many people in the Christian community have demonized this Day of the Dead, but personally I believe there is no harm in celebrating it. They like to blame Satan for everything, and a small minority would love to pick up pitchforks and go on a witch-hunt. These are the same type of people who would burn books and dress up in KKK outfits. Frankly, I'm pretty sick of these individuals, and they give a bad name to the followers of Christ. The scary part about it is they think they are doing what is right, and I am vehemently opposed to them. I've been in their circles and walked amongst them. There's a strange look in their eye, and I can tell it wouldn't take much for them to march in step and turn in Jewish sympathizers.

This Halloween my cousin's band played at an Irish Pub and almost everyone dressed up. There were witches and goblins and sexy sluts. It was fun to let loose for awhile and be free from the fashion police of the workplace. As the Dead Kennedy's once said, "After Halloween we'll be stuffed back into rigged business costumes," so we might as well enjoy our day of liberty while we have the chance. Tomorrow we can always put on our true masks and hide behind the deceptive lies we tell everyday.

22 Romans 8 11/1/11-11/3/11

Paul is not one of my favorite writers in the *Bible* because, in my opinion, he puts us back under bondage after Jesus set us free. Nonetheless, Chapter 8 of *Romans* is liberating. Paul writes about how we are no longer under condemnation after turning to Christ. He even comforts us by writing "that neither death, nor life, nor angels, nor principalities, nor powers, nor things present, nor things to come, nor height, nor depth, nor any other creature" (Rom.8:38-39) can separate us from our Father in heaven. These words have given me great comfort when I've been at my lowest points. And right now these words have edified me because I've been living in darkness lately. I feel like I'm beyond reconciliation, and I should be cast into the abyss with Lucifer and the rest of the unforgiven. But according to the *Book of Romans*, there is hope for wretched individuals like me. That means there is hope for you too. Paul writes, "If God is for us who can be against us?" (Rom.8:31) God is on our side, so we will be victorious. It may feel as if we are in a war that cannot be won, but the victory has already been won at the cross. We are merely the last few soldiers in a war that ended long ago. It's like we're still fighting the last remnant of Japanese soldiers in WWII, and we are bringing words of peace and reconciliation to the unsaved. As for Lucifer and his minions, they've been fighting so long that they've lost their bearings and can no longer differentiate between right and wrong. So rise up, brothers and sisters! We shall overcome! We may suffer. We may die, but we will rise again and live forevermore.

23 Manny, Moe, & Jack 11/4/11-11/7/11

There are hundreds of drunken exploits that I could record from our days in college, but the story of Manny, Moe, and Jack is one of the most memorable tales.

The three friends had been partying all night in San Luis Obisbo. Jack, the drunkest of the three, had a brilliant idea. He jumped out of a moving car and charged up a staircase to one of the Old Town buildings. Manny and Moe followed him and watched Jack jump from rooftop to rooftop like he was James Bond. This was possible because the buildings were built long ago, and the space between the rooftops was only a few feet. Still, if he missed or slipped, he would have fallen to his death or been seriously injured. Fortunately, this did not happen. Instead, he pulled off the feat with great dexterity, and when the buildings ran out, Jack decided to leap onto a nearby tree to make his way down. He jumped, grabbed a branch, lost his grip, and fell on his ass. It looked painful, but he didn't break anything, so he kept going. Manny and Moe didn't follow his lead. They went down the staircase they originally came up. When they reached the bottom, they saw their friend climbing a fifteen-foot fence that led to a dry riverbed. The drunken fool fell from the fence into the riverbed, and it looked like he was dead. Meanwhile, as Moe was observing the fall, his girlfriend called. He answered, "I can't talk right now! Jack is dead! I have to call the paramedics!" and hung up. The girlfriend knew Jack's parents, so she proceeded to call them and informed the father that Jack was dead. The truth was Jack did not die from the fall. He was only banged up a bit, and he only needed a few stitches. Moe, however, never called back his girlfriend to tell her what really happened, and this caused great consternation on the part of Jack's family.

After the fall, Jack was lifted by Manny out of the riverbed and thrown back over the fence because he was semi-unconscious. He hit the ground with a giant thud, but once again, he managed to escape without any major injuries. Eventually, the three friends made their way back to the car to find the doors wide open with beer cans on the seats and two cops standing nearby. They asked, "Whose car is this? Who's driving?" Moe answered, "It's my car." The cop said, "You're going to jail for a DUI." Moe smirked, "Hey, I didn't say I was driving." The cop replied, "Then who was driving? I'm taking someone to jail." No one admitted to being behind the wheel just as Jack was starting to regain his equilibrium. He stood on his feet and cursed, "Fuck you, pigs!" and started making a scene. The cops were about to arrest Jack just as an ambulance pulled up. Manny said, "Wait a second. We're taking Jack to the hospital. He's been seriously injured," and showed the cops the big gauge on his head. One officer looked at the drunkards, shook his head and said, "Either you all get in that ambulance right now, or I'm taking you to jail." The three friends jumped in the ambulance, and Jack received ten stitches at the hospital.

The next morning Jack received a call from his mother. Apparently, she had been up all night trying to get a hold of her son, but he had left his phone in the car, and no one else knew what happened. Moe's girlfriend tried calling him back but his cell phone battery had died, so no one back home knew what truly took place. At last, Jack's mother found out the truth, and I'm relaying that story unto you. As for the tale itself, I wish there was some kind of moral to it, but there really isn't. It's true that drunken behavior is not wise, but in this case, everything turned out alright. As for Manny, Moe, and Jack, they went onto drink for years and years, but they ended up having kids and sobered up a bit. Does that mean that I'm endorsing this behavior? Absolutely not, but I thought I'd share the tale with you anyway because it's always made me chuckle.

There are other renditions of the story that sound much better than mine. In one tale, Jack breaks his neck but is sewn back together by an old maid. Another tale had Jack doing flips from rooftop to rooftop, and I've even heard one rendition where Jack steals the police car at the end. I don't really know which tale is the most accurate because I wasn't there. I wonder though if some of the stories we grew up with as kids were true or not. For instance, do you really think there was a great fish that spit up Jonah on the beach? Was Samson actually that strong? Was the earth destroyed by a great flood long ago? I don't know the answers to these questions, but shouldn't a man of reason question his own beliefs?

24 Clarification 11/8/11-11/10/11

Some critics have suggested that many of my entries are too profane or unacceptable for a follower of Christ. You are probably right. I cannot deny the vial thoughts spinning through my mind. I may present some twisted and disturbing views, but I do believe it's important to be honest with my thoughts and transgressions unto my audience. Telling you about my dark past and current sins is my way of clearing my conscience. Many of you do the same at the confession booth or behind closed doors, but this is my method of coming clean. I may have hurt others in the process of writing these words down, but I figured it would be better if I told the truth as opposed to speaking falsely. Yet even now I'm twisting the facts and hiding behind fabrications. I'm a liar and a deceiver at heart, so you're going to have to read between the lines to discover the real truth. The only person I'm completely honest with is God. And even though I know He sees everything, I still try to hide from Him like a little child. Yes, I see the foolishness in it too, yet sometimes I attempt to cover up my sins like Adam and Eve did in the Garden. To sum up, I know my writings will be banned by much of the Christian community for my depravity. I can't change my fate. Many of them are the same people who have lynched and murdered in the name of God. Their righteous crusades are now frowned upon by history, and one day I believe these same people who are now blacklisting me will accept my writings as works inspired by the Holy Ghost.

25 Veteran's Day 11/11/11-11/12/11

Jose served time in Iraq and Afghanistan. He says it earned him his citizenship. Jose was a former student of mine, and he now works as a recruiter for the army. He came and spoke to my classes. He told some funny stories. He made it sound like joining the armed forces would be a pleasure cruise on the Love Boat. Some of the students bought into his story. Jose divulged that he killed people. He said he lost some close friends. He said he was fighting for his country, and he has no regrets. Jose said that sometimes he can't sleep at night. He said the nightmares can be unbearable. He said he always has the same dream about a bomb going off in the Green Zone. Jose claimed it was a suicide attack. He doesn't like to talk about it. A student asked him if he would do another tour of duty. He said he doesn't know yet. I asked him if he would recommend the service for his own children. He answered, "No, it's too dangerous. I'd rather send my kids to college." After class I asked, "If you think the army is too dangerous for your own kids, how can you recruit teenagers with a clear conscience?" He responded, "It's just my job, Mr. E., and I'm good at it. It's better than being in the front lines." Shrapnel wounded Jose in the leg. He now walks with a limp. Jose was sixteen when I first met him. Now he's all grown up, and I hardly recognize him. Jose said he has six months left of service. Jose misses his friends in his platoon, but he'd rather be at home with his family.

***

I'm a strong supporter of the armed forces, although I'm more of a "speak softly but carry a big stick" (Teddy Roosevelt) advocate. If I were not, I wouldn't permit recruiters to come to my classes. War is a necessary evil in this era, so we need new recruits to support our exploits abroad. Still, I don't back every call to duty by our presidents. For example, I think the Iraq War was a poor decision. I never supported this declaration. In retrospect, I believe the War in Vietnam was a mistake too, but I think WWII was justified. As for today, I like to believe we are fighting for freedom and democracy, but sometimes I wonder if we're fighting for big oil companies instead. If this is the case, I think we need to reevaluate our position. Resources are important but not at the cost of thousands of lives. Wars should be fought for righteous causes not whims by our generals and their constituents. I realize this is not how the world works today, but it's the precise reason why we need to turn things upside down. Is revolution the answer? No, I don't think so, but I do believe we can work from the inside out and turn our fates around.

26 VW Bug 11/13/11-11/15/11

My older brother used to have this beat up VW bug when he was a teenager. My mother made him take my sister and I to school when we were younger, so we would pile in the backseat with other kids in the neighborhood and get a free ride to school. There was no heater in the car, so we would freeze in the morning during winter. The windows would be all fogged up, and we couldn't see anything, so my brother would have to stick his head out the window to see where he was going. As for the car, it wouldn't start all the time, so we'd have to kick start it to get it going. That meant we had to push the car to generate speed as my brother jumped in the car to pop the clutch. It wasn't the most fun in the world, but it was better than walking. The car also had slick tires, so when the car went around corners, the whole back end would slide out. It was a terrifying thrill ride, but no one ever got hurt. One time we were pushed so hard against the back window by one of his turns that the whole window popped out of its slot and went flying out into the street. The funny thing about it was the window didn't even break. When we arrived home, my brother popped the window back in, and we were good to go again.

My father saw how slick the tires were getting on the white bug, so he made my brother buy four new ones. My father thought that it would be safer riding on a new set, but he had no clue how reckless my brother used to drive. As for my brother, he didn't realize that if he took a sharp turn now, the car wouldn't slide out anymore, and he found out the hard way one afternoon when he was out driving with his friends. My brother took a turn like he used to do with his old tires only this time the tires did not give. Instead, the car flipped on its side and skidded towards the curb. Sparks went flying everywhere, and the three passengers in the car screamed like lunatics, "Ahhhhh!!!" Before they knew it, the car stopped, and everyone sat there for a moment in shock. My brother asked, "Is everyone okay?" His friends answered yes and started to laugh hysterically until someone said, "I feel something wet." Another said, "I think I smell gas," and everyone panicked. All of them crawled on top of each other and fought to get out of the bug just as the car started to burst into flames. Fortunately, they escaped with their lives, and no one was hurt.

When the cops pulled up, there was smoke everywhere. My brother had finished putting out the flames with a fire extinguisher. He used to leave it in the trunk with some jumper cables, a small cooler filled with beer, and a set of tools in case of emergencies. He had to be prepared because the car always broke down. As for the VW, it survived the ordeal. My brother and his friends pushed it back on its four wheels and drove away. No one thought that it might be too dangerous, and the cops didn't seem too concerned. They shook their heads indifferently and one said, "Since no one's hurt, we'll let you off this time."

Looking back at that VW bug puts a big smile on my face. It's an old car I'll never forget. I hope when people reflect back on me, they'll do the same. I don't want anyone to weep or feel sorrow because I'll be in a better place. And if I happen to cross your mind, think back on the good times we had together. Tell someone a story about our escapades, and I guarantee you'll feel much better.

27 Bohemian Rhapsody 11/16/11-11/18/11

Life is a Bohemian Rhapsody. There are highs, lows, and exhilarating moments. During the journey there are dramatic windfalls and comical excursions. At times one feels like singing Figaro and playing a guitar solo. Other times life is melancholy; it tastes bittersweet and lonely. During these interludes one feels like nothing matters. It's as if Beelzebub has set aside a devil to terrorize you and me. Yes, life truly is a strange journey.

Sometimes one wonders if it's real or it's just fantasy. All I know is we're all caught in a landslide, but one day we'll escape this reality. One day we'll find a place where it's easy come and easy go, but for now we'll have to struggle through this tragedy. For me, my time is almost up, so I want to say goodbye to everybody. I want to set the record straight and say I'm sorry. I want to give you a hug and express my love before I ascend in a cloud up to heaven.

28 Letter to the Americans 11/19/11-11/21/11

I, Enoch, a prophet and teacher of the Lord, have come to bring one final message before the Apocalypse and coming of the Lord. I entreat you, America, "remember therefore from where you have fallen" (Rev.2:5) and fight for liberty and justice like long ago. It is time to put aside our selfish ambitions of power and glory and reach out to the poor and needy. We need to live righteously once again, so we can see beyond the shadow of darkness. Once we take the "log out of our own eye," (Mt.7:4) we'll be able to see clearly and help others who are suffering. Our hypocrisy has left a bad taste in the mouth of the nations and our sins have been unveiled on the airwaves. With the help of our televisions and knick-knacks, we have plagued every corner of the globe with our lust and wanton needs. The nations of the world have imitated our folly. The Old World is falling into an abyss due to our poor example and even the East is now being pulled into the whirlwind. Oh America, the land of milk and honey, the Lord is about to take away everything that we hold dear. "Judgment will begin at the House of God," (1Pet.4:17) and America is on the top of that list. We will "reap what we have sown," (Gal.6:7) and the fires of hell will be released amongst us. Therefore, my brothers and sisters, it is time to put aside our uncleanliness and live honorably. We need to turn from our evil ways and revive the Spirit of love, kindness, and brotherhood. I know it will not be easy, but if we "draw near to God, He will draw near to us." (Ja.4:8) He will show us a means of escape from our temptations. Our God is merciful, and for decades He has been waiting for us to return unto Him. He has kept our enemies at bay in hopes that one day we will repent and call upon His name. However, our time is short. The prophecies of the end times are falling into place exponentially. If we rise above the ashes, He will care for us during the Days of Tribulation. If not, we will die by fire, plague, famine, and earthquakes.

29 Controversial Issues 11/22/11-11/24/11

Should abortion be legal? Is gay marriage okay? Should murderers be executed? Should taxes be increased? All of these controversial issues and others are discussed in the *Bible*, so I'm going to present the Biblical perspective on these topics and give my personal opinion on the issues as well.

First, I am opposed to abortion. I think a woman has other options; however, I believe there are many reasons why we should keep abortion legal and let each woman decide for herself if she wants to keep the child or not. The reason most of the Christian community is pro-life is because of the prophet, Jeremiah. The scripture reads, "Before I formed you in the womb, I knew you." (Jer.1:5) Most interpret this as meaning that we are alive at the moment of conception. Thus, it makes sense that most Christians would be against any form of abortion, but I'm still pro-choice for the reasons of rape, poverty, and unwanted pregnancies. Adoption is a better choice, but in some cases, it's not an option for some women.

With regards to gay marriage, I could go either way on the issue. Personally, I don't care if gays get married or not. It's not going to affect my life at all. Many of the church folks think permitting gay marriage will give a bad example to our children because homosexuality is considered deviant behavior in the *Bible*. Yes, it will probably make homosexuality more acceptable in society, but in the same breath, I doubt it will bring the wrath of God down upon us either. It's true that Sodom and Gomorrah were judged for their sodomy, but I believe their whole society was guilty of far more evil deeds. Homosexuality may be considered sinful in the *Bible*, but so are drunkenness, fornication, and numerous other sins. To permit homosexuals to get married does not sit well with many Christians because traditional marriage has always been between a man and a woman; still, if we allowed homosexuals to get married it may cut down on some of the promiscuous behavior taking place in the gay community. Then again, maybe it will put them under bondage, and they'll regret ever wanting marriage in the first place.

As for Capital Punishment, I am for it. If someone is found guilty of committing murder, they should be put to death in a timely matter after the verdict of the jury. My opinion is in agreement with the *Bible* that states, "he who strikes a man so that he dies shall surely be put to death." (Ex.21:12) As for the criminals who have been sitting on death row for years, what's the purpose of this? It's costing the taxpayers tons of money to keep these criminals alive. I think our judicial system should give the murderers a few days to clear their conscience, say their goodbyes, and hang them from a rope.

The issue of taxes has been in the press lately, so I figured I should address the issue. I do believe 10% is a fair amount for all Americans (rich or poor) to pay, but during times of war and economic distress, it might be wise to raise the taxes on the population until the crisis is over. That means we might need to pay a bit more until we are out of the red, but once we balance our budget, let's go back to 10% and live within our means. As for the *Bible*, Abraham gave Melchizedek "a tenth of all" (Gen.14:20) he had. Therefore, this pattern has been modeled throughout history and many modern day Christians tithe the same way. I suggest we base our tax code on Biblical doctrine. One thing for sure, it would simplify things.

As for seat belt laws, helmet laws, and curfews, I think we should get rid of all of them. Shouldn't adults and parents of children decide what's right for themselves and their own kids? Why is the government getting involved in this? It's probably wise that we wear a seat beat and helmet, but aren't these laws taking away our rights as American citizens? These issues are not addressed in the *Old* or *New Testaments*.

I've spoken previously on the legalization of marijuana, and I think it would better if we legalized it. We could tax the product, make paper out of it, and use it for medicinal purposes. Yes, I know most people will use it simply to get high, but I don't think prohibition works. It didn't work with alcohol back in the days of Al Capone, and it's not working with marijuana today. As for the *Bible*, there is no mention of marijuana in the text, but it is opposed to being under the influence of another. The *Bible* also suggests that we should be sober minded and alert. Therefore, I believe there is more doctrine in the *Bible* that stands opposed to using marijuana and alcohol. Nevertheless, Jesus did drink wine with the sinners, and Paul exhorts Timothy to "drink a little wine" for his "frequent ailments." (1Tim.5:23) In my assessment there's not enough evidence to convince me otherwise, so I think marijuana should be legalized like alcohol is today.

Gun control has been debated for decades in the States, but I am still opposed to the idea. I own guns. I use them to hunt, protect my home, and for recreational shooting. Also, the Bill of Rights declares that we have the "right to bear arms," so I don't think we should take guns away from our citizens because some individuals abuse the right. On the other hand, I do think it's important to learn how to shoot a gun before the public is permitted to buy one. One option would be to make people who want to buy a gun go through a training seminar before they are allowed to purchase their first gun, but there should be no infringement on the second amendment. Guns did not exist when the *Bible* was written, so the point is mute, but people did use swords and shields to protect themselves.

As for intelligent design versus evolution, the *Bible* definitely leans towards creationism even though most of the scientific community believes in evolution. Even so, what can it hurt to present both opinions to our children? There's no reason to be so dogmatic about either side. By suppressing one side of the issue, it completely undermines free thought. I've heard the complaints that there's nothing scientific about God, but to rule out God completely is illogical. Alternately, let's keep the floor open for debate.

To conclude, I have listed many controversial issues and have given my opinion on each one. I briefly summed up what I think the *Bible* teaches on these subjects, even though many theologians would disagree with me. Just remember, my opinions are not the Gospel truth. Feel free to look up the topics yourself and come to your own conclusions.

30 Prayer 11/25/11-11/27/11

If we really want to make a difference, we need to get down on our knees and pray. The scriptures tell us that wherever "two or three are gathered together, the Lord is there in our midst." (Mt.18:20) God does not require our worship or prayers, but He will honor our petitions. The results may or may not happen overnight, but He will answer our prayers eventually. If it's in His will, we can change the world for the better. As for the way we pray, I think people need to stop using prayers that our repetitive. For example, I grew up Catholic, and we would say the "Our Father" and "Hail Mary" prayers over and over again. I doubt God hears these prayers. Our prayers need to be honest and sincere. We need to speak to God from our hearts as if He's a personal friend. It is wise to be respectful, but we're more likely to be heard if we're like children coming to their Father. As parents, we like to give things to our children and so does God. The Lord's just waiting for us to call upon His name. Now if we ask for a Mercedes Benz and money continually, I don't think He's going to hear those prayers. He can give us material goods, but we must remember God's going to do what's in our best interest, and I don't believe having everything we desire is beneficial. Pray for those around you. Pray for those who are far away. Pray for wisdom, faith, and all the good traits. And please, pray for our country, our leaders, and everyone else in need.

31 Gospel 11/28/11-11/30/11

According to the *Bible*, there is only one way into heaven. You must believe that Jesus Christ is the Messiah. This means you believe that Jesus died on the cross and rose from the dead. If you trust in anything else, you will not inherit the Kingdom of God. The Gospels are dogmatic on this point. It means you can't believe in Buddha and enter into heaven. It means you can't be a Muslim and enter into the Pearly Gates. You can't be a Hindu or a Mormon or a Jehovah Witness or any other religious belief. Even being a good person won't help you at the judgment seat. All that will matter is whether you believed in Jesus Christ or not.

Why do we have to believe in Jesus in the first place? It's simple. He's the Son of God, and He died for our sins. A lot of people don't understand what this means, so I'm going to do my best to explain this basic doctrine.

Long ago when Adam and Eve fell in the Garden of Eden, they committed the first sin. Therefore, as a species we have inherited their sin. It's called Original Sin. That means everyone from the beginning until the end is guilty of sin. As the scriptures read, "Through one man sin entered into the world, and death through sin, and so death spread to all men because all sinned." (Rom.5:12) Jesus, on the other hand, did not commit a sin. He lived a pure, upright life. There is no one in history that has done the same. Even in birth, He was immaculately conceived by the Holy Spirit. It was not the seed of man. If it was, Jesus would have been guilty of Original Sin too, and there would be no hope for mankind.

Due to the fact that Jesus lived a sinless life, death could not conquer Him, and He rose from the dead. Now what does this mean for mankind? It means that we now have access into heaven. The scriptures state, "Through one transgression there resulted condemnation to all men, even so through one act of righteousness there resulted justification of life to all men." (Rom.5:18) This means that all we have to do is repent of our sins and believe in Jesus Christ to inherit eternal life. Our faith in Jesus removes our sin, and it allows us to enter into heaven by riding on the coattails of the Messiah. He is our mediator. He is our propitiation for our sins. He is the reason we do not have to go to hell.

Now I know many of you don't understand the logic in all of this, but it's the truth. It was outlined in the *Old Testament* and fulfilled in the *New*. Research it further if you're still in doubt. It will all make sense if you read the *Bible* from beginning to end. But to simplify it in a few sentences, all you have to do is believe in Jesus Christ. As the Word states,

"If you confess with your mouth Jesus as Lord, and believe in your heart that God raised Him from the dead, you shall be saved; for with the heart man believes resulting in righteousness, and with the mouth he confesses, resulting in salvation." (Rom.10:9)

That's the Gospel in a nutshell, and I'm sharing it with you because it's my duty. Everything else I've said is irrelevant. This is what really matters. This is how your soul will be saved. *"For God so loved the world that He gave His only begotten Son that whosoever believeth in Him should not perish but have everlasting life." (Jn.3:16)*

32 We are the Light 12/1/11-12/4/11

As my days are coming to a close, I long to continue in this earthly vessel, but I greatly yearn to be with the Lord. I know that once I leave this lowly body I will be given a new one that is free from defect and infirmity. Still, I want to encourage all of you to press forward in your faith. Be courageous, patient, and loving for a great reward awaits those who are in Christ. For those outside the faith, I warned you about what's to come. There will be great tribulation on earth, and if you die an unbeliever, you will be separated from God eternally. Please, I entreat you, make peace with God now before it's too late. As for what's imminent, "let no one deceive you, that Day will not come until the man of lawlessness is revealed, the son of perdition, who opposes and exalts himself above every so called god or object of worship, so that he takes his seat in the temple of God, displaying himself as being God." (2Thes.2:3-4) This is a final sign for you. Do not bow down unto him or worship his name. Flee for your life instead and call upon Yahweh, the true and righteous one, to save you. For believers, do not fret. These things must take place, but be alert and sober. The "Day of the Lord will come just like a thief in the night," (1Thes.5:2) so be prepared for His coming. Abstain from every form of evil and do your best to live peaceably with one another. You will prevail. God will finish the good work He started in you. Be aware, these are evil days. There are many who will try to deceive you through "philosophy and the traditions of men." (Col.2:8) Do not be fooled by their reasoning and endless chatter. You know the truth. The Spirit bares witness within you. As *The Alarm* once said, "Hold onto what you believe is right. Don't let anyone turn your eyes." One day the war will be over, and we will have peace in our time.

33 What if... 12/5/11-12/8/11

If the Germans won the war what would have changed? Would we be speaking German and praising Hitler's name? If my uncle hadn't died in Vietnam, would my aunt still have her wits and the kids have grown up strong? I wonder if my old girlfriend had kept our child, if we'd be married now and I would be a father. These are some of the thoughts that spin through my mind when I'm looking back at history and the timeline. How about you? Do you have any regrets? Would you roll the dice again or play the same old hand?   I'm not sure what roads you would change, but I know I would try to avoid the same mistakes. Kiana often wonders if she married that rich boy, if she would have three kids and be a stay home wife. My buddy talks about the girl that got away. He goes on about her curves and her heavenly face. "If I'd gone to college... If I got my degree... I wouldn't be working down at the factory." "If I didn't use drugs... If I could stay clean... I'd be a rich man, and I would own this place." There are so many ifs and doubts that clog our minds, but we can't go back and try to set it right. We must move forward and accept our fates even though the dice are loaded and our lives are vain. Misfortune and heartache will be on our plates, but we'll pull through and reach the pearly gates.

Part C: The Holy Land

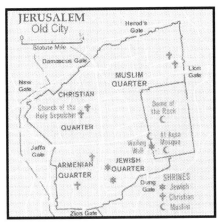

34 (Day 1): Friday, Dec. 9th

Last night the Lord spoke to me in a dream. He said, "Go to Israel and finish your testimony. Do not worry about what you will do or say, for I am with you." Thus, this morning I went to work and prepared substitute lessons plans for the time I will be away. In truth, I don't know if I'll be returning, but who knows, the Lord might grant me more time on earth?

When I returned home, I consulted my wife and told her my intentions. After hearing my plan, Kiana thought I had gone mad, and she objected. A long argument ensued. In the end, she grudgingly went along with my plan, and the two of us booked a flight to Israel hours later. We leave tomorrow afternoon. I also went by my parents' house to say goodbye to them. They told me they would look after the place while I'm gone, but they have no idea I may not be coming back. I also called Conte, my editor and chronicler, and told him I'd be sending him daily updates of my journey. He said he wanted to come along but there was no way he could get away from work on such short notice. He has been my Luke for the last 3 ½ years, and I would like to thank him for everything.

Anyway, that's where I'm at this very moment. I have no idea what to expect, but it's going to be an interesting excursion. I am scared to death but hopeful in the same breath.

35 (Day 2): Saturday, Dec. 10th

After another long flight across the globe, Kiana and I arrived in Israel. From Ben Gurion Airport, we took a taxi to Tel Aviv and recuperated at the hotel. I've learned from so many years of travel that it's best to jump right in with their time zone even if you suffer from jetlag. If it's nighttime, then go to sleep. If it's daytime, barrel through it as best you can even if your head is dying to hit the pillow. There was still sunlight when we checked into our hotel, so we stayed awake and had an early dinner. We then walked up and down the beach and stopped in at a local bar and drank some Goldstar beers. It was relaxing, and we saw a blues band play, but after the second beer, I thought I was going to fall into my mug from exhaustion. To wake up, we stopped at another place and had some tea and a pastry. The caffeine and sugar kept us awake for a couple more hours, but by the time we arrived back at our hotel, we were the walking dead, so we took a shower and crashed hard on our bed.

Tel Aviv was the same as I remembered it back in 2001. Everything is westernized, and if you're traveling around the Middle East, it's a breath of fresh air from the Muslim nations that surround the country. There is still a large military presence everywhere you go, but after a while, you don't even think twice about sitting next to a soldier carrying an M16 while you're on the bus. My perspective might change tomorrow when one of those rifles are being pointed in my direction. I'll explain why tomorrow, but if you don't hear from me in the next 24-hours, I'm probably locked up in jail or my blood has been spilled on a Tel-Aviv street.

36 (Day 3): Sunday, Dec. 11ᵗʰ

Today the wife and I went around to some of the hotspots in Tel Aviv, and I set up and played apocalyptic songs to the people passing by. I tried to keep it relatively tame because I heard it's illegal to proselytize in Israel. I found that rather funny considering it's a democratic government. So I pretty much played songs that wouldn't rock the boat too much. I played "Armageddon," "Misconceptions," "Gog," and "22" by the Faithful Church. I also played some offshoot covers like "Redemption Song" by Bob Marley, "Guns on the Roof" by the The Clash, and "When the Man Comes Around" by Johnny Cash.

As I played to the people passing by, some folks would stop and listen. Others would sing along. One orthodox Jew hissed at me when he heard the song "22." All the lyrics come from Psalm 22 & 23, which is in the *Old Testament*, but he could tell it was about Jesus on the cross. In general, I wouldn't stay too long in one spot, because I didn't want to attract too much attention. At one location, a soldier came up to me and said, "You can't play here" and pointed his rifle at me, so I packed up my mini PA system, my guitar, and went somewhere else. After hitting three locations, we took a break and ate some food. We then went back to our hotel, and I took a long nap.

In the evening, I set up on the beach boardwalk near the other street musicians. Many people came by and listened, but by the end of the last set, a group of zealots came up to me and started heckling me. One of them asked, "Why are you singing these Christian songs? Are you trying to convert us? Do you think you're some kind of prophet?" I did my best to answer the questions as delicately as possible, but these young men wouldn't let up. They started pressing in on me, cursing me, and one of them started messing with my guitar. As soon as he touched my guitar, I got angry and started to push back. This didn't help the situation, and it became even more volatile. Thank God Kiana was there. She helped cool down the situation. She smiled and said, "Boys don't you have something better to do? And Enoch, I'm getting hungry. Let's get something to eat." The group of young men laughed and one mocked, "It's obvious who rules the roost in this relationship." Another man cursed then said something in Hebrew as the group started to head down the boardwalk.

I looked at Kiana with appreciation as I started to pack up my gear, but she rolled her eyes at me. We then went to one of the pubs/restaurants and had a beer with our dinner. Afterwards, we went back to our hotel and watched a movie on television. Tomorrow morning we'll be leaving Tel Aviv and taking a bus to Jerusalem.

37 (Day 4): Monday, Dec. 12th

We arrived at our hotel in Jerusalem around noon. We lounged around for a bit then went down to the Old City to scout out the area. For those who've never been to Jerusalem before, the Old City sits inside greater Jerusalem, and it's where many of the tourist sites are located like the Wailing Wall, the Dome of the Rock, and the Church of the Holy Sepulcher. Kiana and I cruised all over the maze of streets inside the Four Quarters of the city. One section of the Muslim Quarter was being blocked due to unrest by some Muslim men, so we turned around and went the other way. Going up to the Wailing Wall and wearing a yarmulke was an odd experience, but it was culturally enlightening. It's sad that the wall is all that's left standing of the Old Temple. Isn't it time for the Temple to be rebuilt once again, and Yahweh's name to be praised and honored? It's too bad that when the Temple is rebuilt, many of the Jews will worship a false messiah, but there's nothing we can do to change that event in history. It is written. It shall be done. All we can do is try to influence one individual at a time and hope the Man of Lawlessness will not deceive them.

When we returned from the Old City, it was very late, but we did get a good idea of the area and where to set up. We met an old Catholic priest who lived in the area. He gave us a lot of advice on what to do and what not to do. He was very helpful and warned me that there might be dire consequences if I tried to evangelize in Jerusalem. Before we went our separate ways, he laid hands on both of us and prayed. Kiana was all teary eyed, and he gave me a firm handshake. I have to admit he did seem like a good old man. In fact, I've met a lot of holy people in the Catholic Church over the years that are doing good deeds. I'm sorry if I've been a bit tough on Roman Catholicism over the years, but I suppose it's because I was brought up in that denomination. It was like catching someone in your own family lying to you. Consequently, I was highly critical after I came to the light and studied the *Bible* on my own. I learned that the Church had some teachings that were contrary to the *New Testament*. Initially, I was livid, and I thought it was my duty to point out these discrepancies to everybody. Nowadays, I just want to let it all go and find unity within the different denominations. We all believe Christ died for our sins and rose from the dead. Isn't that enough to end the strife and bring the church together?

Later in the evening, we ate dinner and crashed on our hotel room bed. Tomorrow I will continue my missionary journey. I am anxious. Jerusalem is a volatile area. I believe anything could happen.

38 (Day 5): Tuesday, Dec. 13th

We woke up early this morning, and I hauled a table and two chairs with me down to the Old City. It was a long walk. By the time we arrived at our destination, I was dripping in sweat and I had to buy a cheap t-shirt from one of the local vendors to replace the one I was wearing. After cooling down, we set up the table and put up a sign. It read, "*Bible* answer man. Ask any question on the *Bible*, and I will attempt to answer it."

For the first hour, the two of us sat there twiddling our thumbs, but around noon, things started to pick up, and we had a large crowd gathered around us. One woman asked a question about divorce. A man dressed in a suit and tie asked us where Cain's wife came from. A third person asked me a question on hell, and my response angered many. One man protested, "How can a good God cast ones into hell?" so I answered him to the best of my ability. Some were appeased with the answer while others walked away distraught. Finally, someone asked me, "Was Jesus the Messiah?" I answered, "According to Christians, He was. According to many Jews, he was not. And according to Islam, Jesus was a prophet." "Well, what do you think?" someone voiced. I answered, "Jesus fulfilled over 300 prophecies concerning the Messiah, and He backed His claim to be God by performing many miracles and rising from the dead. Therefore, I believe Jesus was the Messiah." One Israeli with a long beard scoffed, but another orthodox Jew inquired further, and the two of us spoke for sometime debating the issue.

After he left, Kiana and I tried setting up in the Jewish Quarter, but the locals kept telling us that we were not permitted to set up there, so we left. I'm not sure if they were telling the truth or not, but we didn't stay around to find out. I hailed down a taxi, and he took us to the Muslim Quarter of the Old City. Kiana was not happy about this, but she grudgingly went along with me. When we arrived in the area, we set up our table and put up our sign. We had no idea what was going to happen. We expected the worst, but we were surprised to find a lot of Muslim men who were curious, and they asked insightful questions. At times I brought up contradictions between the *Bible* and the Quran like the sacrifice of

Isaac not Ishmael, and many people were astounded by this information. One man couldn't believe it was written in the *Book of Genesis*, so I had to show him the actual text and challenged him to check other *Bibles* to see if it was true or not. We stayed in the Muslim Quarter for a couple of hours, and it was fruitful. Afterwards, we ate lunch at one of the local cafes, and flagged down a taxi van to take us back to our hotel.

Overall, I have to admit our outreach was a rewarding experience. People were quite hungry for the Word in the Old City. At times soldiers and merchants would give us the evil eye, but no one was too confrontational. There were some people that debated passionately, but I was able to keep my cool this time because God's Spirit was directing me. Tomorrow I'm going to try a different outreach technique, but for now I'm going to hit the hay and get some sleep.

39 (Day 6): Wednesday, Dec. 14th

After a bountiful breakfast and a successful trip to the toilet, the two of us made our way to some of the hotspots in Jerusalem. I didn't feel like carrying that table everywhere I went again, so I came up with a new scheme. I bought a fishing pole, a bucket, and hung a large sign around my neck. It said, "Fishing for men. Ask me any question on the *Bible*."

I have to admit I had a blast casting out my line near all the shoppers and watching the perplexed look on their faces as I reeled it in. Some patrons stared at me. Others laughed, and some people came up and asked questions. At one point there was a large crowd gathered around us near one of the shopping areas, but it was nothing like the hordes of tourists and locals that gawked at us in the Old City yesterday.

Kiana struck up a conversation with one woman, and the two of them spoke for some time. She's better at showing empathy than me, so I let my wife handle that one. Apparently she was going through some tough times, and Kiana was willing to listen. I wish I had that sort of patience, but it's not one of the gifts I've been given. I can teach and prophesy, but I'm not as sympathetic and caring as my wife. I suppose that's why the Church is a body. We all need one another to survive. Without it, we would simply fall apart.

By late afternoon, the two of us had burned out, so we went and had a falafel at this little café recommended in the *Lonely Planet* Guidebook. Later, we milled about and went back to the hotel because it was getting cold outside. Last time I was in Jerusalem it was during the summer, and the weather was perfect like Southern California, but today the sun didn't come out, and it was quite chilly.

In the evening, we went and saw a comedy at a movie theatre. It was an odd experience because when you wait in an Israeli line, there's really not a line. You sort of have to push your way up to the front to be served. It's annoying as hell. Inside the movie theatre it was assigned seats. Back home, it's first come first served. I like our way better, but there are some benefits to knowing your seat will still be there even if you arrive fifteen minutes late.

Tomorrow is the 15th. I have a sick feeling in my belly. Each click of the clock feels like a time bomb in my bosom. Is my time really up?

40 (Day 7): Thursday, Dec. 15th

It's 2:00 A.M. I can't sleep, but Kiana is snoring away. It's hailing hard outside, and I can hear heavy thumps on the roof. Today might be the last day of my life. I don't know what's going to happen. I'm terrified to find out what's behind the next door. "I have fought the good fight" (2 Tim.4:7) like Paul once said, even though my testimony has been impure. I have prayed for forgiveness and have straightened my ways, but I still feel I've fallen short in many areas. There is so much more I could have done or said, but I wasted my time on unfruitful pursuits. Now it's time for the judgment seat. All I can do is bow my head and lean upon the cross. I hope I make it into heaven. The Spirit is telling me that everything will be alright, but I still have my doubts. Even in my last hour, I'm filled with uncertainty.

When I started this journey, twenty-five years ago, I stood as proud as a mountain. I said, "Send me, send me!" (Isa.6:8) like Isaiah, but I never thought about the consequences. I fell time and time again, but with the strength of the Lord, I kept getting back up. Now I'm on my knees again asking for His strength one last time to bring down these pillars.

Tomorrow, I plan to head down to the Wailing Wall and preach the Gospel. This is against the law in Israel, and if I don't get shot, I'm sure I'll get arrested. I'd rather die than be locked behind bars, but my fate will be decided by God. I'll leave it in his hands. I'm a bondservant to the Lord, and He can do with my life as He sees fit.

If my time is up, I want to say goodbye to everyone one last time. To my friends, I will miss all the good times we had together. We truly did live on the edge. To my family, you have a tender place within me, but don't be sad when I'm gone. I have lived a full life, and soon I'll be partying in heaven. To my wife, I will miss you the most. You have stood by my side during my trials and tribulations, and I love you with all my heart. God bless everybody. May the Lord be with you!

EPILOGUE

Enoch was shot dead in the Old City by a stray bullet. According to eyewitness, there was an uprising as he was prophesying to the crowd. A bunch of radicals started throwing stones down at the worshippers by the Western Wall and security forces opened fire. Enoch was killed in the crossfire. Was he intentionally murdered or was he in the wrong place at the wrong time? In the long run, it doesn't really matter. Enoch is no longer with us, but his story will live on forever.

I hope you enjoyed reading Enoch's exploits as much as I did. His tales were dark, meaningful, and amusing. Over the years, I've often wondered, "Is he telling us the truth or pulling our legs?" At times I really didn't know. If you asked Enoch, he would tell you dogmatically, "Of course, it's the truth," with a grin on his face. This means we'll have to decide for ourselves what's fact or fiction.

In conclusion, these are Enoch's entries in their original form. I did make a few changes here and there, but I did not compromise the content of his journals. I simply edited them or put them in order. At times I wanted to delete whole passages and rewrite the entries, but I decided against it, because I truly believe Enoch was inspired by God. He was a visionary, a great teacher, and a prophet of God.

Sincerely,
Craig Conte

REFERENCES

Prologue
- a. Book of Revelation: Last book in the Bible
- b. Two Witnesses: Rev.11
- c. Elijah: Old Testament prophet; 1Ki.17-22; 2Ki.1-2; Mal.4:5
- d. Enoch: Gen.5:18-24; Heb.11:5; Gen.4:17; Jude 14-15; Book of Enoch; Sirach 44:16; Sirach 49:14
- e. Moses: Book of Exodus in the Bible
- f. John: Apostle and writer of several books in the New Testament
- g. Zerubbabel: Zech.4; Hag.2:20-23
- h. Book of Enoch: An ancient text found within the Dead Sea Scrolls that dates back to 200 BC. This book was considered authoritative by many of the early church fathers. Today it's considered a pseudepigraphical text by most of the Christian community. Today only the Ethiopian Orthodox Church accepts the *Book of Enoch* as the inspired Word of God.
- i. Dead Sea Scrolls: Collection of scrolls found between 1947-1956 that date back to 200 B.C. They include the oldest known surviving copies of the Biblical texts and extra Biblical texts.
- j. Watchers: Fallen angels who slept with women in the Book of Enoch
- k. Nephilim: Gen.6:4
- l. Disciplined Order Chaotic Lunacy by Craig Conte; prelude to 1,260 Days

Chapter 1: Sex & Dying in a High Society
- a. Title: "Sex & Dying in a High Society" by X (Los Angeles punk band)

Part A: Thailand
Arrival in Thailand
- a. Bangkok: Capital of Thailand
- b. *Great Expectations* by Charles Dickens
- c. Buddha: Founder of Buddhism; Siddhartha
- d. Ezekiel 18: *Old Testament* scripture
- e. Romans 2:12-16: *New Testament* scripture

f. "I am the way, the truth, and the life; no one comes to the Father but through Me." (Jn.14:6)

Khao Yai National Forest

a. Title: National Forest in Thailand

b. Millennial Reign: 1,000-year reign of Christ; Rev.20

c. Noah's Ark: Gen.6-9

Ashen Horse of Bangkok

a. Ashen horse: Rev.6:8

b. Chaing Mai: Largest city in Northern Thailand

c. Hancock: Hollywood movie starring Will Smith

d. Universalists: Based on universalism

e. Inner rooms: Mt.24:26

f. "You will be like God." (Gen.3:4)

g. YHWH: *Old Testament* name for God

Phuket

a. Island off the southwest coast of Thailand

b. Patong Beach: Beach on Phuket

c. "A real rain will come and wash all the scum off the street" (Taxi Driver); Red Angel Dragnet by The Clash (British punk band)

d. Karon Beach: Phuket beach

e. Kata Beach: Phuket beach

Bachelor Party in Pattaya

a. Pattaya: Coastal city located in the Gulf of Thailand

b. Las Vegas: City in Nevada also known as Sin City

Pattaya Reflection

a. "Resist the devil and he will flee from you." (Ja.4:7)

Ko Samui Island: The End of a Trip

a. Island in Thailand

Part B: I Must Not Think Bad Thoughts

a. Title: "I Must Not Think Bad Thoughts" by X (Los Angeles punk band)

Back in the U.S.A.

a. Title: Based on "Back in the U.S.S.R." by the Beatles (British rock band) & "Back in the USA" by Chuck Berry (American rock'n'roll artist)

b. "Waiting for the next big thing" Line from U.S. Forces by Midnight Oil (Australian rock band)

Where Am I?

a. "Are we going backwards or are we going forwards?" White Riot by The Clash: British punk band

b. Cloud by day and pillar of fire by night: Ex.13:21

Either/Or You'll Regret It

a. Title: *Either/Or* by Soren Kierkegaard (Philosopher from Denmark)

b. John the Baptist: Mt.3; Lk.1-3; Jn.1,3

c. Kingdom Age: 1,000 year reign of Christ (Rev.20)

d. "I Still Haven't Found What I'm Looking for" by U2: Irish rock band

e. Bono: Lead singer of U2

Economic Meltdown

a. Mark of the Beast: Rev.3:16-18

b. Day of the Lord: Joel 2:31

c. Barrack Obama: 44th President of the United States

Death & Disease

a. Ronald Reagan: 40th President of the United States

b. Flask of oil: Mt.25:1-13

c. Mark of the Beast: Rev.3:16-18

Goodbye Uncle Jim

a. "Put his house in order" (2Ki.20:1)

b. Lake of Fire: Rev.20:10,15

Part C: The Decline of Western Civilization

a. Title: Based on an American documentary on the Punk movement directed by Penelope Spheeris

In the Name of Allah...

a. Title: Allah = name for God in the Muslim religion

b. G20 Summit: Group of finance ministers and central bank governors for twenty major economies

c. "Things fall apart. The centre cannot hold. Mere anarchy is loosed upon the World." The Second Coming by William Butler Yeats

d. Pandora's Box: In Greek mythology a large jar that unleashed all the evils upon the world

e. Muhammad: Prophet of Islam

f. Beast and False Prophet: Rev.13-14

g. Quran: Religious text of Islam

h. YHWH: Hebrew name for God

Lukewarm

a. Title: Rev.3:15-16

b. Asherath: Mother goddess of sex; Queen of Heaven; *Old Testament* god

c. Race: 1Cor.9:24

d. Church of Corinth: One of the early churches in the *New Testament*

e. *Book of Hebrews*: *New Testament* epistle

f. Captain Pickard: Captain on the Next Generation of Star Trek

g. Star Trek: Science Fiction television series created by Gene Roddenberry

h. Peter Stoner: Mathematician and astronomer

i. DKs: Dead Kennedys (San Francisco punk band)

j. Jello: Lead singer in the Dead Kennedys and spoken word artist

k. Holden Caulfield: Narrator in *The Catcher in the Rye* by J.D. Salinger

Running with the Devil

a. Title: "I found the simple life ain't so simple when I jumped out on that road." Running with the Devil by Van Halen: American rock band

b. "Now ain't that special" Catchphrase from the Church Lady on Saturday Night Live

c. King David: 1 & 2 Samuel of the *Old Testament*

A Higher Calling

a. Big Bear: Mountain resort in Southern California

b. Nazarites: Num.6:1-5, 18-21

c. Their blood is no longer required of me: Ez.33:1-20

d. Wash my hands: Mt.27:24

e. Millennial Reign: 1,000-year reign of Christ; Rev.20

f. Know the Lord: Jer.31:34

Pride

a. "Nobody's Hero" by Stiff Little Fingers: Belfast punk band

b. Angels and Orioles: Major League Baseball teams

The Fall of the West

a. The Decline of Western Civilization: American documentary on the Punk movement directed by Penelope Spheeris

b. Friedrich Nietzsche: German philosopher and poet

c. *Beyond Good and Evil*: Book by Nietzsche

d. Millennium: Doomsday television series created by Chris Carter

e. "This is Who We Are." Quote from Millennium

f. Matthew 24: Chapter that speaks about the end times in the *Book of Matthew*

g. Ezekiel 37: Prophecy that speaks about the return of Israel to the Holy Land

h. Day of the Lord: Joel 2:30-32

i. *"Place your order. Place your bet. As you play poker the time clock ticks. The thief ain't coming or summer's near. Roll them dice or flee in fear."* Misconceptions by the Faithful Church

Bob Marley, Joseph Smith, & the Rapture

a. Bob Marley: Reggae artist/musician from Jamaica who propagated the Rastafarian religion

b. Joseph Smith: Prophet and founder of the Mormon religion

c. Caine: Main character on the television series Kung Fu starring David Carradine

d. Rapture: 1Thes.4:13-18

e. Man of Lawlessness: 2Thes.2:3

f. Elijah: Mal.4:4

g Flask of Oil: Mt.24:1-13

h. Left Behind: Those who are not raptured.

i. Rastafarian: Religion formed in Jamaica that believes Haile Selassie was/is god or the reincarnation of Jesus Christ

j. Mormon: Religion based on the teachings of Joseph Smith

k. Jehovah Witnesses: Religious group based on the teachings of Charles Taze Russel

l. Haile Selassie: Former emperor of Ethiopia; worshiped as God by the Rastafarians

m. Scientology: Body of beliefs and practices created by L. Ron Hubbard

Sports Addiction

a. NFL: National Football League

b. NBA: National Basketball Association

c. NHL: National Hockey League

d. Tested by fire: 1Cor.3:12-15; Zech.13:9; 1Pet.1:7

Part D: The Unheard Music

a. Title: "The Unheard Music" by X (Los Angeles punk band)

Post Office Shooting

a. Turn the other cheek: Mt.5:39

Prayer, Meditation, & Loving One Another

a. "Idle time is the Devil's playground" based on H.G. Bohn's "Idle mind is the Devil's playground."

b. "Our Fathers" based on the Lord's Prayer in Mt.6:9-13

c. "In the name of the Lord Jesus" is a common ending in many evangelical prayers

d. Bride at the wedding feast: Mt.25:1-13

e. Reborn spirits: Jn.3:3-8

f. Loving one another: Jn.13:34; Jn.15:17

g. "Love your neighbor as yourself" (Lev.19:18; Mt.19:19; Mt.22:39)

Down There By the Train

a. Title: "Down There By the Train" by Johnny Cash: American country/folk singer and artist

b. Buddha: The enlightened one in Buddhism who reached nirvana; Siddhartha

c. Allah: Name for God in Islam

d. "Way, truth, and life" (Jn.14:6)

The Path of Least Resistance

a. "Walk the road less traveled" from The Road Not Taken by Robert Frost

b. Church of Laodicea: Rev.3:14-22

c. "Fear God and keep His commandments." (Ecc.12:13)

Yin Yang

a. Title: Polar opposites in Chinese Philosophy (One is negative, dark, and feminine, and one is positive, bright, and masculine)

b. Edify, exhort, and console: 1Cor.13:3

c. "I'm not the worst, and I'm not the best" Yet Another Movie by Pink Floyd

d. Hedge: Job 1:10

Pornography

a. Brother George Geftakys: Lead pastor of a Fullerton, CA group of assemblies/ churches that were disbanded after he committed adultery

Infidelity

a. California State University of Long Beach

b. Ten Commandments: Ex.20:1-17; Deut.5:6-21

c. King David: 1 & 2 Samuel: *Old Testament* books

Sex Slaves

a. Isaiah's nakedness: Isa.20:2-3

b. Jeremiah's yoke of bondage: Jer.28:10

c. Asherah: Mother goddess of sex; Queen of Heaven; *Old Testament* god

d. Lot's wife: Gen.19:26

e. Sodom: Gen.19

f. Last Days: Acts 2:17; 2Pet.3:3; 2Tim.3:1

Forty-Two

a. Sheol: Darkness, hell, Hades; Ps.9:17; Ps.18:5; Ps.30:3; Ps.88:3

Suicide

a. Judas' suicide: Mt.27:5; Acts 1:18

b. Mortal sin: Grave, grievous, or serious sins in Roman Catholicism

c. Ten Commandments: Ex.20:1-17; Deut.5:1-21

d. "Thou shall not murder." (Ex.20:13)

e. "Whosoever believes in Him shall not perish but have eternal life." (Jn.3:16)

Baggage in my Head

a. "Doers of the Word" (Ja.1:23)

b. "New self" (Col.3:10)

c. Parable of the Talents: Mt.25:14-30

Attack Upon Christendom

a. Title: Based on Soren Kierkegaard's *Attack Upon Christendom*

b. Big Bang Theory: Cosmological model that explains the early development of the universe

c. Prime mover: Based on Saint Thomas Aquinas cosmological argument for the first cause of existence

d. "How can the deaf, dumb, and blind kid ever be saved?" Based on the songs Pinball Wizard and Christmas by The Who

Usury

a. Law of Moses: *Torah* (Five books of Moses)

b. "You shall not charge interest to your countrymen/brothers: interest on money, food, or anything that may be loaned at interest. You may charge interest to a foreigner, but to your countryman you shall not charge interest." (Deut.23:19-20)

c. Millennial Reign: 1,000-year reign of Christ; Rev.20

Shakespeare, Success, Evil, & the Lord's Return

a. William Shakespeare: English writer, poet, and playwright

b. Lord's Return: Rev.19:11-21; Mt.24:29-31

c. "Will success fail me? Will it make me free? What they tell me I should want; is it what I need?" Success by Linda Perry: American musician, songwriter, and producer

d. O Maranatha, O Lord come: Rev.22:20

e. Son of Man: Mt.16:13; Mt.17:9; Mt.24:30; Jn.12:23: Ezek.3:1-4

Fame, Fortune & Everything Else in Between

a. *Rolling Stone Magazine*: US based magazine devoted to music and popular culture

b. "The Unheard Music" by X (Los Angeles punk band)

c. 1,260 Days: Rev.11:3

d. Mansion in heaven: Jn.14:2

Foul Ball

a. Angels: Major League Baseball team from Anaheim, California

b. Erick Aybar: Shortstop on the Angels

c. Yankees: Major League Baseball team from New York

Scratching the Itch

a. Las Vegas, Nevada: Sin City

b. "Getting faded is a basic human drive like food and water and sex and sleep." Based on the Doggfather in *The Outlaw Bible of American Literature*

c. Snoop Dogg: American rapper, singer, and producer

d. AA: Alcoholics Anonymous

e. Normy: One who can drink or dabble with drugs without getting hooked or addicted

Here's the Rope... Now Swing Away

a. Title: Based on "Wire" by U2: Irish rock band

b. True wisdom comes from the Lord and hearing His Word: Prov.1:7; Rom.10:17

c. Children are covered: 1Cor.7:14

d. Tribulation Period: 3 ½ to 7-year period; Dan.12:7; Rev.12:14

Mercy

a. Jonah and the Whale: *Book of Jonah*; *Old Testament* book

b. Nineveh: Assyrian city on the eastern bank of the Tigres River; The prophet Jonah prophesied to this city

c. *Torah*: Law of Moses; *Old Testament*

d. Noah: Gen.6-9

Chapter 2: 40 Days & 40 Nights in Europe

Lost Luggage

a. Casablanca, Morocco: City in North Africa

b. Marrakesh, Morocco: City in North Africa

The Veil

a. Djema al-fna: Outdoor marketplace in Marrakesh

b. Paul: Apostle and author of many epistles in the *New Testament*

c. John Lennon: Musician, singer, and former member of the Beatles

d. "Woman is the Nigger of the World" by John Lennon

The Moroccans

a. Fez, Morocco: Ancient city in North Africa

b. The Battle of Gog: Ezekiel 38-39 in the *Old Testament*

1992 Vs 2010

a. Lisboa, Portugal: City of Western Europe

b. TAP Air: National airline of Portugal

c. Bairro Alto: District in Portugal with restaurants, businesses, and trendy shops

d. Baixa: Business and shopping area in Portugal

e. Hard Rock Café: Restaurant chain with a rock'n'roll theme

f. Sofitel Hotel: Luxury hotel chain

g. "Fuck yeah" Team America soundtrack; America F**k Yeah by Trey Parker

The Thrill is Gone

a. Title: "The Thrill is Gone" by B.B. King (American blues singer/musician)

b. Millennial Reign: 1,000-year reign of Christ; Rev.20

Lisboa

a. Lisboa: Capital of Portugal

b. Porto: City of Portugal

c. Buenos Aires: Capital of Argentina

d. San Francisco, California: City in the United States

e. Big Bear, California: Mountain city in Southern California

f. Armageddon: Rev.16:16

Welcome to the Machine

a. Title: "Welcome to the Machine" by Pink Floyd (British rock band)

b. Santa Barbara, Monterey: Cities in California

c. *Let's Go*: Travel book for low budget travelers

d. World Cup: Global sporting event in soccer

e. Super Bowl: NFL championship game in American football

f. World Series: MLB championship series in baseball

Purgatory

a. L.A., Orange County: Counties in California

b. Igreja De Sao San Francisco: Church in Porto

c. Great White Throne Judgment: Rev.20:11-15

d. Lake of Fire: Rev.20:11-15

e. Abraham's Bosom: Lk.16:19-31

Church

a. "2 or 3 are gathered together" Mt.18:20

b. Chuck Smith: Lead pastor of the Calvary Chapel Ministries

c. Calvary Chapel: Christian denomination with churches throughout the world

d. "Forsake the assembling of ourselves together" (Heb.10:25)

Highlights

a. Madrid: Capital and largest city of Spain

b. Museo Del Prado: Spanish national art museum in Madrid

c. Goya: Spanish artist/painter

d. El Greco: Painter, sculptor, and architect of the Spanish Renaissance

e. *Lonely Planet*: Travel book

f. *Let's Go*: Low budget travel book

g. Montera Rd. (A street in Madrid)

h. "Legalize It" by Peter Tosh: Reggae artist from Jamaica; Original member of the Wailers

Espana, World Cup Champions!

a. Lakers: NBA basketball team from Los Angeles, California

b. Angels: MLB baseball team from Anaheim, California

c. Darin Erstad: Centerfielder on the Angels 2002 World Series champion team

Running with the Bulls

a. Pamplona: City in Spain famous for bullfighting and running with the bulls

b. Ernest Hemmingway: American author

c. *The Sun Also Rises* by Hemmingway: Most of the story takes places during the San Fermin Festival in Pamplona

d. San Fermin: Two-week festival in Pamplona with the running of the bulls, bull-fighting, and other entertainment

Come on Down and Make the Stand

a. Title: "The Stand" by The Alarm (Band from Wales)

b. Tribulation Period: 3 ½ to 7-year period prophesied in the *Books of Daniel, and Revelation*

Sabbath

a. Title: Shortened version for the name of the band Black Sabbath (English rock/heavy metal band)

b. Barcelona, Spain: Capital of Catalonia in Spain

c. 10 Commandments: Ex.20:1-17

Fade Away

a. Title: "Fade Away" by Stiff Little Fingers (Punk band from Northern Ireland)

b. Friday the 13th: Horror movies with Jason as the murderer/villain

c. "Blaze of Glory" by The Alarm (Band from Wales)

Hangover

a. Title: Based on American comedy/film with the same title

b. Ibiza: Spanish island in the Mediterranean Sea

c. Los Angeles Angels of Anaheim: Major League Baseball team

d. Star Trek: Science fiction television series created by Gene Roddenberry

For Freedom

a. Title: "For Freedom" by The Alarm (Band from Wales)

b. Milano: City in Italy

c. "I got my Bible, and I got my handgun" America by D.O.A (Punk band from Canada)

d. Big Brother: George Orwell's *1984*

e. Superman: Comic book superhero from DC Comics

f. "Truth, justice, and the American way" Quote from Superman

g. "Meet the new boss, same as the old boss." Won't Get Fooled Again by The Who (British rock band)

Love Your Neighbor as Yourself

a. Title: Lev.19:18; Mt.19:19; Mk.12:31; Lk.10:27

b. Venice: City in Italy known for its canals

Post Austria

a. Krakow: City in Poland

b. Vienna: Capital of Austria

c. Auschwitz: Concentration camp during WWII

    d. Bangkok: Capital of Thailand

    e. Saint Christopher: Statues/medals placed in automobiles to protect the driver from death and accidents

    f. *Book of Enoch*: An ancient text found within the Dead Sea Scrolls that dates back to 200 BC. This book was considered authoritative by many of the early church fathers. Today it's considered a pseudepigraphical text by most of the Christian community. Today only the Ethiopian Orthodox Church accepts the *Book of Enoch* as the inspired Word of God.

Krakow, Poland

a. Krakow: City in Poland

b. Holiday Inn: Hotel chain

c. Venice: City in Italy known for its canals

d. Oswiecim: City in Poland that holds the Auschwitz concentration camp

The Holocaust

a. *Book of Revelation*: Last book in the *Bible*

b. "Multitude which no man can number" (Rev.7:9-14)

c. "Be given a mark on their right hand or forehead" (Rev.13:16-18)

d. Mark of the Beast: Rev.13:16-18

e. Lake of Fire: Rev.20:10-15

Eating, Drinking, & Screwing

a. Charles Darwin: On the Origin of Species (Evolution)

Give Peace a Chance

a. Title: "Give Peace a Chance" by John Lennon (Musician, artist, and former member of the Beatles)

b. Prague: Capital of the Czech Republic

c. Berlin: Capital of Germany

d. John Lennon Wall: Wall filled with graffiti near Charles Bridge in Prague

e. "All You Need is Love" by John Lennon of the Beatles

f. Bob Dylan: American folk/rock artist

g. "There will be no peace. The world won't cease until He returns." When He Returns by Bob Dylan

h. "Thy kingdom come, Thy will be done on earth as it is in heaven." (Mt.6:10)

Berlin, Germany

a. Joseph Stalin: Former leader of the Soviet Union

b. Days of Noah: Gen.6-9; Mt.24:37-38

c. Sony Center: Building center located at Potsdamer Platz in Berlin

d. Zoo Station: Metro stop at the Berlin Zoological Garden

Legalization of Pot

a. Amsterdam: Capital of the Netherlands

b. Paris: Capital of France

Unlike Paul

a. Apostle of the early Christian Church and author of many epistles in the *New Testament*

b. San Francisco: City in California

c. Paris: Capital of France

d. 7-Eleven: International chain of convenience stores

e. "All things to all men" (1Cor.9:23)

Hail Mary... Hell No

a. Mary: Mother of Jesus (Mt.1:25; Mt.12:46; Mt.13:55; Mk.3:31-32; Mk.6:3)

b. Louvre Museum: One of the largest and most visited museums in the world

c. "One mediator between God and man" (1Tim.2:5)

d. Caesar: Former leaders of the Roman Empire

e. Adolf Hitler: Former leader of the Third Reich in Germany

e. Napoleon Bonaparte: Former military and political leader of France

Ménage à Trois

a. Jim Morrison: Former lead singer of the Doors (California rock band)

b. Oscar Wilde: Irish writer

Finding Solace

a. Eiffel Tower: Landmark in Paris, France

b. Inception: Hollywood movie starring Leonardo DiCaprio

Lourdes, France

a. Mount Sinai: Place where Moses received the 10 Commandments

b. Bernadette: Saint Marie-Bernarde Soubirous

On the Train to Switzerland Thinking

a. Sinead O'Connor: Singer/musician from Ireland

b. "These are dangerous days to say what you feel is to make your own grave."
Black Boys on Mopeds by Sinead O'Connor

c. Joe Strummer: British singer/songwriter and member of The Clash

d. Johnny Cash: American singer/songwriter, author, and actor

e. "Redemption Song" by Bob Marley

f. Bob Marley: Reggae singer/songwriter from Jamaica

Neutrality Won't Save You

a. Geneva: City in Switzerland

b. Lake Geneva: One of the largest lakes in Western Europe

c. Lake Tahoe: Large freshwater lake in the Sierra Nevada

Modern Conveniences

a. Colorado River: River in the Southwestern United States and parts of Mexico

b. Mississippi River: Largest river system in North America

c. Mary: Mother of Jesus

d. Zeus: Father of gods and men in ancient Greek mythology

The Meaning of Life

a. Florence/Rome: Cities in Italy

b. "The fear of the Lord is the beginning of knowledge." (Prov.1:7)

Caesar's Rome

a. Colosseum, Pantheon, and the Baths of Caracalla: Ruins from the Roman Empire

b. Golden Gate Bridge: Located in San Francisco, California

c. White House: Official residence of the President of the United States

d. Manhattan: Located in New York

    e. Revived Roman Empire: Dan.7:7-8; Rev.13

    f. Daniel: Prophet and author of the *Book of Daniel*

    g. John's *Revelation*: Apostle of Jesus Christ; Writer of the *Book of Revelation*

    h. Flower of the field: Isa.40:6; 1Pet.1:24

Chapter 3: Visions of the Absurd

The Clock is Ticking

a. "Help my unbelief" (Mk.9:24)

b. I Love Lucy: Television series starring Lucille Ball and Desi Arnaz

c. The Twilight Zone: Television series written by Rod Serling

d. "Comfortably Numb" by Pink Floyd (British rock band)

Written in Stone

a. Ahab and Jezebel: 1Ki.16-22

b. Elijah: 1Ki.17-22; 2Ki.1-2; Mal.4:5

c. Ebenezer Scrooge: Character in *A Christmas Carol* by Charles Dickens

Was Jesus a Murderer or a Maniac?

a. Title: "Was Jesus a Murderer or a Maniac?" by the Faithful Church (Orange County, CA band) and written by Conte

Death, Rebellion, & the Unknown Soldiers

a. The Sun Also Rises by Ernest Hemingway: American writer

b. John Steinbeck: American writer

Fall of the White House

a. "I will pour out My Spirit on all mankind, and your sons and daughters will prophesy, your old men will dream dreams, your young men will see visions." (Joel 2:28)

My Only Friend...The End

a. Title: Line taken from "The End" by Jim Morrison of The Doors

Liberty & Anarchy

a. Big Brother: *1984* by George Orwell

The Quest

a. "An eye for an eye" Ex.21:24

b. "Turn the other cheek" Mt.5:38-39

Repentance

a. Solomon: Wise, wealthy King of Israel; 1Ki.1-12

b. Buddha: Founder of Buddhism

c. Siddhartha: Birth name of Gautama Buddha (founder of Buddhism)

d. Kamala: Fictional lover in Hermann Hesse's book *Siddhartha*

Holy Bible Atomic Hell Fire Heat

a. Title: "Holy Bible Atomic Hell Fire Heat" by the Faithful Church (Orange County, CA band) and written by Conte

b. NRA: National Rifle Association

c. Elohim: One of the names for God in the *Bible*

If I had One Year to Live

a. "The Final Message" by the Faithful Church (Orange County, CA band) and written by Conte

Passing

a. Newport Beach: City in Orange County, California

b. "Not my will but Thy will be done." (Mt.26:39)

c. "There's a lot of road ahead. There's a lot of road behind." The Painter by Neil Young

Drought

a. Joseph: Gen.37-50

b. Two Prophets: Rev.11

c. *Revelation*: Last book in the *Bible*

d. "Minutes to Midnight" by Midnight Oil (Band from Australia)

e. *Book of Daniel*: Book in the *Old Testament*

Alternate Realities

a. "Inexpressible" (2Cor.12:4)

b. "Excelled in splendor and magnificence that he could not describe it to us" (1 Enoch 14:16)

c. *Book of Enoch*: An ancient text found within the Dead Sea Scrolls that dates back to 200 BC. This book was considered authoritative by many of the early church fathers. Today it's considered a pseudepigraphical text by most of the Christian community. Today only the Ethiopian Orthodox Church accepts the *Book of Enoch* as the inspired Word of God.

d. "See, hear, or feel" (1Cor.2:9)

e. The Twilight Zone: Television series written by Rod Serling

Gadulsay

a. "No mind has imagined. No eye has ever seen. It has not crossed the heart of man. Ears cannot perceive." 1Cor.2:9

Sick Until Summer

a. "What a drag it is getting old" Mother's Little Helper by the Rolling Stones

b. TEFL: Teaching English as a Foreign Language

c. Death Valley: Located in the Mohave Desert of California

Famine

a. "Quart of wheat" (Rev.6:5-6)

Vanilla Sex

a. "Bowls of Wrath" (Rev.15-16)

b. "A change is gonna come around soon." A Change is Gonna Come by Sam Cooke

Dark Side of Love

a. Title: "Dark Side of Love" by Shakespearean Fool (Orange County, CA band) and written by Conte

b. Lyrics stand juxtaposed to 1Cor.13

The Rebels

a. *Book of Hosea*: Book in the *Old Testament*

b. "Jesus, remember me when You come into Your kingdom." (Lk.23:42)

c. "Rebel from birth" (Isa.48:8)

Roots, Radicals, Rockers, & Reggae

a. "Roots, Radicals, Rockers, and Reggae" by Stiff Little Fingers from Northern Ireland; the song was originally written by Bunny Wailer but was rearranged by Stiff Little Fingers.

b. "Hammer our swords into plowshares and our spears into pruning hooks" (Isa.2:4)

c. "Fight the good fight" (1Tim.6:12)

Grandpa's Dying & It Won't Be Long

a. Lyrics based on the poem "I'm Fine, How are You?" by Maurice Ingram

Environmental Damage: Hawaii 25 Years Later

a. Waikiki: City on the Island of Oahu

b. Beach Boys: An American rock band from California

c. North Shore: Famous surfing spot on the Island of Oahu

d. Jacques Cousteau: Scientist, filmmaker, and marine biologist from France

e. "Water and air, the two essential fluids on which all life depends, have become global garbage cans." Quote from Cousteau

Forever & Ever

a. *Book of Micah*: *Old Testament* book; minor prophet

b. "Need to do justice, to love kindness, and to walk humbly with Him." (Mic. 6:8); "Son of Man" by Jimmy Cliff: Jamaican, reggae singer/artist

c. "Love our neighbor as ourselves." (Mt. 22:39)

d. "Nation will not lift up sword against nation, and never again will we train for war." (Mic.4:3)

The Jester

a. Title: "The Jester" by Shakespearean Fool (Orange County, CA band) and written by Conte

b. "His arm will be withered. His right eye blind. He'll reign for a time, a times, and half a time. He'll magnify himself and will destroy. And cause the rich and poor to be given a mark?" Dan.7:23-25; Dan.8:23-26; Dan.12:7; Zech.11:17; Rev.13:16-18

c. "Hear ye, hear ye but understand not. See ye, see ye but perceive not." Isa.6:9

Zephaniah

a. *Book Zephaniah*: *Old Testament* book; minor prophet

b. "From the face of the earth" (Zep.1:2)

c. "Reckless, treacherous men" (Zep.3:4)

d. "Seek righteousness" (Zeph.2:3)

e. "Be hidden in the day of the Lord's anger" (Zep.2:3)

f. "All our oppressors" (Zep.3:19)

g. "Save the lame and gather the outcast" (Zep.3:19)

h. "Our shame into praise" (Zep.3:19)

Israel, Israel, Israel

a. Regathering of God's people: Ezekiel 34-37

b. Battle of Gog & Magog: Ezekiel 38-39

c. *Book of Haggai*: *Old Testament* book; minor prophet

d. Zechariah: Minor prophet in the *Old Testament*

e. Matthew 24: Chapter in the *Book of Matthew*; first book in the *New Testament*

f. YHWH: *Old Testament* name for God

g. "One hour on one day" (Rev.18)

h. "It's the End of the World as We know It (And I Feel Fine)" by R.E.M. (An American band from Athens, Georgia)

Zechariah, the Prophet

a. Minor prophet from the *Old Testament*; wrote the *Book of Zechariah*

b. *Gospels of Matthew, John* and the *Book of Revelation*: *New Testament* books

c. *Isaiah, Daniel, Ezekiel, Psalms, Proverbs, Ecclesiastes,* and *Zechariah*: *Old Testament* books

d. "Branch" (Zech.3:8)

e. Judas' future betrayal (Zech.11:12,13)

f. Jesus' sacrifice on the cross (Zech.12:10; 13:6)

g. "Arm withered," "Right eye blind" (Zech.11:17)

h. "Fatally wounded" (Rev.13:3)

i. "Mount of Olives," "Bring His holy ones with Him" (Zech.14:4,5)

j. *Millennial Reign* by Craig Conte based on Zechariah 14 and Revelation 20

k. "It will come about that any who are left of all the nations that went against Jerusalem will go up from year to year to worship the King, the Lord of hosts, and to celebrate the Feast of Booths. It will be that whichever of the families of the earth does not go up to Jerusalem to worship the King, the Lord of Hosts, there will be no rain on them." (Zech.14:16,17)

l. Isaiah 53: Prophetic book in the *Old Testament* written by Isaiah

m. Psalm 22: One of the prophetic psalms written by King David

Malachi, Mischief, & my Nakedness

a. *Book of Malachi*: *Old Testament* book; minor prophet

b. "Behold, I am going to send you Elijah the prophet before the great and terrible Day of the Lord." (Mal.4:5)

c. "Messenger," "Clear the way" (Mal.3:1)

d. John the Baptist: Prophet according to the Christian community; Mal.3:1; Mt.3; Lk.1,3; Jn.1

e. "Crying in the wilderness and making straight the way of the Lord" (Jn.1:23)

f. "I am not." (Jn.1:21)

g. "Do not listen or give honor to the Lord's name." (Mal.2:1)

h. "Dealt treacherously with my wife" (Mal.3:14-15)

Miracle Man

a. Woman caught in adultery (Jn.8:1-11)

b. Socrates: Greek Athenian philosopher

c. Gandhi: During India's independence he was a political and ideological leader of the country

d. Siddhartha: Founder of Buddhism

Restraint

a. Big Bear: Mountain resort in Southern California

Politics

a. Democrat, Libertarian, Green Party, Republican: Political parties in the United States

b. Thomas Jefferson, Abraham Lincoln, Teddy Roosevelt, Franklin Delano Roosevelt: Former presidents of the United States

c. Jello Biafra: Former lead singer of the Dead Kennedys, a San Francisco punk band; spoken word artist

d. Bill Maher: Political comedian with liberal beliefs

e. Rich Marotta: KFI Radio (Inducted 2011, Southern California Sportscasters Hall of Fame)

f. Henry Rollins: Spoken word artist & former singer of Black Flag

g. Ron Paul: Politician with Libertarian/conservative beliefs

h. Dennis Miller: Political comedian with conservative beliefs

i. Chuck Smith: Lead pastor of Calvary Chapel in Costa Mesa

Rich Man's Blues

a. "It's easier for a camel to go through the eye of the needle than for a rich man to enter the Kingdom of Heaven." (Mt.19:24)

Witch Hunt

a. Title: "Witch Hunt" by Rush (Canadian rock band)

b. "The righteous rise with burning eyes of hatred and ill will. Madmen fed on fear and lies to beat and burn and kill." Witch Hunt lyrics by Rush

c. "He who is without sin, let him cast the first stone." (Jn. 8:7)

Laughlin

a. Laughlin: Located in Clark County, Nevada on the borders of California and Arizona; place to party and gamble

b. Lake Havasu: Large reservoir on the Colorado River; place to party

Chapter 4: The Philippines

Abraham Lives!

a. "I am the God of Abraham, Isaac, and Jacob." (Ex.3:6)

b. "God of the living not the dead." (Mk.12:26-27)

Life of Leisure

a. Waikiki Beach on Oahu Island in Hawaii

Sunshine, Rain, & in the Middle of Nowhere

a. "The harvest is plentiful but the workers are few." (Lk.10:2)

b. "A fool will return to his own folly." (Prov.26:11)

c. "Dogs who are eating their own vomit." (Prov.26:11)

d. "Last state has become worse than the first." (2Pet.2:20)

Tequila Bob & Risk Takers

a. Aerial's Point: Off Boracay Island in the Philippines

A Cebu Story

a. Ferdinand Marcos: Former president/dictator of the Philippines

The Class

a. Dennis Hopper: Actor/director

b. Easy Rider: 1969 film directed by Dennis Hopper

Life in the Fast Lane

a. Title: "Life in the Fast Lane" by the Eagles (Band from Los Angeles, CA.)

Hypocrites & Unbelievers

a. Peter's denial of Jesus (Mt.26:69-75)

Under the Weather

a. Harbor Blvd. in Orange County, CA

Gambling in the Backroom

a. Sopranos: HBO television series about Mobsters from New Jersey

b. Waterfront Casino: Hotel/casino on the Island of Cebu

Kawasan Falls & Burning Charcoal

a. Kawasan Falls: Waterfalls on the Island of Cebu

Jeepney Accident

a. Manny Pacquiao: Famous boxer in the Philippines

b. "To be on the alert for we do not know the day nor the hour" (Mt.25:13)

c. "No one knows the day or the hour not even the angels of heaven." (Mt.24:36)

d. 5 virgins/flask of oil: (Mt.25:1-13)

Eastwood's Tale

a. Manny Pacquiao: Famous boxer in the Philippines

Ashen & Rashes

a. "When the Man Comes Around" by Johnny Cash (Musician, singer, and actor)

b. "And I heard a voice in the midst of the four beasts. And I looked and behold a pale horse. And his name that sat on him was Death. And Hell followed with him." (Rev.6:8)

Hash Run

a. Hash House Harriers: Drinking, running, and social club

Luke & the Lost

a. Luke: Author of the *Gospel of Luke* and the *Book of Acts*

The Prodigal Son

a. Parable of the Prodigal Son: Lk.15:11-31

So Far Away

a. Title: "So Far Away" by Social Distortion (Orange County punk band)

Certified & Saying Goodbye

a. Sodom and Gomorrah: Gen.19

Angeles City

a. City of Angeles in the Philippines

Highway to Hell

a. Title: Album/song by ACDC (Australian rock band)

b. Days of Noah: Gen.6-8

Chapter 5: The End

Part A: Anger, Analysis, & Anarchy
   The Bluffs
     a. The Bluffs: Fairview Park in Costa Mesa, CA
   Good will Follow Bad
     a. Big Bear, California: Mountain resort in Southern California
     b. Millennial Reign: 1,000-year reign of Jesus Christ; Rev.20
   Beyond Good and Evil
     a. Title: *Beyond Good and Evil* by Friedrich Nietzsche (German philosopher/ writer)
   Fresh Pussy
     a. "When's this God of 'ours' going to show up?" Line taken from the movie Forrest Gump; "Where is the promise of His coming?" (2Pet.3:4)
   Writing Wall Memorial
     a. *Disciplined Order Chaotic Lunacy* by Craig Conte; Prelude to *1,260 Days*
     b. Zzyzx Road: Located in San Bernardino County near the California/Nevada border.
   Deism
     a. *The Adventures of Tom Sawyer* by Mark Twain; Rush (Canadian rock band) with a song titled "Tom Sawyer."
     b. "One way" (Jn.14:6; Acts 4:12)
   Sickness Unto Death
     a. Title: *The Sickness Unto Death* by Soren Kierkegaard
     b. "70 x 7" (Mt.18:22)
     c. "Sin no more lest a worse thing come upon you." (Jn.5:14)
   Harvest Time
     a. "Wedding feast" (Mt.22:3)
     b. "O Lord come!" (Rev. 22:20)
   Questioning the Omnipotent
     a. "Remember how it all began, the apple and the fall of man." Thick as Thieves by Natalie Merchant
   True Sounds of Liberty
     a. *An American Demon* by Jack Grisham (Singer, author)
     b. T.S.O.L. and Vicious Circle: Punk bands from Los Angeles and Orange County, CA
   Sex, Marriage, & Multiple Relationships
     a. "Angels of heaven" (Mt.22:30)
     b. Star Trek: Science fiction television series created by Gene Roddenberry

Part B: Broken & Parting
   Freedom of Speech
     a. Paul: Apostle of the early Christian church and writer of much of the *New Testament*
     b. Kingdom: 1,000 year reign of Christ after His return; Rev.20

Overcome

a. 3 ½ year testimony: Rev.11:3-7

b. "Lake of Fire" (Rev.20:10)

It's a Wonderful Life

a. Title: It's a Wonderful life directed by Frank Cabra and starring James Stewart

b. Hezekiah: His seed bore King Manasseh after he prayed to be healed on his deathbed; 2 Kings; 2 Chronicles

c. King Manasseh: One of the wickedest kings to reign in Judah; Hezekiah's son; 2 Kings; 2 Chronicles

Halloween

a. Title: "Halloween" from Plastic Surgery Disasters by the Dead Kennedys (San Francisco punk band)

Romans 8

a. "Neither death, nor life, nor angels, nor principalities, nor powers, nor things present, nor things to come, nor height, nor depth, nor any other creature" (Rom.8:38-39)

b. *Book of Romans*: Epistle written by Paul to the Roman Church

c. "If God is for us who can be against us?" (Rom.8:31); gospel song

Manny, Moe, & Jack

a. Title: Manny, Moe, & Jack from Pep Boys Auto Parts

b. San Luis Obisbo, CA

c. James Bond: Secret agent in movies

d. Jonah and the Whale from the *Book of Jonah* in the *Old Testament*

e. Samson from the *Book of Judges* in the *Old Testament*

f. The Flood from the *Book of Genesis* in the *Old Testament*

Veteran's Day

a. Love Boat: 1970s television show; it was a cruise ship

b. Green Zone: Relatively safe and fortified area during the Iraq War

c. "Speak softly but carry a big stick." Quote by Teddy Roosevelt (26th President of the United States)

Bohemian Rhapsody

a. Title: "Bohemian Rhapsody" by Queen (British rock band)

Letter to the Americans

a. "Remember therefore from where you have fallen." (Rev.2:5)

b. "Log out of our own eye" (Mt.7:4)

c. "Judgment will begin at the House of God." (1Pet.4:17)

d. "Reap what we have sown" (Gal.6:7)

e. "Draw near to God and He will draw near to you." (Ja.4:8)

Controversial Issues

a. "Before I formed you in the womb, I knew you." (Jer.1:5)

b. Sodom and Gomorrah: *Book of Genesis* in the *Old Testament*

c. "He who strikes a man so that he dies shall surely be put to death." (Ex.21:12)

d. Melchizedek: *Book of Genesis*; type of Christ

  e. "A tenth of all" (Gen.14:20)

  f. Al Capone: Mobster during the prohibition of alcohol in the 1920s

  g. "Drink a little wine" (1Tim.5:23)

  h. "Frequent ailments" (1Tim.5:23)

  i. Right to bear arms: 2nd Amendment in the Bill of Rights

Prayer

  a. "Two or three are gathered together, the Lord is there in our midst." (Mt.18:20)

  b. "Our Father" (Mt. 6:9)

  c. Hail Mary: A Catholic prayer

Gospel

  a. "Through one man sin entered into the world, and death through sin, and so death spread to all men because all sinned." (Rom.5:12)

  b. "Through one transgression there resulted condemnation to all men, even so through one act of righteousness there resulted justification of life to all men." (Rom.5:18)

  c. "Mediator" (1Tim.2:5)

  d. "Propitiation" (1Jn.2:2)

  e. "If you confess with your mouth Jesus as Lord, and believe in your heart that God raised Him from the dead, you shall be saved; for with the heart man believes resulting in righteousness, and with the mouth he confesses, resulting in salvation." (Rom.10:9)

  f. "For God so loved the world that He gave His only begotten Son that whosoever believeth in Him should not perish but have everlasting life." (Jn.3:16)

We are the Light

  a. Title: "We are the Light by The Alarm (Band from Wales)

  b. "Let no one deceive you, that Day will not come until the man of lawlessness is revealed, the son of perdition, who opposes and exalts himself above every so called god or object of worship, so that he takes his seat in the temple of God, displaying himself as being God." (2Thes.2:3-4)

  c. The "Day of the Lord will come just like a thief in the night." (1Thes.5:2)

  d. "Philosophy and the traditions of men" (Col.2:8)

What if...

  a. Adolf Hitler: Former dictator of the Third Reich in Germany

Part C: The Holy Land

  Day 1: Friday, Dec. 9th

  a. Luke: Author of the *Gospel of Luke* and the *Book of Acts*

  Day 3: Sunday, Dec. 11th

  a. "Armageddon" Faithful Church song based on Rev.16:16; band from Orange County, CA

  b. "Misconceptions" Faithful Church song based on Rev.18; band from Orange County, CA

  c. "Gog" Faithful Church song based Ezekiel 38-39; band from Orange County, CA

d. "22" Faithful Church song based on Psalm 22-23; band from Orange County, CA

e. "Redemption Song" by Bob Marley (Jamaican reggae artist, musician)

f. "Guns on the Roof" by the The Clash (British punk band)

g. "When the Man Comes Around" by Johnny Cash (American singer, musician)

Day 4: Monday, Dec. 12th

a. Man of Lawlessness (Antichrist, false messiah); 2Thes.2:3-4

Day 5: Tuesday, Dec. 13th

a. Sacrifice of Isaac: Gen.22:6

Day 6: Wednesday, Dec. 14th

a. "Fishers of Men" (Mt. 4:19)

b. *Lonely Planet*: Travel Guidebook

Day 7: Thursday, Dec. 15th

a. "I have fought the good fight." (2Tim.4:7)

b. "Send me" (Isa.6:8)

Map References

a. Thailand = http://d-maps.com/carte.php?lib=Thailand_map&num_25605&lang=en

b. Europe = http://d-maps.com/carte.php?lib=Europe_map&num_car=13147&lang=en

c. US = http://d-maps.com/carte.php?lib=united_states_of_america_usa_map&num_car=11849&lang=en

d. Philippines = http://d-maps.com/carte.php?lib=Philippines_map&num_car=583&lang=en

e. California = http://d-maps.com/m/californie/californie25.gif

f. Israel = http://d-maps.com/carte.php?lib=Israel_map&num_car=26289&lang=en

g. Old City = http://wikitravel.org/en/jerusalem/old_city

Oddities, Coincidences, Patterns

a. Chapters based on song titles or lyrics: Sex & Dying in a High Society; I Must Not Think Bad Thoughts; Back in the USA; Running with the Devil; The Unheard Music; Down There by the Train; Here's the Rope…Now Swing Away; The Thrill is Gone; Welcome to the Machine; Come on Down & Make the Stand; Fade Away; For Freedom; Give Peace a Chance; Was Jesus a Murderer or a Maniac; My Only Friend…The End; Holy Bible Atomic Hell Fire Heat; Dark Side of Love; Roots, Radicals, Rockers, & Reggae; Witch Hunt; Life in the Fast Lane; Loss for Words; So Far Away; Highway to Hell; The End; Halloween; Bohemian Rhapsody; We are the Light

b. Musician/band references: X; Beatles; John Lennon; Chuck Berry; Midnight Oil; The Clash; Joe Strummer; U2; Bono; Dead Kennedys; Jello Biafra; Van Halen; King David; Stiff Little Fingers; Faithful Church; Bob Marley; Peter Tosh; The Wailers; Pink Floyd; The Who; Snoop Dogg; B.B. King; Trey

Parker; The Alarm; D.O.A.; Bob Dylan; The Doors; Jim Morrison; Sinead O'Connor; Neil Young; Rolling Stones; Sam Cooke; Shakespearean Fool; Beach Boys; Jimmy Cliff; Conte; R.E.M.; Rush; Eagles; Social Distortion; ACDC; Natalie Merchant; T.S.O.L.; Vicious Circle; Jack Grisham; Queen; Black Sabbath

c. X song titles: Sex & Dying in a High Society; I Must Not Think Bad Thoughts; The Unheard Music

d. Bands/singers in titles: Bob Marley, Joseph Smith, & the Rapture; Sabbath; True Sounds of Liberty

e. The Alarm song titles/lyrics: Come on Down & Make the Stand; For Freedom; We are the Light

f. Soren Kierkegaard: Either/Or You'll Regret It; Attack Upon Christendom; Sickness Unto Death

g. Prophets in titles: Zephaniah; Zechariah, the Prophet; Malachi, Mischief, & My Nakedness

h. Movies as titles: The Decline of Western Civilization; Hangover; It's a Wonderful Life

i. Faithful Church/Shakespearean Fool titles: Was Jesus a Murderer or a Maniac; Holy Bible Atomic Hell Fire Heat; Dark Side of Love; The Jester

j. Running titles: Running with the Devil; Running with the Bulls; Running Death Dream

k. 40: Pattern for each five chapters

Author Information

Craig Conte is a writer, musician, and teacher. He earned a Bachelor's Degree from the University of California, Los Angeles and a Master's Degree from California State University, Long Beach. Conte has also written *Revelations, Disciplined Order Chaotic Lunacy, Millennial Reign,* and *Abraham's Abode.* He lives in Southern California.

YHWH Books & Records
P.O. Box 3922
Costa Mesa, CA 92628
U.S.A.
Email: faithfulchurch@hotmail.com
www.yhwhbooksandrecords.com
www.craigconte.com